LAST STAGE TO EUREKA

ALSO BY JOHNNY GUNN

Brookside, Oregon Territory Series

Ezekiel's Journey Series

Jack Slater Series

Slim Calhoun, Bull Morrison Series

Snake and the Dog-Man Series

Terrence Corcoran Series

LAST STAGE TO EUREKA

A Terrence Corcoran Western

JOHNNY GUNN

WOLFPACK
PUBLISHING
EST 2013

Last Stage to Eureka
Paperback Edition
Copyright © 2025 Johnny Gunn

Wolfpack Publishing
1707 E. Diana Street
Tampa, FL 33610

www.wolfpackpublishing.com

Paperback ISBN 979-8-89567-310-2
Ebook ISBN 979-8-89567-309-6

LAST STAGE TO EUREKA

CHAPTER ONE

THE SPRING of 1880 in the Diamond Valley of central Nevada was magnificent unless you had to be on one of the roads or trails leading in or out of town. Then, it was just muddy. By the middle of May, the magnificent lands of high mountains and lush valleys were drying out, and roads were full of ruts, but things no one had seen for months were growing. Daytime temperatures brought sweat to workers' brows, and cold beer was advertised in several saloons.

A lone rider on a mud-caked horse loped up the road from the Eureka and Palisades rail station and into Eureka. Tired and sweaty, the young man nodded to a couple and let his eyes search for his destination.

Eureka—the name should tell you it was a mining and ranching community and county seat of Eureka County. The mines were active, producing gold, silver, and lead. Ranches had fine herds of cattle, sheep, and hogs, businesses in town were active, and many had *Help Wanted* signs in the windows.

The single rider rode up to the sheriff's office and stepped off his horse. He was tall and thin, tired from a long two-day ride, and stepped through the door. "You Ed Connor?" the man asked, stopping in front of the pot belly stove, almost out of habit since it hadn't been lit in over a week now. He shucked his dust-covered coat, doffed his hat and turned to the sheriff.

"I am," Connor said. He saw the bright tin badge, noticed the man's gun belt carried a Remington revolver, and there was a sheathed knife on his other side. "What can I do for you?"

"I'm Lander County Deputy Sheriff Dirk Mallory, sent here to tell you about a recent problem. Sheriff Kemp wants, that is, needs a little help."

"Tell me all about it," Connor said as his chief deputy, Terrence Corcoran, walked in. "This is my chief deputy, Corcoran, Terrence Corcoran." He turned to Corcoran. "Say hello to Lander County Deputy Dirk Mallory."

Everyone shook hands, Mallory and Corcoran pouring themselves coffee. "Wells Fargo stage coming east was robbed just outside Austin three days ago."

Corcoran nodded. "Got the word. Heard they stole the horses, everything the passengers had, and left them to make their way back to Austin," Corcoran said.

Sheriff Connor nodded his head. "That stage was a day late coming into Eureka. We got the wire on that. How can we help?"

"How does that affect us? I've known Lander County Sheriff George Kemp for several years now." Corcoran said.

"Our investigation indicated the outlaws rode off with

the Wells Fargo horses toward Eureka, not south toward Belmont. Sheriff Kemp wants to know if you have heard anything, or if you would do some investigating as well."

Connor sat back in his chair, reached into his shirt pocket for a cigar, and strummed his fingers on his desk after he got it lit. *Kemp didn't send him to ask for help. Could have done that with a simple wire. He's here as an investigator but doesn't know that, he thought.*

"How many in the gang?"

"It looked like there were four, Sheriff."

"Interesting," Corcoran said. "Four men leading four horses would have been noticed. This is spring, and that valley out there is filled with buckaroos taking care of calves and mamas, getting set up for branding. Four men driving four horses would have been noticed."

"Particularly if they were harnessed, not saddled," Sheriff Connor said. "From the looks of you and your horse, it took a couple of long days to get here. Ride on back and tell Kemp we'll do some nosing around and keep you up to date on anything we uncover." Connor looked at Corcoran.

"Why don't you and Mallory step over to the Bonanza and have something to eat before he takes off." He didn't have to say anything else. What he implied was, *find out everything you can about what happened.* Corcoran nodded with a smile.

"Good idea. You hungry, Deputy?"

"Could eat a buffalo, Corcoran. Won't even need to cook it."

The two walked the short distance to the Bonanza Club, and Connor stood at the door of his office. *Those two just met, and I think they're already a team. Corcoran's taller and heavier, but good money would say Mallory is one hell of a fighter.*

————

SHORTY DUGGAN, all five feet and three inches of him, swaggered into the Flint Brothers Saloon, located next door to the Eureka Opera House, loudly slapped a Double Eagle on the hardwood bar, and glared at Justin Flint, the younger of the two brothers. The brothers had been rowdy troublemakers growing up, and their saloon was an extension of themselves.

"You drinkin' or just showin' off, Shorty?" It was not meant in jest.

"Gimme a beer, and mind your mouth. Put that beer in a clean glass." Duggan was a cocky little fellow who demanded respect even if none was due. Neither of the Flint brothers had ever offered the least amount of respect to the man.

Flint was a big man, heavy through the shoulders and chest, strong legs and arms. He took great pleasure in never asking for help lifting beer and whiskey barrels around. He had a quick temper and wasn't well-liked by many because of it. He had no tolerance for nonsense. "My business is selling beer and whiskey. You want fun and frolic, go next door," was his attitude, spelled out often.

"You gonna buy a ten-cent beer with a Double Eagle? You ain't had twenty dollars in a year, Shorty. Who'd you rob?"

Three old men at the end of the bar, nursing those ten-cent beers, laughed at the comment. Shorty whirled on them, scowled, and turned back to the barkeep. This kind of disrespect could not be tolerated. "I've said it once, this'll be twice, and there won't be a third, Flint. Watch your mouth!"

"Or what, Shorty?" Flint topped a pint glass of his own brewed beer and shoved it across the bar, scooping the twenty-dollar gold piece. Flint won't tolerate nonsense, but that doesn't include himself, and he held the gold coin up to the light, pretending to inspect it.

"Go ahead, Flint. Bite it." Shorty laughed. It wasn't filled with humor. "You need to learn how to treat your paying customers, Flint."

Flint scowled and flipped the coin into the money tray. "You'll have to come back later for the change. Too early to have that much money available."

"You ain't taking that coin and not giving me change, Flint. Give me my change, now." Duggan's eyes were narrowed. Twenty dollars gone? No, no, he thought, the idea scaring the hell out of the man. It had been months since he held a Double Eagle, and he wasn't going to let this one get away. His hand moved quickly to the big iron hanging on his hip.

"Or what, Shorty?" The look on his face was pure hate carried by a wry smile. "You ain't man enough to talk to me that way, little man. And your fingers move another half inch, and your head will be splashed all over my clean little saloon."

He saw that Shorty Duggan had already taken a long drink of the beer. "You just come back in a few hours and

I'll have your change." Flint never took his eyes off the hand near the holstered gun, and he smiled when Duggan saw the double barrels of a shotgun aimed at his head.

Justin Flint enjoyed having a bad attitude, enjoyed being the biggest man around, and took great pleasure in making those around him uncomfortable. He went out of his way to never throw the first punch, but worked hard to get that first punch thrown. Shorty Duggan wanted to be an outlaw, wanted people to get out of his way because of his outlaw attitude. He called it the swagger of defiance.

Move it or lose it, was his way. He swaggered down the streets of Eureka, his Colt riding a bit low on his short legs, glowered at everyone he met, but had never been arrested for anything since leaving Virginia City as a teenager. He robbed a candy store, injured the lady who ran it, and his father paid to keep him from jail. That brought him to Eureka.

The idea of jail scared the youngster. Everyone on both sides of the bars was bigger and meaner than he was. Arriving in Eureka, a mining town like Virginia City, he adapted the outlaw persona. Almost all the men in town were bigger than he was, stronger than he was, and willing to kick his butt at any time.

He wore his gun as a threat, carried a skinning knife as a threat, and was known to pull either at the least threat. Local women and young girls shied away, and the working girls wanted to see the cash first.

He did odd jobs around town for a dollar here and a quarter there. Having a Double Eagle was out of character, and he wasn't going to lose it to Flint. "Gimme the twenty back," he bawled it out and heard chuckles from the three old men at the end of the bar. "You shut up," he yelled, shaking his fist at them.

Was he losing control of the situation, of his own self? Why hadn't he pulled his gun? Was it because Flint had the shotgun and knew that ugly monster would kill him? Where was all that outlaw attitude?

He turned back to Flint. "Gimme it back now."

"Or what?"

Shorty stood back from the bar, pulled the Colt, and went down on the floor, his gun un-fired, his head bleeding hard. Flint smiled."Thank you, Amos."

Amos Diddy was one of the old men at the end of the bar, was near sixty, maybe even more, and had worked for Wells Fargo, riding guard sometimes, working for Wells's police agency most of the time. He still carried the oak baton that just opened a long gash on the back of Shorty Duggan's head.

"Still got it, Mr. Flint. Saw that coming and moved right in, I did. Might even be worth another cold beer, eh?"

"Might be. Amos." Flint laughed. "If you help me drag this fool out of here." Flint set the shotgun down and walked out from behind the bar, and the two dragged the little man toward the batwing doors, swinging gently in the early morning breeze.

"Just leave him in the dirt, Amos," Flint said. "Then go get the doc. You got a couple of cold ones coming." Mr. Diddy was smiling as he walked toward Dr. Whidby's.

CHAPTER TWO

THE SUNRISE WAS BEAUTIFUL, the air warm, and the cold water splashed across his craggy face felt good. Terrence Corcoran stood on the back porch of his small cabin on the eastern outskirts of Eureka, admiring what Mother Nature was providing. He was watching a couple of ducks hightail it toward the sun. Spring along the canyon was blooming. He smiled at the scene and walked toward the corral.

"Stand quiet, Dude. We'll get you all brushed out and saddled in just a short time. That young deputy from Austin could sure put his whiskey away. You checkin' to make sure I got my head on straight?" Corcoran chuckled, brushing more of winter's hair from the stud horse. He had more conversations with Dude than any other person in the village.

"Ready to work out the winter kinks, old man?" He stepped into the near side stirrup and settled into the well-worn saddle. Instead of riding west into town, he turned Dude east, let him settle into a beautiful trot, and after a few minutes, stepped him up to a lope, and within minutes they were tearing up the acres at a full-out run.

Corcoran loved to feel the muscles ripple as the long-legged stud ran at full speed, the wind tearing at his face. He had the hurricane strings tight under his chin, the brim of his hat flattened out by the speed, and the grin on his face would have charmed the hardest of women.

Not many in town ever saw this side of Terrence Corcoran. Riding at a full racing gallop, Corcoran was howling, almost like a wild Indian chasing down an enemy. *Damn this feels good.* He was a ten-year-old boy again, without an obligation to his name.

Corcoran eased the big boy back to the trot, and after a couple of miles, turned him around and let him walk back toward the cabin. "Wish I had that kind of energy," he all but whispered. "I'd be a panting and wheezing, old man, Dude. Let's ride through the town, say hello to whoever's out, and then stop at the Bonanza Club for breakfast, eh?"

He could feel the day's heat wasn't far off and enjoyed the cool air he was moving through. Grasses and early flowers were blooming trailside and off across the open plain east of the Eureka Canyon. The Diamond Mountains still had a mantle of snow across the top ridges to his north.

"It's a beautiful morning, Dude. Be nice if we could just ride off into those mountains. You could find some spring grass, and I could find a sprightly trout or three. Sure as I'm talkin' to you, somebody's gonna get all messed up, and I'm gonna have to be a deputy sheriff. You watch, Dude. You just watch, somebody's gonna mess up this fine day."

As Corcoran rode into the village proper, he found Dr. Whidby, Amos Diddy, and Justin Flint standing over the inert body of Shorty Duggan. Corcoran patted Dude along his neck. "Told you so."

He stepped down and walked over to the scene. "What'd he do this time?"

"Morning, Corcoran," Whidby said. "Old man Diddy smacked him on the back of the head as he went for his gun. Better talk to Flint. Duggan will suffer a nasty headache for the next few days but he'll survive."

"That true, Flint? Duggan pulled a gun on you?"

"Looked like he was gonna," Flint said. "Amos saved his life by smashing his head in. I was holding the big scatter gun."

"Kinda early for all this, ain't it?" A wry smile crossed the deputy's face. "Didn't know you opened up this early. What brought all this on?"

"You might want to ask the fool where he got a twenty-dollar gold piece when he wakes up. Ain't never seen Duggan with that much gold. Just another little piece of trash if you ask me."

"Help me get him in the back of my buggy, Corcoran. Then follow me and help me get him in the office. You can have the rest of the day to do your investigatin'."

Corcoran laughed, picking Shorty Duggan up and placing him in the buggy. "At your service, Doc."

On the quick ride to Whidby's office/hospital complex, Corcoran wondered about that twenty-dollar gold piece. *Duggan lives on quarters and silver dollars. That bunch he hangs out with do the same. Interesting.*

———————

"HEARD what happened to Shorty this morning?" Jake Hubbard was talking with Pete Chambers outside the Eureka Stables, where Hubbard worked shoveling droppings and feeding those staying there.

Chambers was the old man of the group that hung around with Shorty Duggan. Chambers being almost twenty-five. He spat out a mouthful of tobacco juice, pulled his hat brim down, and leaned against the corral fence. He was imitating what he saw from time to time when a group of buckaroos got together to spin a few stories.

"I'm gonna do my best to stay away from Shorty for a while. He ain't got brain one. What I hear is, he tried to spend one of them gold coins. Ain't that just the damndest?"

"Kinda thinkin' the same thing," Hubbad said. "Corcoran's sniffin' around now. Can't trace them coins, though," Hubbard said, snickering some. "Heard it was some old guy snuck up behind Shorty and dropped him with the butt of his gun. Shorty said he's gonna kill him when he sees him again."

"That'll bring the roof down." Chambers stood up from leanin' on the fence rail, grabbed a square-nose shovel, and handed it to Hubbard, who headed to the barn. "See you and the boys later. At the cabin?"

"Yeah. Hope somebody brings some beer," Hubbard

said. "Plans for makin' some more money, with or without Shorty Duggan."

Chambers stepped onto his horse, a black gelding with four white stockings, and rode off to the west. Hubbard made the slow, rambling walk into the barn, wondering why it was that the four of them let Shorty Duggan tell them what to do. "I ain't no dummy," he said, right into the face of a fine white trotter sticking its nose over the stall gate.

"Fact is, it should be Jake Hubbard running things." He kept on talking, almost in a whisper, as he cleaned the stalls and filled the wheelbarrow many more times than once. Hubbard was about five foot ten and was always ready to belittle Duggan. Chambers was almost six feet tall, and if he stood a side to you, you might have trouble seeing him. Hubbard was paid a dollar a day, had a stall of his own, and ate once or twice a day when he remembered. He and Chambers were a pair.

"My ma made me finish the third grade. I know my numbers, damn it. Ain't no reason for me to be followin' that smart alec Duggan. Him and his big plans. He ain't sold a horse yet." It never dawned on Hubbard to wonder where Duggan tried to sell those horses.

———————

"NOT EVEN EIGHT o'clock and I'm covered in sweat," Corcoran said, sitting down at the side of the sheriff's desk. "Shorty Duggan got himself mixed up at Flint's place this morning. He keeps it up, and he'll be living in the back room, Sheriff."

"Yup," Sheriff Ed Connor said, stretching his bad leg out to the side. "Watching that play out. Man ain't got sense enough to come in out of the rain. Flint get hurt?"

Corcoran laughed. "Not a scratch. Old man Diddy smacked Duggan pretty hard on the back of the head with that battering ram of a club he carries. Both Diddy and Flint were sure Duggan was going for his gun. I got their statements, but Shorty wasn't talking at the time. Here's the kicker, Ed. Shorty was flashing a twenty-dollar coin. Where would he come up with one of those? Two-bit coin, you bet. A twenty-dollar one? Horse pucky, my friend."

"How did your evening go with that young deputy from Austin? Seemed like a nice fellow."

"Oh, he was nice all right, but damn near drank me under the table. He's a bit of a tanker, Ed."

"My money would have been on you."

"You would have won, but I know I was with a good one last night. Maybe you should join us next time he's in town. Did learn a few things from him, though. That gang that robbed the stage never said anything at all, just used their weapons to make their points. All their horses were sweaty and muddy, and one of the men, the only one to speak, made crude remarks to the woman who was on the stage."

"That deputy have any descriptions? Anything we can use from our end?" Sheriff Connor stuck his empty tin cup out, and Corcoran filled it with hot coffee for him.

"On the men? Nothing. Wore masks, and like I said, they never said a word."

"Looks like you have your work cut out, Corcoran."

Sheriff Ed Connor sat back in his chair and chuckled. "Just find a muddy horse ridden by someone who can't talk."

"Let's go to the Bonanza and get some breakfast, eh?" Corcoran said, not taking Connor's bait, but had to hold in a chuckle. *Old man's still got it. Hope that leg heals soon. This is his kind of crime.*

CHAPTER THREE

"Do you plan on riding out to the scene?" Eureka County Sheriff Ed Connor was settled in at a table near the window at the Bonanza Hotel and Casino restaurant. His chief deputy, Terrence Corcoran, sat across from him. Both had a good view of the main street, which on a fine spring morning was coming to life.

Women in spring colors, men in shirt sleeves instead of buffalo robes and bear skin jackets. Storekeepers were sweeping the wooden sidewalks instead of shoveling snow and mud. The two men wearing bright tin badges weren't able to take all that in, what with people dead following the holdup of the last stage to Eureka.

"I pretty much know that country, and it's been almost a week since the robbery, but even with all that, I do want to ride out there. I want to do some circling, see if I can pick up where those boys rode off to. Is it an Austin bunch, a Nye County group, or bandits from right here in Eureka?"

The sheriff nodded. "With eight horses, they should

leave some sign, even after a few days. What did Mallory think?"

"Never said, Ed. Tells me he don't know." Corcoran and the sheriff chuckled. "Gives me a bit of an edge," Corcoran said, his eyes dancing with humor. "That stage runs once a week, Ed. If this is a local gang, they just might hit again."

"That run doesn't carry much of anything but people. Bank money is carried, for the most part, on trains," the sheriff said. "Bank money comes south from Battle Mountain to Austin. Austin's gold and silver goes north to the main line. Why did that gang hit the stage to Eureka?"

"Got me thinkin' too, Ed." Corcoran was about to go on when an explosion blew into the dining area. The explosion was named Cindy Cook, a redhead filled with the desire to be Corcoran's number one love. She was also the waitress at the restaurant.

She landed on Corcoran's lap, her arms wrapped around the big man's neck, and gave him a wonderful good morning kiss. "I knew you couldn't stay away from me for very long, Terrence. Oh, I love you so much."

Sheriff Connor was laughing, Corcoran was trying to extricate himself, and the owner of the Bonanza Club walked up to the table. "Interesting," is all he said, pulling up a chair and settling in. "Maybe you could take their order, now, Cindy."

She gave Corcoran one more kiss, stood and straightened her skirts, and smiled. "What can I get you gentlemen this morning?" She acted as if this happened every morning.

"Steaks and eggs, darling, for both of us," the sheriff said. "Lots of fried potatoes, too."

"Coffee around first," Jimmy Henderson said. Henderson built the Bonanza Club as one of the first businesses when the gold strikes were made in the canyon. It started out as a tent saloon and is now a two-story hotel, casino/bar, and full-service restaurant.

"You look like you have something on your mind, Henderson. What's up?" Corcoran pinched Cindy as she poured his coffee, and she almost spilled it.

"Oh, you," she said, but there was a definite smile attached. "More later?"

Corcoran gave the impression that he was ignoring her, but she caught the quick little nod and danced her way into the kitchen.

"I do have something on my mind, Corcoran. That stage robbery has me baffled." Henderson said. "The Eureka and Palisade Railroad brought a gold shipment from the Carson City mint for the mine's payroll and for the bank last week, as you know. That would have been my choice, not a stagecoach filled with people and little money."

Corcoran smiled, nodded to both the sheriff and Jimmy Henderson. Those were his thoughts, exactly. "Even someone who didn't think too well would go for a train car filled with gold and silver coins over a coach full of people and small change."

Henderson took a sip of hot coffee and looked at the two lawmen. "So, even the foulest of criminals has a motivation for the crime. What's the motivation?"

Sheriff Connor coughed softly as he put his coffee

cup down. "Answer that, Corcoran, and you solve the case. If it wasn't a large cache of money, what was it that brought those four men to kill and rob for pennies?" He shook his head and looked at his chief deputy before continuing.

"Lander County Deputy Mallory said he didn't think those robbers got any more than two hundred dollars," Connor said. "And the four horses."

Corcoran was slowly wagging his head back and forth. "Four men willing to kill, robbed the stage instead of the train." He looked at the sheriff. "You said I had my work cut out, and you were right as rain. How's Lou Foster doing?"

"That young deputy is as tough as you, Corcoran. He's begging to come back on full duty. His arm is out of its cast, and his head is all healed up. He'll be back on duty tomorrow morning."

"Good. I want to take him with me when I go over the scene of the robbery."

Foster, just a year into being a deputy sheriff, busted up a fight between some rowdy cowboys and some equally rowdy miners at the Bonanza saloon several weeks ago. His arm was broken, he took a gambler's chair across the side of his head, and quieted the disturbance with two shots from his Remington revolver. One into the biggest miner he'd ever seen, and the other into the cow boss from the XY outfit. Both men lived, but the party ended.

"If you're only going to be gone a few days, fine," Connor said. He turned to Jimmy Henderson. "Do you have any ideas of why this little gang hit the stage?"

"I don't think this was a one-time hit, but don't know why I think that way. Could be they thought one of the passengers was carrying a load of cash."

The conversation carried on through the meal, and Corcoran slipped out to pack up for his run out to the scene of the robbery. "I'll tell Lou Foster to get packed," Connor said. "If you find anything, ride on into Austin and let the sheriff know."

———

"GLAD YOU BOYS ARE HERE. I got the word that our little Miss Goody will be on the next stage. She spent an extra couple of days in Reno, and that's why she wasn't on the last one." He was sitting at the table of a cowboy line camp in the Diamond Mountains north of Eureka. The Diamonds are a high and rugged stretch used for summer range for many ranchers in the valley.

"That raid of yours has the sheriff, Corcoran, even Henderson talking to themselves," the tall man wearing a buckskin pullover shirt said. "They can't figure out why you hit the stage."

"Let 'em think about it, Chambers," the leader said and laughed. "You got all of fifty bucks and four horses instead of ten thousand."

"Who knew she wasn't gonna be on that stage? Old man Jackson didn't even know. He was in a panic when the stage didn't show up."

Enid Jackson owned the Eureka Bank and had interests in two of the mines pumping out gold and silver. His daughter, twenty-three-year-old Louisa, had been attending college south of San Francisco, and was going to spend her summer break with her family in Eureka. Instead of taking the train east to Palisade, she got off in Battle Mountain and came south to Austin to visit a friend, then take the stage to Eureka.

The girl had spent all of her youth roaming the Diamond Mountains, was an excellent horse rider, a fine shooter with rifle or shotgun, and could whip most of the boys she grew up with. Louisa stood a tall five feet nine inches and was fully developed and easy on the eye. The leader of the gang was sure she would bring at least twenty thousand dollars from that fat old banker. He'd take ten, and the boys could split the other ten. All they got was a hundred and four horses.

"We need to know she will actually be on the stage this time. That damned deputy Corcoran is already snooping around too much." He stood up and straightened the buckskin shirt, pacing around the small cabin.

"That's true," Chambers said. "But the hit we made was a good one. We learned a lot, too. It was hours before anyone knew the stage had been robbed. Those people had to walk back to Austin. Taking those horses worked out well."

"Yeah," the leader said. "We still have 'em, too. Tried to sell one, but when that buckaroo saw where the horse wore a harness a lot, he backed off right away. These cayuses we got ain't never seen a cow, don't know nothin' about ropin'. We're gonna be feedin' 'em a long time, I think."

"If someone tried, could he pick up our trail because

of those horses? Our four and their four would leave a pretty good trail to follow."

"We ain't here to talk horses," the tall one said. "Let's build a good plan for when our little bundle of cash comes through." He wasn't angry but glared some at the man talking horses. "It would be my idea to do exactly what we did, except for one change. We need to know that girl will be on the stage, and two, let the horses go after we're several miles from the scene."

The tall one looked around the table, and the other three nodded. He was wondering about them. Duggan, who liked to think he was the smartest of the bunch, sitting there nursing a broken head, Chambers, probably the smartest, scowling, and Jake Hubbard, an out-of-work, out-of-ideas, no-account.

"You been doing a lot of talkin'," Duggan said. "You got some better ideas?"

The tall one smiled. "I think I have." The scowl that followed shut Duggan down immediately. "I let you make some of the plans, Shorty, and you left out something that led to the failure, so don't get that high and mighty look on your face with me. I'll bash the other side of your skull in. Now, about making sure we know our bird will be a passenger."

"It'll drive Corcoran nuts trying to find anything out there," Jake Hubbard laughed. He was overweight and laughed at everything that was said. "How do we find out if that girl is on the stage if we're out on the road waiting for it?"

"Got to have someone in Austin. She'll have to be in

Austin for a day or two before. If she's there, she'll surely then be on the stage," the tall man in the buckskin shirt said. "Might be time to have a fourth member of the group."

"That kid, Jonas Johnson been hangin' around," Shorty Duggan said. "Give him a hundred dollars to let us know she's in town. He's not very smart, but I think he could handle this. We'd have to dump him after, though. He's got a big mouth."

"Everyone okay with that?" Chambers asked, and all nodded. "Does he know all of us?"

"Afraid so," Shorty said. "That's why he has to die when this is over."

"Set it up and get him off to Austin. That stage runs in two days. She should be there, and we need to be out there and ready, too. Remember, Jake, we need food, water, and whiskey for the next two days. Let's ride out separately like last time."

Chambers watched the man in the buckskin shirt walk toward the door. *He's got a terrible hate for that banker, but it's going to line my pockets with plenty of gold. He wants ten thousand for himself, and we split ten thousand.* Chambers chuckled softly as he got to his feet and headed for the cabin door. *He ain't never going to see his ten thousand.*

CHAPTER FOUR

"WE DIDN'T LEARN MUCH, did we?" Lou Foster and Terrence Corcoran were making the long climb to the summit from where the road leaves out at the north end of the Smokey Valley. At the summit, they faced a long ride down into Austin, the Lander County seat. "We rode a wide circle, but we still don't know where those jaspers went."

"There's two sides to that, Lou," Corcoran said. "We know they didn't ride off for the Monitor Valley. We know they didn't ride off for the Smokey Valley, and we're pretty sure they didn't ride off for Eureka."

"So where did they take those horses?"

"After we have a chat with Dirk Mallory we'll follow those tracks, me boy. My guess is they'll lead us into the Diamond Range."

"Makes sense," Lou Foster said. "They could just dump the coach horses and go anywhere."

"Or," Corcoran said with a smile. "They could lead us

to a line camp in those rocky old hills and we'll find four horses in a brush corral."

They snaked down from the summit into Austin and rode up to the International Hotel. "We'll get a room, find Mallory, eat a big steak, and get back on the road at first light," Corcoran said.

"I always wondered why there isn't a rail line on this road," Foster said. "Never get one of those smoke-belching locomotives over this pass. It ain't a pass, is it? Just steep to the top and steep down into the canyon."

"They built the towns where the gold was not where they could run a rail line," Corcoran said. They both were laughing when they pulled up in front of the hotel. "I've heard stories of runaway wagons and teams coming down this canyon. Can't imagine trying to stop a train."

———————

IT WAS a half hour before they were able to track down Deputy Mallory at the Buckhorn Saloon. "Glad you're here, Corcoran. Have anything new to pass on? I know I don't."

"We spent a bit of time at the scene, Mallory, but wanted to get into town before doing anything. Truth is, we wanted a cold beer," Corcoran joshed.

That brought a chuckle from Mallory. "What's your plan?"

"We'll leave out at first light and try to pick up that trail. What's going on at your end?" He wanted to ask why the Lander County Sheriff hadn't already followed that trail, but didn't.

"Wells Fargo detective is here. Gruff old bastard who doesn't drink. Goes by the handle of Smoky Pierson. Lives the good life in San Francisco, hates these hills we have that he has to climb to get from the hotel to our office. You should hear his gasping."

"San Francisco has hills," Lou Foster said.

"At sea level," Mallory said. Austin's six thousand and some feet above sea level. Pierson swears there ain't no oxygen in this air. You staying at the International? You'll run into him. Sheriff know you're in town?"

"Doubt it," Corcoran said.

"I'll let him know what you found out. Gotta get back before you and me get tangled up in a bottle, Corcoran. Don't think I sobered up for a week last time we got together."

"We gotta do it again, old man. Can't have too much fun, you know."

They whapped each other on the shoulders, and Corcoran signaled for the bartender to set him and Lou up again as Mallory made a hustle for the bat-wings. "He's a good man, Lou, and sharp. Got himself a good mind."

"I thought Wells Fargo detectives were supposed to be among the best," Lou said. "This Smoky fellow doesn't seem to meet those standards."

"We'll probably meet him at supper. Let's finish these beers and head back to the hotel. When we signed in, I thought I saw a name on the register I wanted to check out."

It was downhill on the walk back to the International, and Corcoran pointed out a young man sitting on a bench outside the hotel. "Recognize him, Lou?"

"Don't know his name, but he spends a great deal of time at the Bonanza Club in Eureka." He shook his head, trying not to stare at the man. "Don't think he has a job. Hangs around with Shorty Duggan."

"He's Jonas Johnson," Corcoran said. "Like us, he's a long way from home. Let's walk right on past him and see if he says anything. Don't mention why we're here if he does say something." Corcoran was wondering just why Johnson would be here.

Been trying to figure out why that stagecoach was robbed, knowing it wasn't carrying anything but people, and here's Johnson sitting from where the stage would leave. Is he looking for or waiting for someone? Was that gang looking to kidnap someone? Is that why Louisa Jackson is in town?

They walked right by Johnson, and he didn't look up, and Corcoran wondered why. He knew Johnson had seen them coming. They walked into the hotel, and Corcoran spotted Louisa Jackson sitting by the large window that looked out onto a garden in the back of the hotel.

"Hello, Miss Jackson. This is a pleasure running into you," Corcoran said.

"Terrence Corcoran," she exclaimed, almost loudly. "What a surprise. Oh, my, and Lou Foster, too. You're a deputy now? Oh, my. I'll be leaving on the next stage. I missed the last one by just a few hours."

"Heading home, are you?" Lou Foster's cheeks were a bit redder than when he walked into the hotel.

"I'm going to be spending the summer with Dad then heading for Philadelphia. My schooling is over, and I'll be going to work in an office full of lawyers. Scary. Will we see each other while I'm home, Lou?"

Lou Foster had a hard time swallowing, tried not to look at Corcoran or Louisa, tried not to remember how wonderful it had been dancing with the lovely lady, having picnics alone with her, sitting alone in their backyard, kissing and talking.

"I would like that," Foster whispered. "We'll be having supper here at the hotel. Will you join us?"

"Oh, my yes."

"We'll come get you at seven, Louisa," Corcoran said, giving Foster an interesting glance. "What room?"

"Two-twelve, Lou," she said to Foster in answer to Corcoran. Foster nodded along with a broad smile and bright eyes.

The two deputies stood and watched the lady walk toward the stairs. "Sounded like you two have a bit of history, Lou. She is lovely, and her father is rather wealthy. She missed the stage that was robbed. Am I seeing something?"

"I missed that, Corcoran. Too busy looking at her."

"You're a lawman, Lou. All day and night, every day and night. Don't let things like this get past you. Was that stage robbery supposed to be a kidnapping? Let that roll around in that big head of yours."

Foster stood, red-faced, watching Corcoran walk away. "I got a lot to learn," he whispered, hurrying to catch up.

CHAPTER FIVE

THE KNOCK at the door was more like a pounding, and both Corcoran and Foster had their guns in hand that fast. "It's open," Corcoran said. He was standing at the wall alongside the door and Foster kneeled down beside one of the beds. "Best to come in with open hands."

"They're empty," a gruff voice said as the door swung open. A man in a herringbone suit, white bib-front shirt, and no hat, walked into the room, his arms out to the side and his hands spread open and empty.

He was burly, had his suit coat open, and Corcoran saw the big sawed-off double-barreled shotgun hanging from his shoulder. The gun hung in such a manner that it could be brought into play with very little movement on the part of the wearer. A big gun carried by a big man.

"Name's Detective Pierson, Wells Fargo. You Corcoran?" He was looking right into Corcoran's eyes.

"Terrence Corcoran, Chief Deputy, Eureka County Sheriff. Don't think we've met before." Corcoran slipped his iron back in its holster.

"Why should we have?" Pierson said, as he walked over to the window and took a look out, also seeing Foster slip his gun away.

Corcoran tightened up just a bit at the crude comment and didn't bother to answer. "Something I can do for you, detective?"

"The coach was robbed in Lander County, Deputy, not Eureka. What do you think you're doing here?"

"Coach was headed for Eureka, Pierson. Lander County Sheriff asked for a little help. If this bothers you, just take a deep breath and stuff it. You might work for the company that was robbed, I work to solve every crime that's committed in or around Eureka County. If you don't like that, you can turn around and walk right out of this room." Corcoran heard his young deputy take a deep breath. *You're learning, Mr. Foster. Stay sharp.*

Corcoran smiled at the heavy but strong Wells Fargo detective. "On the other hand, if you're looking to work with me, welcome. Your choice."

"No," Pierson said. "I'm in charge of this investigation, and don't forget it. You don't make a move without clearing it with me. Got it?"

"I work for the Eureka County Sheriff, Detective. Only the Eureka County Sheriff. I'll pass on to the Lander County Sheriff what information I gather." Corcoran saw Foster's hand hovering close to his weapon, saw the Wells Fargo detective's hand inching toward his terrible weapon, and knew he had to calm things down.

"It's time to leave, Pierson. Don't make me say it twice, and don't get in my way. You have your job to do, and I have mine. Stay out of my way."

Pierson's eyes narrowed to just slits, the scowl filled that face, and Corcoran watched the man slowly pull his hand away from his side. Pierson stood about five feet and ten inches but weighed a hefty two hundred pounds with very little fat. He had a barrel chest, wide and strong shoulders, and legs like oak trees. Corcoran wondered how much of the hotel room would exist if it came to fisticuffs. He wore a wry smile when he turned to Foster.

Pierson slowly made his way through the hotel door, not bothering to close it, and walked down the hallway. Corcoran pushed the door closed and nodded to Foster. "Don't think we'll get much help from that gentleman, Lou. Everything all right with you?"

"Just fine, Corcoran. Just fine." Foster was breathing hard, and sweat was beading on his upper lip. "I don't think Detective Pierson had ever been talked to that way. He really wanted to shoot you." He took another deep breath and thought to himself, *and me.*

"I was safe," Corcoran said. "You were backing me up."

Foster turned bright red thinking about that. It was true, of course, and Lou realized he had done that more than once. Maybe, he thought, he really would be a fine lawman like Corcoran. "You planning on giving Pierson any of your thoughts?"

"Thoughts?"

"Well, like maybe that gang was looking to kidnap someone. Maybe Louisa Jackson?"

"That's between us only, Lou, and it's just a thought."

MORNING FOUND the two riding out of town to where the stagecoach had been robbed. "Ain't a whole lot to be seen, Corcoran," Lou Foster said. The coach had been recovered, and only horse prints and people prints were left, etched in the ancient desert dust. The crime took place on a busy highway, and there had been some traffic since, making it even more difficult to find something significant.

Corcoran was off his horse, looking down at where the coach teams would have been standing. "Quite a lot to be seen, Lou." He motioned the young deputy to come over. "See, here is where one of the gang held the horses while they were cut loose from the coach."

Foster walked over. "Looks like they didn't unharness them," he said. "So, does that mean they led the horses off harnessed?"

Corcoran smiled. "Good. I'm sure they left them harnessed. Now, get back in the saddle and let's see if we can find out which direction they went." He rode out, away from the roadway, away from all the tracks, maybe fifty feet or so, and turned to ride in a circle around the scene.

"We saw their tracks yesterday, you remember, but didn't determine which way they lit off," Corcoran said.

It was when they were two hundred feet or so after crossing the roadway to the east that Corcoran stopped and stepped off Dude. "Here we go, Lou. Can't miss sign like this."

Lou Foster, still in the saddle, looked at where eight horses had ridden through the sage and brush. "Won't be hard to follow this bunch," he said.

"It's days old, hasn't rained, so these tracks should be easy to follow. We'll pick up on that bright and early tomorrow morning. Let's get back to the hotel. I'd like to get a few answers from Miss Jackson and see if that young Johnson boy is still in town. That'll be your job. Find him and try to find out what he's doing here."

"Probably looking for a job," Foster said. "He don't have one in Eureka."

Corcoran had some thoughts about that. *No job? At his age in a mining camp? Not a drunk or I'd know it. Not staying at the hotel, or if he is, not under his own name. I checked the register.* Corcoran looked at Foster and thought about Louisa.

"You and Louisa about the same age, Lou?"

"We are. In fact went to school together. Didn't want nothing to do with a rancher's kid, being a banker's kid. I worked some to change her thoughts," and he chuckled, remembering some of their time together.

"How about Mr. Johnson? He about your age, too?"

"Yup, but dumber than a snake shaking its skin off. Not sure if he made it to seventh grade or not. Didn't finish, I know that. He'd come to school with bruises a lot. His old man was mean, and his ma didn't do much cooking either. He ain't very smart, Corcoran. If you're trying to match him with Louisa Jackson, it won't fit."

"I wonder if he's here to make sure she is. She missed the last stage, remember? He would be smart enough for that. See what you can find out."

————

It was late in the afternoon when they got back to the hotel, and Foster went off to see if he could find Jonas Johnson. Corcoran caught a glimpse out the back window and walked out to the back of the hotel, where a small lawn was established and found Louisa Jackson sitting at a table with another young lady.

"Beautiful day, isn't it," Corcoran said.

"Oh, look who's here. Deputy Corcoran. It's good to see you," Louisa said. "Daddy always says he wouldn't even have a bank if it wasn't for you. Your reputation keeps the bad guys away. Will you join us?"

Corcoran smiled, doffed his hat, and sat down. "I'm Deputy Sheriff Terrence Corcoran," he said to the other woman before sitting. He looked at Louisa. "You've been away for a while."

"Three years, Terrence. All grown up and ready to take on the world." Her laugh was just a tinkle. "This is my friend Samantha Jordan. She used to live in Eureka. Her father has the Owl Hoot Saloon here in Austin."

"Glad to meet you," Corcoran said, standing and offering his hand. "Your father would be Joe, often called Trader Jordan?"

"Yes. Do you know him? He's the best father ever."

Corcoran remembered the trader well. "He and I had a few issues, but I know he kept his family well." There was more he could tell, but not today, not with these two lovely ladies. He turned to Louisa. "Going to be with us for a while?"

"Most of the summer, I hope. Moving to Philadelphia before fall." She gave him a wonderful smile before continuing. "What brings you to Austin, Terrence?"

"Don't want to frighten you, but the stage you missed last week was held up. I've brought Deputy Lou Foster along, and we're going to find the robbers."

"I heard about that. I sent Daddy a wire that I was here, and he wanted to send a carriage, but I said no, the coach will be fine. They wouldn't rob it twice in a row, would they?" Both girls twittered some, and Corcoran frowned.

Would they? he wondered. "I certainly hope not. I'd best be moving. Have a good trip, and it was nice meeting you, Miss Jordan."

Corcoran ambled his way into the hotel's barroom and ordered a beer. Looking around, he spotted Wells Fargo Detective Pierson at the end of the bar. *Interesting. I'm sure Mallory said he doesn't drink.* Corcoran ignored the man and his mug of beer, and spent some time studying others by way of the mirror behind the bar.

There were a couple of miners, a couple of local businessmen, and a few buckaroos standing at the long bar. The two barmen were kept busy. It wasn't just a minute or two that Pierson moved down the bar to stand next to Corcoran.

"Ain't gonna find stagecoach robbers drinking away an afternoon," Pierson said. His voice was an angry growl, and he shoved Corcoran a bit, moving in next to him.

"Said the pot to the pan. I'll drink when I want, Pierson. You ain't got much room to complain, I see." Corcoran shoved an elbow out, moving Pierson's arm.

"What did you find on your little trip this morning?"

So, big-time Detective Pierson is keeping track, eh? Corcoran smiled. "You'd be surprised what one can find when one spends time at a crime scene. Coat buttons, hairpins, horse hoof prints. Amazing. Wells Fargo, all right with you spending the afternoon at the saloon?"

The almost empty mug slammed down on the bar, and Pierson bellowed, "I'll drink when I want, Corcoran. None of your damned business." He stepped back from the bar, almost inviting Corcoran to take a swing.

"I've met a lot of different people in this business of law-keeping, Detective, but you are unique. Have you even been out to the scene of the crime? You like to push people, eh big guy? Push me one more time." Corcoran couldn't tell if that double-barreled shotgun was tucked under the coat or not.

Corcoran could see Pierson puff up like he was going to wipe the bar with the deputy's face when a big arm came between the two men. "Maybe you'd like to push a Lander County deputy, too, Detective. We don't hanker to have fights in our saloons, mister, so cool your heels."

Corcoran's almost six feet stood shoulder to shoulder with Mallory's almost six feet, and the two glared down at Pierson's shorter stance. The two wore badges, one said Eureka County, the other, Lander County.

Pierson slammed the empty mug on the bar, turned, and walked toward the swinging doors. Mallory nodded to the barman, who produced two mugs of goodly chilled beer for the lawmen.

"Find out anything this morning?"

"You keeping track, too?"

"I was checking up on Pierson only to find him checking up on you." He laughed. "It could have been a circus."

"Well, we did find the trail the outlaws left us. We'll be on that first thing in the morning. Anybody talking about the robbery? Maybe throwing names about?"

"Just the regular after something like this. Forcing the passengers to walk back was unusual, and running off with the teams. The killing was unnecessary, too. Those boys were more than robbers, they killed and didn't care if others died. Mean, nasty people, Corcoran." Mallory motioned for the barman to bring another couple of mugs of beer.

"Let's take a table, Corcoran. You've got something on your mind. Don't want some of these fine folk at the bar listening in." He smiled, looking left and right. More than one head ducked down quickly.

Lou Foster joined them as they took to the chairs. "I had a long talk with Johnson. He just simply answered my questions. Dumb as horse crap. He was paid to be here but doesn't know who paid him. Got a note and twenty bucks to be here."

"Watching for someone?" Corcoran hoped so. "A lovely lady we both know?"

Foster nodded his head. "He sent a telegram to Eureka saying so. It was addressed to somebody named Butch. Just Butch. No last name. I don't know anyone named Butch."

"I don't either," Corcoran said. "You're sure it's Butch? Somehow, I was hoping that Johnson was sent by Mr. Jackson, but now, I'm worried."

"Mind telling me what this is all about?" Mallory said.

Corcoran looked about as casually as he could before he said anything. "I don't think this was a simple stagecoach robbery. I think those four men were looking to kidnap Louisa Jackson."

"Oh, oh," Mallory said. "The banker's daughter? She would certainly bring a hell of a lot more money in than what they got. And she's in town right now," Mallory said. He looked first at Corcoran and then at Foster, before taking a look around the hotel saloon. He wasn't looking for anyone, just needed a few seconds to let all that information soak in.

"We've got some work to do, I think." Mallory leaned back in his chair, looking up at the ceiling, covered in embossed tin. "You have a plan?"

"Working on one," Corcoran said, adding a chuckle. "You?"

"Sticking like mule hoof glue to your butt, Corcoran. Have you made Miss Jackson aware of the danger?"

"Not yet. She's determined to take that stage out of here, tomorrow. I'd like to send her out tonight in a carriage, and you and me take that stage tomorrow."

"Splendid. That would be my plan, for sure."

"And, as I see this, I spend the night on the open desert with the lovely Louisa," Lou Foster said. There was a well-defined smile on his young face. *How many times, so few years ago, did I wish for that opportunity? Me driving a small buggy and Louisa sitting beside me, wrapped in a warm wool blanket. Yes, Corcoran,* he thought, *I will be pleased to escort the lady home.*

"We gonna tell Pierson?" Mallory asked. He drained his beer and motioned to one of the barmen to send more over. "You gotta know he's watching us closely right about now."

"I've asked Louisa to join us for supper," Corcoran said. "He'll probably put it together. I just hope he's a professional and lets this play out. And..." Corcoran smiled and chuckled. "No, Louisa has not been approached on this. It might get iffy."

CHAPTER SIX

"YOU LOOK LOVELY, MY DEAR," Corcoran said when Louisa answered her hotel room door. "Ready for a splendid supper?"

"Miss Jackson won't be having supper with you, Corcoran. She'll be with me." Smoky Pierson gently pulled Louisa back into her hotel room and stepped to the door. "Her father wired me, and I'll be escorting her on the stage tomorrow, so take a hike, deputy."

He slammed the door in Corcoran's face, and the big man was able to step back before it hit him. Corcoran stood still for just a moment, collected his anger, and let it pass. He wanted to put a foot through that door, put two, maybe three shots in the heavy detective, and reined in his thoughts, turned, and walked back to the restaurant to join Foster and Mallory. The look on his face told the two there was trouble.

"Change of plans, gentlemen." He sat down as the waitress brought steaks to the table. "Detective Pierson contacted Emil Jackson and will be riding in the stage tomorrow morning with Miss Jackson. We're pretty much left out of the picture right now. Outside our own jurisdiction, and no real evidence that the stage will be held up."

The sour look on Corcoran's face gave shudders to the folks at the surrounding tables. Three deputy sheriffs sitting at a table, glowering at what looked like each other, was enough to kill one's appetite.

"Think they would hit it at the same point as before?" Mallory asked.

"Who knows?" Corcoran looked over to Lou Foster. "Did young Mr. Johnson say anything about a Wells Fargo detective being in town? Or did you bring it up?"

"I didn't," he said. "And I don't recall any mention of him being here. That means the gang might not know."

"That just bothers the hell out of me," Corcoran said. "What can your department do, Mallory?"

"As you said, we can't go to a judge and try to protect Louisa, particularly if she's already being protected by a Wells Fargo detective. And we have not a shred of evidence that the stage run is in jeopardy. No, Corcoran, all we can do is watch."

"Can we ride out with the coach?" Foster asked.

"Not a bad idea," Mallory said. "What do you think, Corcoran?"

"Not a bad idea, but I think I'd rather be where the coach was robbed before. If it's going to be hit, that gang would almost have to be there tonight. Bah!"

"What?" Foster asked.

"Pierson has us pinched in. If that gang is already out there, we can't go. To escort the coach would cause the gang not to attack, and yet if we do escort it, it would just be a nice, long ride home."

"By escorting, as Foster suggests, at least Louisa would be safe," Mallory said.

"There is that," Corcoran said. Corcoran was looking for a fight, not just to save Louisa Jackson, but to catch and or kill the gang that attacked the stage last week. One person dead was more than enough to get the lawman's blood up.

Mallory's eyes lit up, and he stood up. "Sheriff. You going to join us for supper? You know Chief Deputy Terrence Corcoran from Eureka County, and this is Deputy Lou Foster from Eureka."

"I do," Lander County Sheriff George Kemp said. "Corcoran. Foster. Got some bad news for you fellows. May I sit?"

"Of course," Mallory said.

"That Wells Fargo detective has put the clamps on your working with us on the stage robbery. He got the district judge to issue a *do not interfere* edict. My department and the Eureka department are forbidden to continue our investigation, not just of the initial incident, but of the possibility of a second attempt." Kemp was more than angry as he sat shaking his head.

"I just left the man," Corcoran said. "He's escorting the girl on the morning stage. Never said a word about that. We're out?" He sat quiet, looking at his cold steak, shaking his head slowly, back and forth. Foster, Mallory, and the Lander County Sheriff could see the anger building.

That's what the smirk was when that fool slammed the door

in my face. The Johnson kid being here makes it all but certain that the stage will be held up. Can Pierson, in the coach, protect that girl? I have to be there. That's final, judge or no judge.

"He claims that we have destroyed evidence and that we are interfering in his investigation. The damned old judge bought it." Sheriff Kemp looked at Dirk Mallory. "You're out. And I wired the order to Sheriff Connor, Corcoran, and you're out. There is nothing I can do about it, either."

"What's Pierson's point in all this?" Lou Foster asked.

"Pride," Kemp said. "Not going to let someone else solve the robbery."

"He's going to be inside that coach with Louisa Jackson, Sheriff," Corcoran said. "I'm not able to present any kind of evidence, but I believe that coach will be hit again tomorrow in a second attempt to kidnap the girl. As you know, her father owns the bank in Eureka. She was supposed to have been on the coach last week." Corcoran's anger was more than evident. "Pierson can't save her."

"Our hands are tied, Terrence," Kemp said. "On the other hand, if you two left out right now, you could be well past where you think the robbery would take place and wait. If the coach doesn't go by when it should, you could ride back and maybe do some good, at the least."

"You are one cagey sheriff," Corcoran said. "Let's go, Lou. At least we had a good supper." Kemp and Mallory both had smiles as the two men headed upstairs to get their gear and check out of the hotel.

CHAPTER SEVEN

"WE'LL MAKE camp where the road south to the Smokey Valley cuts this one," Corcoran said. "There's a rocky ledge just southwest of the intersection. Get a good breakfast in the morning and wait for the coach. Not move until we know something."

"Will we be close enough to hear anything?" Lou Foster asked.

"That canyon narrows along the natural springs, Lou. The stage has to slow and that's only about half a mile from where we are. If guns are used, we'll hear 'em." Corcoran got busy with the pack animal, and Foster undressed his horse, both thinking about tomorrow morning.

It turned dark as the two were seen by Pierson riding out of town. He smiled, getting his little victory by way of the judge. He might even get a nice little present from the banker when he safely delivers the girl.

"Sleeping in the sand," Lou Foster griped. "Going to miss that mattress."

"Well, old son, we'll have a fine breakfast cooked over an open fire. There's your compensation. We're considerably less than a mile from where that coach was robbed. If there's gunfire, we'll hear it. The canyon will direct it right to us."

"Not really close enough that we could ride in and break it up."

"No, we're not, but we will be able to get there quickly, possibly follow the outlaws, and hopefully save Miss Jackson. Pierson really made a mess of this by going to the judge. We, at least, won't be in contempt of court."

It was some time before Lou Foster could get to sleep. Remembering the few times he was able to be alone with Louisa during their high school years shoved the shades of sleep aside. She was from a monied family, and he was the son of a small rancher. He knew she liked him but also knew she fended him off, at first because of his lack of a monied family.

Would things change if he was one of those who saved her? He had a hard time putting those questions aside. It seemed that he had just laid his head on his rolled-up pants while Corcoran was stomping around getting a fire lit.

"Up and at 'em, Mr. Foster. Sun's gonna be beating on us shortly."

The sky was clear, the air was chilly, and the lack of clouds and wind told the men it would be a hot day ahead. The fire was warm, and Corcoran was right, Foster was just shoving his foot in a boot when old Sol broke the far horizon. Shafts of springtime warmth made the morning grand, warm, and friendly. Friendly until Foster remembered why they were there.

"What time does that stage leave?" he asked, warming his hands over the fire.

"Eight o'clock," Corcoran said. "Be at least two hours getting here. Where the road dips into that narrowing canyon, where the spring water was running, should be where the bandits will hit. If there's gunfire, we'll hear it."

"Do you have a plan for if the coach just races right on by? Considering the judge's order, that is."

"Well, Mr. Foster, we will be riding on a public road for home. That we just happen to be a mile or so behind a stagecoach is just happenstance," Corcoran said, almost laughing as he finished. Smoky Pierson pulled a fast one on us, but we're pretty sharp, too."

The two men had a nice breakfast, took care of their horses, packed up their bedrolls, and waited for the stage. The horses were saddled, and Corcoran checked his pocket watch for at least the third time when a volley of gunshots echoed down the canyon.

"Let's go," Corcoran yelled. He swung into the saddle, Foster right behind him, and lit out for the main road. More gunshots were heard and then it was quiet as they raced the last half mile for the coach. A trail of dust could be seen heading northeast as they pulled up to the stopped stage.

Both driver and guard were slumped in the high seat, and screaming could be heard inside the coach. "Keep the team under control, Lou," Corcoran yelled, bailing from Dude's back. He raced to the coach and jerked the door open. Smoky Pierson's body, riddled with gunshots, slowly rolled out and into the dust. Corcoran knew the man was dead and looked inside to find another man, badly wounded, and two women, one screaming her head off.

Corcoran got one woman out of the coach, coaxed the other to calm down, best he could, and got her out, as well.

"Either one of you hurt?"

Neither one answered the question and then just started talking about the hold up. "They just ripped that poor girl away from that man, hit her really hard, and threw her on a horse," the non-screamer said. "It was horrible. They shot that man over and over. They killed Martha's husband, too, when he pulled his gun."

Corcoran yelled at Foster. "The team's okay?"

"Spooked, but they're fine. No injuries."

"We gotta get these people back to Austin and chase that gang, too. Can you drive four-up?"

"I'm an old farm boy, Corcoran. No problem." He climbed up into the seat and eased the driver and his messenger off the seats, being as gentle as he could. "Now that they're calmed down, they'll almost drive themselves." He chuckled.

Corcoran was trying to get Pierson's body back into the coach when two riders were heard coming on fast. "Company," Foster yelled. He was off the coach, gun in hand, as Sheriff Kemp and his deputy Dirk Mallory rode up in a storm of dust.

"That Pierson?" Kemp asked.

"Yup," Corcoran said. "Girl's gone, too. We gotta get on their butts, Sheriff."

"Go, Corcoran. Me and Mallory will take care of this mess. I'll wire Connor. Find 'em and kill 'em."

Foster leaped from the coach and was on his horse that fast, and he and Corcoran headed out in the direction they had seen the dust. It was Foster who picked up the trail. "They must have brought a horse for Louisa. We've got at least five horses we're following."

The two were at a strong lope, cutting across the open desert of the far north of the Smokey Valley. "No sense killing our horses," Corcoran said. "Those fools are racing full out and their horses will give out on 'em. Just keep a steady pace, Lou." They slowed their horses to a mile-eating trot.

The gang seemed to be heading mostly east and slightly north as they cut through open desert. There were deep cuts in the desert from runoff created during spring and summer thunderstorms, and the two had to be careful crossing them. "Seen some serious down-pours in this country, Lou. Seen these gullies run full to overflow. Might find mud in the bottom, and your horse will go right out from under you." Corcoran said as they negotiated their way through one gully that was at least nine feet deep. They saw where the gang had to fight their way out through a steep bank that was also muddy from spring runoff.

"Prints are much clearer, Corcoran," Foster yelled as they topped off. "Think we're getting closer?"

"Might be. They've been pushing those nags pretty hard. Haven't seen any dust, though. Have you?"

"No, and I'm looking for it, too." Foster grew up on a horse, moving cattle with his father as a youngster. "If they've been riding as hard as they were leaving that stagecoach, those horses are about worn out. They're probably walking them."

Corcoran brought Dude down to a slower trot, and Foster rode up beside him. "If they are, they might also know we're behind them," he said to the young deputy. "We gotta be aware of a possible attack. They may get themselves hidden in some rocks and wait for us."

"We're more than a day from crossing that range into the Diamond Valley. That would be where they might camp up. Since we aren't on a road or trail, they could hide out in that range and wait for us."

"Let's keep riding, Mr. Foster, and keep our eyes as wide open as we can. We have lots of daylight left in this day. Those mountains are still some way off. You know that girl. Will she put up a fight?"

"She's pretty headstrong, Terrence. One fine horseman, or should I say, horsewoman, too. I think we can plan on her doing what she can to get loose from them."

"Hope she's careful. They're killers for sure. Both Wells Fargo men driving the stage, the detective, and that one passenger, all shot to hell. She gets too rowdy, they might just shoot her." Corcoran was looking at the trail they were following, wondering just who these four outlaws were.

They've now killed five people in their kidnapping adventure, apparently without any kind of remorse. Would they kill their golden goose? Her father would pay thousands of dollars to get her back, and that's a lot of money.

His reverie was broken when Foster yelled out. "Dust, Corcoran. Way out there."

"We've made some good time, Foster. They had a good head start on us and we've closed up. Their horses must be in bad shape. If they see our dust, they might just hole up and wait for us, or they might try to race out for those hills and the safety of the rocks."

"Do you have any idea where they might be heading?"

"I'd bet several gold coins on a line camp somewhere in the Diamond Range. It's to their benefit to keep Louisa alive so they would have to have someplace where they could cook, not just over a campfire, and someplace they could defend as well."

Foster looked out across the prairie. "That range we're looking at has a valley on the other side, and there's another smaller range to cross before dipping into the Diamond Valley. I'd put money on them planning to spend the night in that little valley. There's springs, too." He said, pointing at the mountains a few miles in front of them.

"I'll bet her father will be screaming when he finds out. Would he pay a ransom?" Foster asked. "How big would it be?"

"He's been challenged before, Lou. How big? Many thousands would be my guess. He'll pay good for her return, and there will be a few men in town who will interfere in our attempt to get to her to get a big reward. We'll be tested, I'm afraid."

"Looks like we're gaining on them," Foster said. "Should we keep up this pace?"

"You bet. Drive 'em until their horses quit on 'em."

CHAPTER EIGHT

"WE GOT PEOPLE BEHIND US," the tall, thin man, Pete Chambers, said. "I thought you said that heavy man I emptied my gun into was the Wells Fargo detective? You said Corcoran rode out of town last night, too. Who are these people?" It was a challenge that the rest chose to ignore.

Any little change from what he thought was the plan would set Chambers off. First, the range they were looking to cross was much farther away than he'd been told, and now, there are riders coming up from behind. Would they make that range? Their food and water was on the other side.

Jonas Johnson, now riding with the gang, shook his head. "I saw Corcoran and Foster ride out of town, Pete. I don't know who that might be." Johnson rode out less than ten minutes behind Corcoran, leading a horse for Louisa to ride. Did that mean they planned from the start to kill everyone on that coach? That they did not plan on taking the coach teams?

Chambers took a quick look all around and shook his head. "Can't stop, get hid, and ambush those jaspers. Ain't no place to hide. Ain't across that ridge where our food is. Where we planned to stop for the evening," Chambers continued. "But we can't push these horses too much more. They'll just quit on us. Gotta fort up somewhere, I'm afraid."

"We'll be in those hills, yonder, soon enough. There's plenty of rocks to get behind." Shorty Duggan pointed at the hills, still a good five miles in front of them. "I know we wanted to be on the other side of those hills before stopping, but those men behind us are moving right along."

"Let's trot easy for as long as we dare, hoping the horses will have a little bottom to them if we need to make a dash for a rock outcrop," Chambers said. "Keep a good hold of that woman's horse, Jake. Let's go." The tall one had taken control of the gang and liked how things were working out.

Even if those yahoos following us catch up, we'll kill them just like we killed every single person on that stage. He seemed to forget there were several survivors, witnesses. He wasn't aware that the screaming woman had not been shot, she was just passed out when they ran off. *No one knows who we are, what we look like, or even how we sound. Get rid of those following, get ten thousand dollars from old man Jackson, and Mexico here I come.* He had no plans on sharing that ten thousand with the others. Was he aware that the stranger in buckskins was asking for twenty thousand?

In the back of Chamber's mind was a not very well put together plan that included killing the other gang members and Louisa. Banker Jackson would be paying for a dead daughter. Chambers almost chuckled, thinking about that. *I'll take the train to San Francisco and catch a nice sea-going ride to Mexico. I'll live like a king, drink the best tequila, smoke Havana cigars, and have women beg for my pleasures.*

Each of the outlaws spent time looking back over their shoulders at the dust being kicked up by the two horsemen following them. "We better be quick about finding some rocks to get behind," Shorty said. "Those two are catching up."

"See those rocks that look like spires, off to the left a bit? I make them about three miles."

"Closer to four, Chambers," Shorty said. "You thinking of making a hard run for them?"

"If we don't, we'll be in the open when those two behind us catch up. Let's go." He put the spurs to his tired horse, made sure Jake and the girl were with him, and hoped that Shorty and Johnson were too.

The horses had spent a long two days being ridden hard from Eureka to where they planned to rob the stage, and then a hard ride up to this point. They had been at a full run for way too long a period and weren't up to another two-or three-mile race, uphill, to those spires of rock.

Johnson's horse was in the best shape, but he rode so seldom that it really wasn't at all. Jake Hubbard's horse and the one Louisa was riding were leading as the gang bolted for the rocky hillside. Chambers could feel his horse try to keep up, but it just didn't have anything left in the tank. He fell behind and saw that the two followers were catching up quickly.

Shorty Duggan was in the lead along with Johnson. Hubbard and Louisa were twenty or so yards behind, and Chambers fell to about fifty yards behind. Shorty saw the problem, gave up on the tall spires, and rode for a group of rocks just up the slope, bailing off his horse when he got there. Hubbard led himself and Louisa into the rocky area, and Johnson followed. Johnson, as planned earlier, took control of the horses and led them behind a group of rocks out of where bullets might fly, and tethered them on some bushes.

Pete Chamber's horse was down to a slow walk by the time he got to the rocks, and he jumped off and ran to where the others were. Men were checking their rifles and handguns, making sure everything was loaded and ready.

"That horse is gonna give us away," Shorty yelled. "Get it put away, Chambers. Quick, man. Damn. Run that horse behind some rocks."

It didn't really matter, as Foster and Corcoran seemed to see what was going on and had spurred their horses into a hard charge, closing fast. Did they see Chambers? Did they see the lone horse on the hillside? Chambers couldn't get the horse to move. It stood still, shaking all over. Too tired to care while Chambers screamed at it, kicked it, and whipped it with the long reins.

At the sound of the two horses pounding closer, Chambers turned and ran for the rocks, ducking in next to Hubbard and Louisa. She had her scarf off and was waving it in the air, and Hubbard turned and drove a fist into her nose, knocking her to the ground. She cried out, and he snarled at her to be quiet or get another fist to the head.

"You bastard," she screamed. "You'll hang for this. My father will see to it that you hang."

Hubbard slapped her again, and Jake grabbed her. She tried to kick him, and he kicked her in the head. She slumped, passed out. "Don't kill her, Jake. She's worth thousands to us. Keep her alive."

"Damned spitfire is what she is. Got a lot of fire, that girl does. Gonna be fun tonight, eh Chambers?"

She whimpered, not fully out, curled up on the sand and dirt, wiping blood from her nose. *I hope that's Lou and Corcoran following us. These men will kill me, and I gotta fight them until Lou and Terrence can get me out of this.* Her eyes were blazing as she wiped away some blood and tears. She fought Jake Hubbard off as he tried to jerk her to her feet.

Hubbard shoved her behind a big jutting rock, told her to sit and not move as he drew his weapon. "No," she cried out, but then saw all the men had their weapons out and knew that Corcoran had to be close. All the others found their own rock and had weapons in hand. Shorty had the only rifle and watched the two riders come on fast. "They'll be in range soon, boys, and we can take a much-needed rest."

Hubbard struggled to get Louisa behind a rock, and she reached out and scratched his face, over and over. The fist slammed her across the side of the head, and she fell to the ground, unconscious. "Damn you, girl," Jake said, wiping blood from deep scratches. He dragged her to the side of a rock and took up a position to be able to shoot and keep an eye on his hostage.

———

"THEY'RE MAKING for those rocks, Lou. Let your horse follow me, and you keep your eyes on the men. We will need to know almost exactly where they are. They are sure to have rifles, so we'll find some rocks of our own. Let's get as close as possible," Corcoran said, kicking Dude into a full gallop.

The distance closed fast, and when Corcoran saw the white smoke from a rifle, he brought Dude to a halt and ran for some rocks. Foster followed and found a rock twenty or so feet to Corcoran's right. Both men had their rifles and saddlebags with them. They already had canteens hanging from their shoulders. Saddlebags had extra ammunition and some food.

"Only the one shot, Terrence," Lou called out. "They're all bunched up around that big boulder. They're behind busted-up rocks at its base."

"I see where you're saying. We gotta get closer. I'm gonna break for that big rock in front of me." He was running hard, Foster put three shots into the outlaws' lair, and there was no return fire.

Interesting, Corcoran mused, looking at the three hundred yards slightly uphill. *Only the one shot has been fired. Only one rifle among 'em?* He chuckled at the thought. When he turned, he saw Foster taking a long, slow aim at something. *Long shot, but that boy's got a good eye.*

Foster's Winchester barked, and Corcoran saw a man crumple a second or two later. "Good shooting, Lou. Best if we get a little closer. I'm going for that moss-covered rock."

"I'll cover," Foster yelled back, and Corcoran made the sprint, sand being kicked up around his feet. Sliding behind the rock, he rolled and fired two or three rounds toward the higher rocks, and he felt Foster plow in next to him. "Okay, are you?"

"One of those bullets was close enough to sing to me, but I'm fine. How many people are we talking about?" Foster asked.

"I'm sure I counted five horses," Corcoran said. "You took one down, and Louisa would have been riding one, so we're probably looking at three men up there. Something to remember, Lou. These men have no use for someone's life. They are sure to use Louisa if they think they can get away."

"Kill her? No!" Lou barked. "Won't allow that. Won't happen if I'm around." He looked up hill into those rocks. *She's in there, somewhere, and she knows that Corcoran and I are out here. Does it mean anything to her that it's Lou Foster here to save her? Does she remember me opening my heart to her just a few years ago?*

He gritted his teeth, trying to see if there was a safe way of getting up and into those rocks. There was no movement that he could see, just rocks heating up in the springtime sunshine. "We have water, Corcoran. I hope Louisa has some."

Corcoran smiled, thinking about that. *That boy's been in love with that girl for a long time. Maybe she'll find out when this is all over.* His mind clouded quickly as he knew just how much danger that girl was in.

Would they use her to make an escape? Would they violate her if this stand-off goes into the late night? How can we bring this to a safe end quickly?

CHAPTER NINE

"HE DEAD?" Pete Chambers called out as Shorty Duggan pulled Jonas Johnson's limp body back behind a rock.

"Saves us the trouble," Shorty yelled out. "One of those jaspers is a fine shooter. Let's keep that in mind. We're down to three. Gotta kill those two and get the hell out of here. Our food and water cache is on the other side of this mountain. Shouldn't have run those horses as hard as we did."

"Ain't the right time to argue about that," Chambers called out. "You got the rifle, kill those two. No way these handguns can reach out there."

Shorty growled something and turned back to where he could see where he thought the two men were. His head throbbed, and he was well aware he was bleeding again. That long ride took all his energy, and he was hungry, thirsty, and angry. This isn't what he would have planned, and now the great planner, Chambers, was suggesting he was responsible.

Shorty shook his head slowly, trying to ease the pain,

and turned in time to see one of the men down slope sprint for a rock. He brought his rifle up when the second man broke and ran. Shorty fired, but knew right away he had missed. *Oh, damn, that hurts.* The recoil and blast from the rifle brought intense pain, and Shorty almost dropped the rifle. *So that's how they're gonna do it. My best bet is to let that first man go and concentrate on killing the second man. They don't know where I am, so anything that first man sends my way won't be close.* He sat down behind the rock, cradling the rifle, and gently rubbed the bloody bandage at the back of his head.

It was still spring, but out on the plain like they were, hiding behind rocks, it was hot. The sun beat down on everyone, the only good being that Corcoran and Foster had water and limited food. "Any one of you bastards bring water?" Chambers knew he didn't, and when no one answered, he split the air with some foul words.

It was Shorty who said we should ride light, and so we cached food and water in a canyon on the other side of this range. Just a few hours ride from here, damn. Chambers was one of those men who rarely offered a plan of his own but was first to criticize one if it didn't prove out. He was sweating hard, the sun was past its zenith, but there were still several hours before it might cool off some.

There wasn't a ledge to hide under, a tree or bush either, and Pete Chambers knew they had to kill those two men out there and move out soon, or they would die. He had to blame someone for not having water, blame someone for not having rifles, blame someone for not having food. *Shorty is responsible for this. He'll not live to see any of that ransom money. Got to get out of this mess he's led us into.*

Both Corcoran and Foster had canteens strapped across their shoulders when they jumped from their horses, and they also had food in their saddlebags. Some venison jerky, a few biscuits, even an apple or two from the hotel. Like the outlaws, they weren't prepared for this long ride.

The heat built fast as the afternoon wore on. Shorty took one shot at Corcoran after Foster made the first move, and missed long. "Damn it. I'm shooting downhill. Forgot that. I'll get him next time." The toughness he was always so proud of was worn thin, his head ached, and he just wanted to lay down in the sand and gravel and go to sleep.

Sweat was running down his forehead, and he spent time wiping it away. Finally, he untied his bandanna and retied it around his head, pushing his hat back. The pain from his bashed-in skull was fierce, but he got the rag tied loosely. He turned and saw that Chambers had done the same thing.

Jake Hubbard was tucked behind a rock with Louisa who was crying, moaning, making a real scene. On purpose? To drive that fat bastard crazy? She vowed he would never hurt her again. The heat was intense, and she knew that without water, these men would soon collapse. *I have to be ready when this man collapses. I don't dare move around, use up my energy. Quit antagonizing this man and save my energy.* She was much younger than any of them but had lived a relatively easy life, going to school south of San Francisco.

Her strength came from all those years growing up in Eureka, playing in the majestic Diamond Mountains, and enjoying the benefits of a wealthy family. Will she be strong enough to fend this man off?

Each of the men was far stronger than the girl, but she knew she was in fine physical shape, would last at least as long as they, maybe longer. *I have to stop crying, stop being a baby, and be ready to fight.*

Shorty's stomach was beginning to give him serious grief, and he knew he would have to move Jonas Johnson's body. The sun was having a field day, and there was bloat and foul air in the immediate area. Flies by the hundreds were gathering, laying their eggs. It was going to get worse, and soon. He got up and started to move around and away from the body when a bullet whizzed past his head, splashing into the rock. He was stung by pieces of the rock being blasted away and fell back into the sand. "Damn."

"Thought I had him," Corcoran muttered. "He moves like that again, and I will." He wiped the sweat from his face and scrunched down into the sand. "We need to get a little closer, Lou. Whoever that is shooting at us every time we move has worked out that after I run, you run. We gotta do it different. After I run, you stay put for some time, and maybe I'll have a shot. Cover me," he yelled and sprinted another ten yards closer to the outlaws.

"Ow!" he yelled, hitting the dirt and rolling into position behind some jagged rocks.

"You hit?"

"No," Corcoran answered. "Fell onto a sharp point of

rock. Damn." He got as much behind the rock as possible and pulled his shirt open, seeing a long laceration on the side of his chest. He pulled his bandana off and used it to stop the bleeding. "Might as well have been shot. Rock took a fine gouge out of me. I'll be okay."

Foster put three rounds into the rocks where Shorty was and then settled down, reloading his Winchester. Corcoran waited and watched, knowing that the shooter up in those rocks was waiting for Lou to make his run.

There he is. Corcoran leveled his rifle, adjusting for shooting uphill, and squeezed the trigger. Both he and Foster saw the man get thrown back from the impact and fall out across the rocks. "Nice shooting, boss. They're down to two now."

"Yup, and one of them has a rifle trained on Louisa, you can bet on that. This is one hot day, Lou. We gotta use that against them. We don't know what they have with them. If we can't make a move on them before sunset, we're in for a miserable night. Any ideas?"

"I'll think on that, Terrence. You?"

Corcoran laughed. "I'll think on that," he called back.

Foster looked left and right, hoping maybe to see a runoff culvert, an actual stand of rocks, or trees, and found nothing. "Except for these few rocks we're in, there ain't nothing to help us," he called out. "I was hoping for a ditch or something."

"Me too." Corcoran rested his back on the rock he was behind and tried to work on a plan. *Best bet is to wait for dark. There are two of us, and there are two men up there, but they have Louisa with them. That should help us, but sure as hell, whoever is holding her will use her as a way of getting out.*

"I'm moving, Lou. You follow. About ten yards at a time unless we draw heavy fire." He unfolded, all six feet of him, and had two steps under him before he was upright, made two more steps and slid behind a jumble of rocks on the hillside. Lou didn't see any movement higher up on the ridge and raced to slide in next to Corcoran.

"No shots fired, Lou. Let's do that again," and he was racing up that hillside to the next scramble of rocks. Again, no one fired, and Lou slid in next to him.

"We're coming close to where those two men should be. At least one of them must be with Louisa."

"The only shots that have been fired at us were rifle fire, Terrence. I wonder if those fine gents only had that one rifle? Even so, we're within pistol range now."

———————

CHAMBERS, long and lean, was suffering from the heat, the sun beating down and reflected from the rocks. "Shorty," he called out. "Those men are moving. Kill 'em." He didn't get an answer and called out to Jake Hubbard.

"Jake, can you see Shorty? Was he hit? We gotta stop those two." Jake wondered if he heard panic when Pete called out. He was having some trouble seeing, sweating so hard, and listening to that girl's constant crying. He checked to make sure Louisa's legs were still tied and crawled out from his lair to look for Shorty. He found the man sprawled on his back, his chest covered in slowly drying blood.

"Shorty's dead," Jake called back. *This ain't good. Just me and Chambers now, and that screaming girl. Those two that followed us have rifles. We gotta get out of here.* "He's got the only rifle, and I don't think I can get to him without getting shot." Both men were now showing signs of panic.

"You gotta try, Jake. Get to him and get that rifle. This heat is gonna kill both of us if you don't."

Why me? Jake thought. *Why not you? Who put you in charge?* Jake being overweight was having its effect, as well. Sweat rolling off him, his energy level at its lowest, and the fact that he had been hearing mean talk from their hostage for hours, combined to make the man weak.

He was no more than twenty yards from the rocks where Shorty was sprawled, but the way there was wide open to the men out on the plain. They'd nail him after his first step. Even if Pete Chambers fired a couple of shots first, they were out of range.

"Ain't gonna do it, Pete. I wouldn't make the first step." As he spoke, he saw Corcoran and Foster move another ten to fifteen yards closer to where he was. He pulled his revolver, put that sixth bullet in, and settled down to get a good, stable shot in. He saw the rock Corcoran was crouched behind, and waited for the man to make his move.

Corcoran jumped up and dashed forward, while Hubbard fired twice with that forty-five pistol, and saw the sand spray well in front of the man as he dived behind some rocks. Foster followed immediately.

"Damn it, Pete. They are out of range of my pistol. Why haven't you shot at anything?"

"Get that rifle, Jake. Get it and kill those men." Chamber's voice was cracking, which told Hubbard that a lack of water and the heat was having its effect on the man. He knew he, too, was weak, tired, hungry, and trapped behind this rock. His only salvation was that rifle, and when Louisa cried out, his plan came together. *That girl is gonna get us out of here.*

CHAPTER TEN

"It's been several minutes without a shot, Foster. Those last shots fell short, so let's move forward quickly. Don't wait, just follow me, and we'll get as close as possible to that ridge." Corcoran braced his foot for the race and took off, covering a long twenty yards, slid under some jumbled-up rocks, and felt Foster slide in behind him. No shots were fired.

What are we dealing with? Sweat was running down his face, his shirt was stuck to his back, and Corcoran was frustrated. *Obviously, the purpose behind all this is to trade Louisa Jackson for money from her father, but there's something missing. There has been almost no planning from whoever is running this show, and now they're trapped in a jumble of rocks on the side of a hill.*

"We have to get this shut down, Lou," Corcoran said. "They have to know they're trapped, can't get out, and their next step is panic."

"Think they'll kill Louisa?" Foster asked. "I'd hate for

that to happen. She's changed since growing up. Has big plans for the rest of her life, and these ugly bastards have her trapped with them."

Corcoran gave his young deputy a long look. "I'd say you've changed a bit, too, Mr. Foster. No, I think they'll do everything they can to keep her alive. She's not only worth money from her father, but right now, she might be worth their lives. An exchange. They want the banker to pay them big money, but when it comes down to living through this current problem, they might use her in exchange for them getting away."

"Would you do that?" Foster's eyes were wide as he turned quickly to look at Corcoran, who simply cocked his head, not really giving an answer. *So many people are already dead because of these two that are left. The first holdup, the second, and the kidnapping. These men here. I can't let Louisa die out here.*

"Let's hope we don't have to answer that question, Lou. Right now, we have men up on that ridge who are desperate, have a woman hostage, and have killed other men. Let's put all our concentration on getting them."

The hillside was a long, gentle slope to a rocky ridge along the spine. It was the first in a stair-step series of ridges that would eventually allow one to look down on the long valley where the outlaws think their food and water are waiting for them. "We've got to get this ended, Lou," Corcoran said. "This early spring heat is draining our energy fast. Louisa is up there with those killers, and sure as we're sitting here, they'll use her to get out."

Foster pointed out a cleft in the rocks. "That's where

the man with the rifle was. We're more than within pistol range." He wiped sweat from his face. "I wonder where they have their horses stashed? Ours are well down there behind us. Think they're setting up for a getaway?"

"I'll say. I don't see any movement, and I'm sure we'd be close enough to hear if they were yelling back and forth. How far is that cleft? Fifty yards?"

"At least," Foster said. "I can't run uphill for fifty yards, Corcoran, not in this heat. How about if I worm my way, rock to rock, bush to bush, and you keep their heads down?" Foster said. "We haven't heard anything from Louisa, either. No yelling or screaming. God, I hope she's still alive."

Corcoran had his rifle reloaded, his pistol fully loaded, and nodded for Foster to make his move. "Don't know where fire might come from, Lou, so make short, quick moves. It's not that late in the afternoon, so let's hope the heat's got to them, too." *That boy's been holding thoughts for that girl for a long time. Those thoughts will drive him up this hill better than anything I could say.*

Foster took a deep breath, saw his target, sprinted, dove, and took a quick look. No shots were fired, and he ran again and dove. Still no fire coming his way, and he did it again. This time, he heard Corcoran fire his rifle twice.

"Run, Foster, run," Corcoran yelled.

He did and kept going, that last fifteen to twenty yards into the cleft in the rock wall, and almost falling on Shorty Duggan's swollen body. The flies were thick, making a lot of noise. Lou saw Shorty's rifle and grabbed it, moving quickly away from the body.

He was out of breath, taking deep gulps of hot, foul air. His head was dripping sweat, his shirt soaking wet, and his legs felt like dead logs. *Lordy, lord, that was a run. Shorty Duggan,* he thought, looking at the body. *I should have known.*

He spent a fast couple of moments orienting himself, trying to figure out where those shots earlier were coming from, and trying his best to see someone. *Where are those two men? Where have they got* Louisa *stashed?* He knew he had to move, but which direction? He didn't want to rush right into someone with a gun pointed at him.

"Tired," he whispered. "This heat is fierce." The heat in that little rock-walled den was stifling, and coupled with the beginnings of Shorty's body starting to rot, was motive enough to move forward. He spun around when a small cascade of gravel slid down behind him, followed by the hefty Jake Hubbard. Foster fired the rifle from his hip, driving hot lead deep into Jake's chest. He levered another round into his Winchester, waiting for that second man, who never appeared.

"You get him, Jake?" Pete Chambers called out, and Lou turned to where the voice came from and didn't try to answer. *You're mine, mister. Damn, I wish I knew where Louisa is.* He slowly climbed out of the cleft of rocks, took a long look at the dead man and recognized him immediately. He looked down the slope to where Corcoran was kneeling behind a rock, his rifle at the ready, and Corcoran pointed off to his left. Foster nodded and looked in that direction, saw Chambers sitting behind a boulder with a handgun.

Why didn't that guy shoot at me as I ran up the hill? Why isn't he shooting at Corcoran? It was Chambers himself who gave his place away. "Answer me, Jake. Did you get him?"

Foster now knew where the last man was but couldn't see him now. He had ducked down behind those rocks. Was Louisa with him? He also saw that there was no other movement in or around where they were. His first thought was to call out for Louisa but he knew that was the wrong thing to do.

"Something's wrong here," Foster whispered, moving further away from Shorty's festering body and away from where Jake Hubbard lay bleeding and dead. "Very careful now, old man." Sometimes crawling, sometimes on hands and knees, Foster moved silently toward where that voice was calling for Jake.

Foster had to chuckle just a bit. "Losers," he whispered to himself. "Jake Hubbard and Shorty Duggan. I wonder if that's Pete Chambers doing all the calling-out?"

As he moved around a rock, something off to his right moved, and he jerked the rifle to shoot and saw Louisa, her feet and wrists tied together, slumped behind a rock. He quickly moved to her side. "Quiet now, Louisa. It's Lou Foster. No noise now. We'll get you out of this."

She was only about half conscious, but her eyes flickered up to meet his, and she nodded that she understood. He got the ropes off, and she flung her arms around the big man, holding on for dear life, sobbing, and trying to be as quiet as possible.

"We'll have all the time in the world to talk, Louisa, but I have one more man to get before you're safe," he whispered. "Just nod yes or no. Are you hurt?" She shook her head but held out her arms and pointed at her feet. The ropes hadn't been kind, and she was skinned and cut.

"I'll live," she whispered back. He had to gently remove her arms from his neck, didn't want to, wanted to put his arms around her and carry her off, but there was that last man to get before they were safe.

"Don't move," he whispered, slowly getting to his feet. "Use this if you have to," he said, and handed her Shorty's rifle. He cradled his and slowly made his way toward where that voice had called out. She never took her eyes from him, and he couldn't hide the smile despite the danger.

He slipped back to where he first saw Louisa and tried to figure out where that last man was.

———

CHAMBERS WAS SWEATING PROFUSELY, partly from the spring sun, partly from seeing Corcoran coming on fast. He had drunk all his water, didn't know where his compadres were, and watched almost helplessly as Corcoran slowly moved, rock to rock, up the hill toward him. Waves of heat could be seen out and across the open plain, having an effect on the man's vision. *All these people,* he thought, *I helped bring together to accomplish one thing. Kidnap Louisa Jackson and hold her for ransom. Where is Mr. Big, the man with the plan? He's strutting around somewhere, wearing that buckskin shirt, waiting for word that we have her. Am I the only one left?*

His anger had risen almost to the same level as his panic as he continued to watch Corcoran come for him.

What went wrong? Mr. Big had this so well planned. Leave food and water cached, get the girl, contact Mr. Big. Get our money. What went wrong?

He wiped the sweat away, saw that Corcoran was well within the range of his revolver, but still hadn't heard from Jake, who wouldn't answer. *Why? Was he dead? Or, did he run off and leave the tall, thin man? The girl,* he thought. *Is she with Jake?* The panic brought as much sweat as the springtime heat, and Pete Chambers could feel the end coming. "I ain't gonna die on this stinking rock," he muttered.

He spent several minutes taking in the landscape, searching for a way out. He would not be alone, either. That girl will be his partner in escape. He spotted the small cavern, not big enough to be a canyon, where the horses were picketed. He slumped, knowing that Corcoran was between him and the horses, and it dawned on him, he didn't know where Jake had the girl hidden.

"I've got to get out of here. All the others have either run off and left me or..." he said, as he slumped down onto the dirt and rocks. "Got to get out of here," he cried softly. All those wonderful plans of having oysters in San Francisco and tequila in Mexico, of ten thousand dollars filling his pockets, and pretty women wanting to be with him. "Gone," he sobbed. "Gone."

Corcoran was close now, hadn't drawn a shot for some time, and moved toward a large stand of rocks. Chambers fired three shots at the moving man and didn't come close. His vision was washed away by sweat, panic, and fear.

"I gotcha," Foster whispered as the shots were fired. He was just a few short yards from whoever fired them, but there was a rock wall in between. *He don't got no idea where I am.* Foster smiled. *Easy now, nice and easy.*

Chambers took another shot, giving Foster the idea that the man was totally involved in looking down the hillside. Foster stepped around the rock wall and saw Chambers about to take another shot.

"Drop it," Foster commanded. Chambers swung around, and a rifle slug tore through his shoulder. He dropped the gun, grabbed for his shoulder, and Foster stepped forward and slammed his rifle into the outlaw's head, knocking him out cold. The bullet did terrible damage to the man's shoulder but didn't hit any of the major blood arteries.

"I got him, Corcoran. Come on up. I've got Louisa, too." Foster yelled it out, saw Corcoran move uphill, and almost ran back to Louisa. She heard his yelling and was on the move. They met halfway. When Corcoran finally joined them, they were still holding on to each other, with her sobbing and him smiling.

"That can wait," Corcoran said. "Any others alive up here?"

"No," Foster said, still smiling, still holding onto Louisa. He looked closely at Corcoran. "I know all these people. Every single, stinking one of them."

"I know that man back there, Lou. He's a loser. How about those you've seen?"

"Same thing. Losers. They all hang out together, along with Shorty Duggan. Only one has a full-time job."

"It's going to take us a while to get back to town, but

somewhere in that beautiful little village of ours is a person who planned all this," Corcoran said. "That's our job, Mr. Foster. Shake him out."

"Does that mean we're spending the night out here?" Louisa was shaking her head.

CHAPTER ELEVEN

"WE DON'T HAVE ANY CHOICE," Corcoran said. "We gotta spend the night here. Let's gather the horses and see what kind of supplies we might have."

"I know we have some food and some medicines," Foster said. "We got one wounded and three dead, though. We're going to need a lot more water than we have." He looked at Louisa and remembered from years ago what a strong person she was.

She's tough, and if she's still the girl I remember, she'll come through. "We're looking at limited food and water, Corcoran, but we'll have all those horses, too. We'll need to find water as soon as possible."

"We'll take it one problem at a time, Lou." Corcoran chuckled, looking around. "The wounded man is Pete Chambers. Let's get him down here and get some kind of camp set up."

It took a few hours to find all the horses and get them back to a small camp. Louisa had a fire going and was cleaning the wound to Chambers's shoulder. "Touch me

wrong once more, mister, and you'll wish you were dead."
She jabbed the wound to make her point, and Chambers
cried out in pain. "I think you understand," she growled.

Corcoran watched the little play and had to chuckle.
"He's lost a lot of blood, Terrence. That bullet did a lot of
damage." All she had was the remnants of the wounded
man's shirt to clean the wound. "We need some hot
water."

"Do your best. We'll ride out in the morning."

"What about those bodies?"

"We'll cover them with rocks the best we can.
Couldn't dig a grave in these rocks even if we wanted to."
Corcoran saw the effects of the comment as it wrinkled
across her face. "This life of a lawman isn't easy, Louisa,"
Corcoran said. "Some of these men have relatives and
friends in Eureka, and they might come out and retrieve
the remains. The rock cairns will keep coyotes and
wolves away."

He paused for just a moment, watching the emotions
work through her pretty face. "The heat we've already
had today will continue for the next several days. It will
probably take us at least two, maybe three days to get
back to Eureka. In this heat, those bodies will deteriorate
rapidly. We can't bring them with us."

"It sounds cruel, Terrence, but I know it isn't. I've
lived a rather protected life, I guess. Daddy wouldn't even
clean a deer or antelope. Mama always took care of that.
I hope I'm more like Mama. I know I miss her. She
always liked Lou."

Corcoran saw her eyes go soft at the thought and
turned to the fire, reaching for the coffee pot. "Mr.

Foster's pulling all the saddlebags from the horses to see what we might find for supper. It's going to be a nasty ride back to Eureka."

Corcoran scowled at the thought of so little food. "Even if we'd seen a deer or antelope, we wouldn't have shot it," he muttered. "Would have brought a hail of bullets our way. I do hope that a really dumb jack rabbit wanders by."

No, Mr. Corcoran, it's going to be a wonderful two or three days. I hope Lou doesn't hold it against me the way I treated him when we were so much younger. What a man he is now.

Corcoran used the last of his water to make the coffee and knew that there was some water left in Foster's canteen. He had rounded up the canteens from the outlaws and had enough for them to have a drink in the morning. "We'll ride east, over the top of this ridge. There's a small valley and another ridge, and then we'll drop into the Diamond Valley."

"Is there water?" Louisa asked.

"Maybe in that small valley, a spring or two, but for sure when we dip into the Diamond Valley." He was trying to remember that small valley. "It isn't that small, really. A full day's ride across it. The horses will be forced to suffer some, I'm afraid. Some were ridden awfully hard today." He took a minute to look around at the sky and shook his head. "We're not lucky enough to face a spring thunderstorm, either."

Lou Foster came back into camp carrying a bunch of saddlebags over his shoulders. "I brought everything, Terrence. Might be some food, might even be something from whoever these fools worked for."

"Good thinking, Lou. I've always hunted in the Diamonds, but didn't you and your father run cattle in that next valley we'll have to cross?"

"All this country. We'll probably see a few old steers when we cross that next ridge. There's always one that'll get away." He chuckled at the thought.

"How about water?" Corcoran asked.

"Limited, but this being spring, there will be some. Watch for a cottonwood or two, and we'll find water." Most of those who traveled the open country of the west knew that. Do a little digging in a wet spot near a cottonwood, and you'll probably have some seepage. "We've got all of their horses plus ours. We're going to need an open spring with running water."

Louisa was going through the saddlebags, finding small packets of jerky, dried-up biscuits, and even some old slices of dried fruit. "These men didn't eat very well," she said. "I guess that means we won't either."

"Did you know any of the men who abducted you?" Corcoran was seated, leaning against a rock. Foster was stomping on uprooted sagebrush for the fire, and Louisa was sitting on the ground, her traveling gowns filthy and torn.

"Only Jonas Johnson. I remember him from when I went to school. He's younger than us, Lou," she said. "He wasn't very smart, either. I saw him in Austin, and it really surprised me when he was with the outlaws, stopping the stage."

She sucked in her breath, her eyes wide open. "Did they really have to kill all those people? Why, Lou? Why did they kill all those people?"

Foster moved over and sat down next to her. She grabbed his hand and squeezed it hard, and he saw tears form and run down her cheeks. "If I could answer that," he said. "They thought that would keep them from identifying them. It didn't have to be. There were a couple that survived, I'm sure."

Foster turned to Corcoran. "Do you suppose Mallory or Sheriff Kemp are following our trail?"

"You bet they are. And I would imagine when Sheriff Connor gets the wire about the holdup and kidnapping, that he'll be coming this way, as well." He scratched at some rocks and dirt and gave Louisa a big smile. "I imagine a certain banker we all know will be riding with Connor's posse."

"No, Terrence, he won't. He might hire somebody to ride with the sheriff, but he won't. He won't do anything if he can hire someone else to do it instead." She wiped away the tears, gave Lou Foster the saddest look he'd ever seen, and squeezed his hand even harder.

There was more silence than Corcoran had ever heard, and he stood up, grabbed some of the broken-up sage, and fed the fire. *So sad. She knows her father rather well. He hunted but wouldn't even clean his catch, and his daughter is kidnapped and he might hire someone to ride with the posse. No wonder she's leaving town.* He chuckled slightly, only to himself. *There are times I just don't like people.*

The sun was slowly falling into the majestic mountains to their west as the three nibbled on some jerky, chewed on tough, stringy dried fruit, and thought about what tomorrow might bring. Despite the heat of the spring sun, the chill in the air reminded those spread out around the fire that they weren't that far from winter. The high mountain desert could be frighteningly cold, helped some by a strong easterly wind.

———

"DID YOU GET THAT WIRE OFF?" George Kemp almost snarled as Austin Deputy Dirk Mallory stepped into the office.

"I did. Tex is packing a mule now, Sheriff. Ready to ride out whenever you are. Think that girl will survive?"

"Hard to say, Dirk. She's worth a lot of money alive, and it don't matter to them outlaws, as long as banker Jackson believes she's alive. You thinking of us riding out and have Tex follow us with the mule?"

"No, I think it's best if we all ride together."

"That's best. Let's get it on, then. We'll be riding into evening before long. We'll go as long as possible." Sheriff Kemp was a heavy man, not all from muscle and bone but from fine beef, pork, and potatoes. Men talked about how Kemp had never missed a meal and often added to his day's take with trips to the sideboard.

The Kemp ranch was in a canyon on the other side of the mountain from Austin, and the sheriff came into possession of his badge after killing off a gang of rustlers and thieves. As a younger man, he was a tall, tough wrangler and horse trainer at the family ranch.

As a sheriff, Kemp let his deputies handle the drunks and burglars, spending his time glad-handing his way up and down the main street in Austin.

"Don't want to kill the horses, Dirk. We'll ride at a

decent pace. Make sure Tex understands that. He sometimes gets all fired up and wants to run that horse of his right into the ground."

Dirk Mallory fought to hold in a snicker, listening to the sheriff. This will be a rather slow chase they'll be on. "We'll catch up to Corcoran. Have any ideas on who these outlaws are?"

"No, but their killing of Smoky Pierson will guarantee their hanging. Killing a Wells detective? 'Bout as dumb as I want to know."

Mallory kept his mouth shut but not his mind. *Pierson didn't have to die, either. If he'd let Corcoran's plan play out, none of this would have happened. Now, Pierson's dead, the girl is in the hands of outlaws, and Corcoran's on the chase. At least I'll be giving that hard-drinking Irisher some back up tomorrow.*

CHAPTER TWELVE

"I NEED YOUR HELP, HENDERSON," Sheriff Ed Connor said. He held a wire that had just come in from Austin. "It looks like Corcoran couldn't stop the young Jackson woman from taking the stage, which was held up. Several people were killed, but Louisa was taken hostage. Corcoran's on their trail."

"That ain't good," Jimmy Henderson said. He was standing behind the long bar in the Bonanza Club's saloon. "How can I help?"

"I'm putting together a posse and will need supplies for three days. You can bill the county," Connor said, a gleam in his eye. Henderson built the hotel, café, and saloon, and generally knew where every dime was. "Jake, our night jailer will have a mule over behind the café for you."

"I'll have it packed and ready for you, Ed. Who's going with you?"

"I've got Amos Lorenzo ready to ride, and looking for

at least one, maybe two more. That gives us five or six men, with Corcoran, Fowler, and me in the fight."

"With the outlaws, that's a lot of mouths to feed, Sheriff. You sure one mule full will be enough?"

"You have a point, but from what Kemp wired, we'll probably all come together forty miles or so north in the Diamond Valley. We can snare some grub from one of the ranches if we have to."

Connor left to get his people put together as Henderson worked to get the mule packed. Conner wanted his posse ready to ride out within the hour. Connor was pleased that Amos Lorenzo volunteered to ride with him. In his younger days, Lorenzo was a scout for the Army and was known for being able to find and follow signs left by animals and men.

"Interesting," Connor muttered, "that Enid Jackson himself isn't riding out with us. If that was my daughter being held by those killers, I'd be screaming to ride with the posse." His muttering was interrupted when Enid Jackson walked into the office.

"I'm glad you're still here, Ed," Jackson said. "I just received this wire. Came from Austin." He handed the paper to the sheriff.

Connor read the page quickly and then read it again. "Just came in?" The banker nodded. The sheriff shook his head. "That stage was hit, and your daughter was abducted hours ago, Enid. This says, quote, We have your daughter. If you want to see her again, you'll need to make twenty thousand dollars available, pronto. The next note will tell you exactly where to put that money. One mistake, Mr. Big Shot Banker, and you'll never see your daughter again. Unquote."

Ed Connor folded the note. "I want to keep this, Enid. This complicates the matter, I hope you know. It adds someone to the picture. This was sent by a member of the gang who wasn't a part of the robbery and massacre." He looked at the wire again. "Sent from Austin, but that doesn't mean this new person actually lives in Austin."

Connor walked to his desk and sat down. "You'll be getting instructions on where and how to deliver that money. I would suggest that you don't. Put it off. Let Corcoran and me get your daughter back safely."

Jackson snapped it out. "No, Sheriff. I'll give them the money. Money is just something we use, my daughter is why I live."

Connor stayed at the desk and frowned. *A group of killers has the girl, and according to Sheriff Kemp, they are racing across the desert for the Diamond Valley. Now, hours after the hold up, Jackson gets a wire. Who sent the wire? Is that person the boss of the gang? Or just somebody they paid to send it off?*

"I have to get the rest of my posse put together, Enid, and get on the trail. I wish you'd change your mind."

"I brought my best man to ride in your posse, Ed. He's outside now, packed and ready to ride. Heck Heckman's a good man, will serve you well."

"That's wonderful, Enid. With Amos Lorenzo and me, we'll ride out as soon as we pick up the pack mule from Jimmy Henderson. Try not to worry too much. We'll catch those bastards and bring Louisa home."

Enid Jackson thanked the sheriff, brought Heckman into the office, and headed back to his bank. "Have a cup of coffee while I finish up here, Heckman," Connor said.

Jackson is one strange fellow, Connor thought to himself. *Not a word about riding with us. No plea for us to save Louisa. Not even a question about this wire.* He tucked the wire in a desk drawer along with some other papers and got to his feet.

"Well, Heckman, let's get on the trail, eh?"

———

"EVERYBODY ARMED, GOT YOUR BEDROLLS?" The two men nodded. "Good. We'll ride north about forty miles, and then turn west into that range where I think we will probably find Corcoran and the killers.

"Today will be a hard ride, and tomorrow might be even harder. Amos, you take the mule, and Heck, you ride alongside me. Mount up."

"Forty miles is a long ride," Heckman said.

"Not really," Connor said. "We're getting a late start, so we might not make where I'd like to be. We'll camp at sundown. Corcoran's facing five killers who are holding a young girl hostage. That's why we're riding. Let's go."

What have I got, a sniveler? Wish I knew something about this Heckman feller. Connor was in the saddle first despite his bunged-up leg, and turned to see Amos Lorenzo give him a scowl. He chuckled. *Good old Amos. He'll keep this Heckman feller in shape.* And Connor led the group out of town. "When we catch up to those men, remember that they killed almost every person on that stagecoach. They need catching."

The road north followed the Eureka and Palisades railroad tracks and was well used. The first ten miles was easy and then they got into some hilly country. Connor took a bullet from an Indian cattle rustler several years ago, and the wound never healed properly. "How's that leg, Ed?" Lorenzo called out.

"Doing fine, Amos. Riding's good for it. It's walking that's difficult. How's the mule coming along?"

"Henderson's got her loaded down, but she's doing fine. How steep will that climb be in the morning?"

"We'll take it as slow as we dare," Connor said. "How about you, Heckman?"

"I'm ready to stop, Sheriff. I haven't ridden this far in years."

"Well, better get used to it. We're riding until sunset, and that's still a few hours away. I'd like to make Spender's Creek our camp. Good feed, good water, and wood for the fire."

"Looking at these tracks, Sheriff, I'd say those killers drove their horses mighty hard. They aren't going to make it as far as they might have thought if they keep that pace up."

"My thoughts, too, Mallory. Corcoran and Foster are following, not trying to chase 'em down. Corcoran's a good man, knows he'll catch up, probably finding killers with their dead horses."

Tex spat a glob of 'backy juice and cussed some. "What's that for, Tex?" Kemp asked.

"Driving these horses like that. Killing offense if you

ask me. Them horses are gonna be gaspin' if they keep it up. Man treats his animal like that needs a good killin'. Them horses ain't gonna be worth nothin' when we catch up. I'm lookin' forward to killing me one or two of them bastards."

"It's all right to be angry about that, Tex, I am too, but we ain't riding to kill. We're riding to capture. Let's keep that in mind."

"We got a late start, Sheriff, but we are making good time." Dirk Mallory said. "That ridge out there has to be crossed, and we'll ride into a nice little valley where we can camp if we don't catch up first."

"I've been in that valley, often," Tex said. "Usually, a couple of springs running full. We'll have water. I doubt they'll get there, though. Not the way they're pushing their horses. My money says we'll be camping with Corcoran this side of that ridge line. We have plenty of food, just have to hope there's water."

Dirk Mallory kept his eyes on the ridge for the next couple of hours, hoping to see some kind of sign that there was something going on. *Two deputies chasing five killers. When the two groups get together, there's going to be dust or smoke, and when that happens, we need to be there.*

Mallory saw the sheriff keep looking back over his shoulder. "Expecting someone, Sheriff?"

"No, Dirk. Watching the sun. Old Sol is diving for those mountains rapidly. We're going to have to start thinking about finding a place to camp. We're not going to be over the top of that ridge out there before dark like I'd hoped."

"I've been thinking the same thing," Tex said. We're several miles away, yet."

"That's what I've been looking for," Dirk Mallory said. He was pointing east. "Look along the base of those hills. Off to the right, just a bit from this trail. Is that smoke?"

"By god, it is," Tex almost yelled. "That ain't shooting smoke, neither," he said. "Wonder which side's got a fire going?" There were no chuckles among the men.

"We better damn well keep that in mind," Sheriff Kemp said. "We don't want to ride into a nest full of killers. Let's pick it up some, Tex, but keep our eyes wide open. Looks like that smoke's about three, maybe four miles away." He looked at Mallory.

"This is your kind of play, Dirk. Ride out there and find out who's making the smoke. We won't be far behind you. Tex, you ride with me, slowly."

Mallory had to chuckle at Kemp's word to the man with the mule, and put his horse in a nice trot that would eat those three or four miles in no time. As he got closer, he slowed the horse to a walk and did what he could to stay in behind rocks and brush until he got a couple of hundred yards out. *Ain't been seen that I can tell. Ease up as close as I dare and hope I can see someone.*

He stepped down and tied his horse off to some brush. It was an easy stalk as rocks and brush hid him well. Mallory spent a great amount of time in the great outdoors, was an excellent hunter, and moved through the desert as quiet as a snake. He was less than a hundred yards out when he heard a twig break behind him.

"Howdy, Dirk. Looking for a beer, are you?"

Mallory whirled around and came face-to-face with Terrence Corcoran, grinning at him. "Well, just damn me all to hell. Nice to see you, Corcoran. You have beer?"

CHAPTER THIRTEEN

SHERIFF KEMP and Tex rode into Corcoran's camp and
tied off their mounts. "I hope that mule has some food
under that canvas," Louisa said. "The last thing I had to
eat was a bowl of boiled oats at sunrise."

"Food and water, young lady," Sheriff Kemp said. "It's
good to see you alive." He turned to Corcoran. "Bring us
up to date, Corcoran. I only see one other person here."

Corcoran gave him a side-long look. *What was he
looking for, the entire gang, alive and well?* "It's been one very
long day, Sheriff," he said. "That's Pete Chambers, the
only survivor of the gang. He's shot bad, but he'll live.
The others are buried under rocks. They put up a hard
fight." Corcoran moved back to the fire and sat down.
"These people seemed to have no plan at all, and that just
doesn't sit right with me. All the men are from Eureka,
should know this country well, but did not have any real
plan."

"In what way?" Kemp asked.

"Specifically, in how to get away after kidnapping

Louisa. They ran their horses into the ground, couldn't get over that ridge there, had no food." He shook his head slowly back and forth. "There isn't any water this side of those hills," Corcoran said. "This was a mix-match, Sheriff. I'm seeing one person who did the planning and others who were supposed to carry it off. The planner isn't with the gang."

"That and the trail they left that could be read by a blind man, done 'em in," Lou Foster said. "From where we are, it's another two days to Eureka, and they had no food with them."

"Have you talked with this Chambers fellow?" Sheriff Kemp said. He was watching Tex put together a pot of coffee and smiled. "I think we can all use some of that, Tex."

Corcoran and Foster both nodded in agreement before Corcoran answered the question. "Not yet, Sheriff," Corcoran said. "It's possible they have food cached somewhere, but not close. We'll be topping that ridge in the morning. It is possible they have food on the other side."

"Not really sure about moving out in the morning," Kemp said. "The stage holdup, the killings, and the kidnap, all took place in Lander County. You can take Miss Jackson home to her father, but I'm afraid Mr. Chambers is now a prisoner of Lander County."

"I'll not argue territory with you, Sheriff. Saving Louisa Jackson was our only goal in the first place." Corcoran sat with his back to a rock. "I'm almost sure there's a hell of a lot more to this than we see. I'll work on that."

"More?" Dirk Mallory asked. "How would there be more?"

"Somebody put this all together," Corcoran said. "Somebody knew Louisa would be in Austin and would ride the stage home. Think about it. Taking the train from San Francisco, most people would have taken it all the way to Palisade to connect with the line to Eureka."

He stopped long enough to catch his breath. "Knowing when she was supposed to be in Austin and putting this so-called gang together was not done by any of the dead men or Chambers there. The dead men and the prisoner are not capable of this kind of thinking or planning, Sheriff."

Kemp warmed his hands over the fire and stared off into the distance. The sun had dipped below the horizon, and the chill in the springtime air moved in quickly. "You got any ideas who that person might be?"

"Not a one," Corcoran said and chuckled. "I'm going to start by looking at some of the banker's customers who might have a reason to get even with the man. Also, look to see if someone has been fired and wants to get even. There have been robbery attacks in the past, but this seems rather personal. Someone feels that they have been hurt by Jackson's bank."

"Sounds like a good plan. Chambers might have something to say about that," Sheriff Kemp said.

"He's in pain tonight, and it will be worse in the morning," Lou Foster said. "That shoulder's a real mess, Corcoran. You'd probably be best talking to him tonight. He might not be with us in the morning."

"We got medicine," Tex said. "I'll keep him alive.

How about you fine people move away from the fire, and I'll stir up vittles for us. Meat, taters, onions, and coffee comin' up. I'll work on the wounded man after supper."

First things first, Corcoran thought to himself and had to smile. *Old Tex is the kind of man to fit right in on a ride like we're on. Kemp must be up for re-election, wanting to make sure he keeps everything in Lander County.*

———

SHERIFF CONNOR SAW the sky lighten up dramatically as he added some wood to the fire and set the coffee pot on a rock sitting right in the flames. "Get up, boys, and shake 'em out. Sun's already halfway through the day."

Amos Lorenzo groaned but had to chuckle as well as he threw the blanket aside. "Lord, it's early, Ed. A man needs his sleep."

"You've had more than enough." Connor chuckled. "Heckman," he yelled at the other man, still wrapped tightly in a wool blanket. "Get up before I start kicking."

"I don't think I can," he wailed, but not moving. "Hurts."

"Gonna hurt worse if I have to kick you out of those blankets. Up, man, and I mean now." Sheriff Connor took two steps toward the inert Heckman, who saw him coming and wrestled free of the covers.

He fought his way into pants and boots and got to his feet, but not standing up straight. "I think I hurt my back," he said.

"Gonna hurt worse before this day's over," Lorenzo

said. "Shake it off, have some coffee while I mix up breakfast."

Connor walked off into the brush and relieved himself. *Just what we need on a ride to capture outlaws and save a young girl. Damn softy. I wonder if he knows where he is? Ain't been in the saddle for a long time, and that means he don't get out in the great outdoors very often.* "Dam it," Connor said right out loud. "That means we can't just ride off and leave him."

The Eureka County Sheriff was almost yelling by the time he got back to the fire. "You're riding with us, you'll keep up, and any cry-baby stuff will get you bruised and sore. Got that, Heckman? Got that?" He was right in the man's face, and Amos Lorenzo knew he had to step in before there was bloodshed.

"Easy, now, Ed. Let's get breakfast and coffee down. Everybody will feel better with full bellies."

Connor had to smile. "Glad you're with us, Amos. I'm gonna need you as the day wears on."

It was a quiet breakfast around a warm spring morning fire, the kind of morning Ed Connor would love to enjoy more than he is. The cold was being washed away by bright sunlight, big, white, puffy clouds off in the distance, not threatening, but indicating the possibility of thunderstorms later in the day.

This would be a perfect morning except for the moans and groans adding to the atmosphere. "All right, men, let's get saddled up." Connor kept a close eye on Heckman, but the man did a good job. Lorenzo got their camp taken down and packed on the mule, and it was time to ride. It was quiet as the three men began their long ride up and into the wide, high mountain valley. They weren't on a well-used trail as they made their climb. It was rocky, they had to make U-turns constantly in steep country. Heckman spent most of every minute complaining about everything.

By mid-morning, the springtime warmth of the morning turned to early summer heat. "Glad we filled all the canteens this morning," Connor said. "This day is gonna put blisters on rocks, I think."

It took more than two hours to make the climb to the ridge, and the horses were sweating profusely as they topped out. A stiff breeze met them, and they stopped to let the horses cool off, as well as themselves. "Feels pretty good, eh, Mr. Heckman," Amos Lorenzo said. "We'll lose this fine breeze as we make our way down into the valley."

Amos Lorenzo was a hunter, had been a guide in years past, and took great pleasure in being out. He let his gaze follow the terrain down into the valley, and cast long looks across the wide expanse and smiled gently. Stands of piñon and stunted cedar were mixed with sage and rabbit brush. He saw gatherings of cottonwood, hoping that might mean water, and what, to this old gent, a fine place to graze a herd during the summer.

Heckman didn't answer, he just groaned. "Sit up straight, Heckman. Put some weight in them stirrups, and enjoy the view. It'll take several hours before we make a stop. Your boss's daughter is depending on you," Connor shouted.

"Watch for springs, Amos. When we meet up with Corcoran, he'll have a mess of horses and people with him." Connor was riding lead with Lorenzo, the mule, and Heckman behind.

"You've already decided that Corcoran has captured that gang and saved Miss Jackson, eh, Ed?" Lorenzo was chuckling but also casting his eyes across the wide valley, seeing if there might be a copse of cottonwood trees guarding a spring.

"Looks like it'll be a hot one, again," Connor said. "What are we looking at, Amos? About fifteen, maybe twenty miles to that ridge out there? If what Kemp said in his wire about where the gang lit out to, they would be heading for that ridge and this valley. Haven't seen any smoke."

"I don't think they made it this far, Ed," Lorenzo said. "I don't see any smoke either. No camps that I can see." *This isn't the way I would have come if I was leading the gang,* Amos Lorenzo thought. *They left out from the bottom of that canyon east of Austin, they could have taken the main road for ten miles or so and snuck into the Monitor Valley. Coming north and east put them in mighty dry country.*

Lorenzo was speculating as a man who spends a lot of time in the outdoors. Did the gang have a mule packed with food? Did they know where fresh water might be seeping out of the ground? *We don't know the first thing about that gang. Hope Corcoran and that young deputy with him remember to be smart.*

Connor was watching Heckman sway in the saddle and shook his head. "Why did Jackson send you, Heckman? Why didn't he come himself? You're a wreck, but we can't let up, and we can't just ride off and leave you, either."

"You're as bad a man as Mr. Jackson, Sheriff. No feelings for other people. Jackson finds somebody down, he makes it worse. I work for him because I have to, not because I want to. Almost everyone who works for the man hates him. He'd drive a stake through your heart if he felt it would be in his best interest."

Connor sat back in his saddle and thought about that. *Is this what led to the kidnapping of Louisa? An employee hates the old man, puts together a gang and kidnaps her? Twenty thousand dollars ransom would do wonders for a man's feelings if he was a disgruntled employee.*

"Let's keep our eyes open. Watch for smoke from a campfire or dust from some riders. We'll stop in an hour or so for a midday break," Connor said, riding off from Heckman. "You get tough, Mr. Heckman. We might still end up in a gun fight with a gang of killers."

"Sure wish we knew what was going on on the other side of that ridge, boss," Amos said.

CHAPTER FOURTEEN

TEX WAS PUTTING everything away following breakfast. "I don't think you folks was ever gonna stop eating. Sheriff, you remember telling me I was bringing too much? Well, damn me, but I don't think I brought enough."

"All we need is enough for breakfast, Tex." Sheriff George Kemp scowled as he poured some more coffee.

"Well, no, that ain't true," Tex said. He cocked his head and gave the sheriff a long look. "We got to give Corcoran and Foster enough to make a two-day trip back to Eureka. And that pretty gal, too."

Kemp scowled even more as Tex talked and broke it off. "Connor will be bringing food for them. No need for us to be feeding them."

"You're angry at something more than my packing, Sheriff. Want to talk about it?" Tex had worked at the Kemp ranch before Kemp became sheriff and has been with the sheriff all these years as well. Kemp was one of those men who became angry about one thing and then let his anger carry on to two or three other things as well.

"Ain't nothin' Tex." The sheriff started to turn away, halted, and turned back on the night jailer. "Damn right I'm upset. Corcoran just rides into our county and takes over. I'm the damn sheriff, Tex."

"Well," Tex drawled it out, "I seem to remember you sending out seeking his help. Now, you get his help and you're all buffaloed. Man shouldn't ask for help if he's gonna get upset gettin' that help, Sheriff."

Kemp snorted and stood up as tall as he could. "Get to packin'. We're gettin' out of here. Only give 'em enough food for one meal."

Tex was an old-line Texas lawman who simply couldn't just retire on a ten-acre spread by a lively stream. He had to keep his hands in the game and gladly took the job of night jailer for Lander County when Kemp was elected. His background in Texas justice was solid, and George Kemp often called on Tex to discuss crime in Austin.

"You were a good man on my ranch, Tex, and you've been a fine deputy, but don't be trying to analyze me or what I'm thinkin'."

Not this morning. Sheriff George Kemp was a private man, far from what a politician might be, but he was vulnerable to criticism. He didn't like it, struck out at those who dared criticize the man, and there had been some recently. Cattle had been stolen, and those who did it have not been caught. Land had been sold fraudulently, and those responsible had not been found. And now, two stagecoach holdups with people dead and a banker's daughter kidnapped. Too much talk and too much of it of the negative sort.

"You're right, Tex, I've got more than just something

on my mind. Corcoran's taking this kidnapping and killing right out from under me, and I need it." He looked at the old jailer and realized he had said too much. None of Tex's business.

Tex shook his head and gave the sheriff just the slightest of smiles. "Election worries, eh?"

"Yeah, and that Corcoran spent a lot of time with our prisoner last night."

Tex stirred what was left of the fire and poured a bit of coffee into his tin cup. "He did and you could have. You could have had Dirk Mallory sit in on the talk, too. That Chambers fellow is the only one alive who participated in both robberies. Corcoran's sure there is another person involved.

"Sometimes, Sheriff, it's better to put aside your own wants and join in on others' pursuits in order to learn things. Right now, you've got a gravely wounded outlaw who might die before you talk to him, and you could have been in on the discussions last night."

"You do come right to the point, Tex." The sheriff hadn't been talked to that way in years, and the scowl proved the point. *I hired him, and I can fire him. Damn old fool knows what he's talking about, though. I could have been in on that talk with Chambers and wasn't. It ain't Tex's place to talk to me that way.*

"Right now, I'd like to smack you across the side of the head, but I know you're right. Help me keep Chambers alive so I can talk to him."

The two men stood next to the dwindling fire, looking at each other but not willing to continue the conversation.

CORCORAN WAS STANDING NEXT to Dude, tightening the cinch when Dirk Mallory walked up. "I don't think Chambers will make the ride back to Austin. He was rolling around all night, ripped the bandages off, and did a lot of bleeding. Did you talk much with him after I left?"

"Not as much as I wanted to," Corcoran said. "There is another person, he alluded to that, but wouldn't go any further with it. They've been paid a small amount from that first holdup, with half the kidnap money going to the gang."

"Meaning somebody's getting the other half. Ten thousand dollars is a chunk of change, Terrence. Chambers didn't give you any hints?"

"I'm not sure he knows. Like Chambers, he's tall, I got that much out of him. And that it's a man who dresses more like a frontier guide than a buckaroo or gambler. Wears buckskin shirts."

Dirk Mallory smiled as he kicked some dust around. "We have a few people in Austin still wearing buckskins. Mostly old guys living in the past. I saw one or two while I was in Eureka."

"Yup," Corcoran said. "Old Army guides, old guys who still try to live the old way. None of 'em would fit as a person willing to kidnap the banker's daughter." Corcoran made sure the cinch was tight and looked at Mallory. "I got the feeling from Chambers that our man might not be much older than any of the gang members."

He looked over at the wounded outlaw, still wrapped in his blanket.

"I really hate to give him up to your sheriff, Dirk. Try to follow up on this buckskin-wearing fellow and let me know what you find out."

"I will, Terrence. I'll bring it to you personally, and then we'll find a bottle or two to share."

Corcoran was laughing as he stepped into a stirrup and mounted Dude. "Have a good ride back. When we top that ridge, I hope we'll find Sheriff Connor." As Sheriff Kemp got his group underway, Corcoran was still thinking about the man in the buckskin shirt.

I wonder if there is a little more to it than I've allowed. Maybe it's more than just kidnapping the girl for money. What if it's revenge? What if old man buckskin feels he's been wronged and this is his way of getting even? I've got a lot of work in front of me when we get back to Eureka.

He looked around as Sheriff Kemp, his deputy Mallory, and the rest from Austin rode off in a cloud of dust. He was trying to put some kind of handle on Kemp. He was a rancher with good land and good stock but wanted to be a good lawman, too. *I wonder why? Maybe it's like what Tex was saying, that the man has too much of an impression of himself. Ego.* He spotted Lou Foster and Louisa getting ready for the morning's ride.

He's going to be a fine lawman and soon, if the love bug don't take him off somewhere. I almost gave up the badge, think I would have, actually, if Crazy Hair hadn't got killed. I love being a lawman, take great pleasure in bringing outlaws hard to earth, but that girl had me roped, and was dragging me to the fire. Corcoran reached up and let his fingers dust off the bent and well-worn tin badge. *I would have given it up, bought some land, and been a married man. I miss that lady.*

Corcoran had a smile on his face as he rode to where Lou Foster was helping Louisa into the saddle. *How many people has this lovely lady's father wronged? He is, after all, holding mortgages on a lot of property in the Diamond Valley.* "All set, are we?"

"Looks like it," Foster said. "Them taking all those horses with them back to Austin sure makes it easier on us. Think the sheriff will be in that little valley?"

"Hope so. Kemp gave us enough food for a midday break and that's all. He ain't the nicest man I've dealt with." He smiled at Louisa. "You look well this morning. How do you feel?"

"Bruised and sore, Terrence. Those ropes really hurt, and riding so fast for so long..." and she let it trail off. "I'm fine."

"Let's ride, then," Corcoran said, leading off at a trot for the mountains and rocky ridge they'll have to cross. The same ridge they were fighting in yesterday. Foster and Louisa rode together at least for the first few miles.

"What happens if Sheriff Connor isn't in that valley?" Louisa asked.

"We'll be on short rations for sure. It's at least two days to Eureka, after we get in the valley," he said, "and we have a pouch full of snacks." Foster tried to smile. "Might get a chance to shoot a jack rabbit or two, maybe get lucky and see some antelope. Otherwise, short rations and what little water we might find."

Corcoran led them up the steep hillside, around the rocks they fought in the day before. There were stands of brush to get through before reaching the spiny ridge. He stopped at the top and looked down across the wide prairie. The other two stopped alongside. "See anything, Foster?"

"Not yet." He slowly scanned the brush and trees, rises and troughs, and shook his head. It was mid-morning, and the heat was already rising. Heat waves altered the scene, and made the far-off trees do little provocative dancing. "Don't see any movement at all, Corcoran. The best way down on the other side is right where that pointed peak is. There's a trail just to the south of that peak."

"I remember it well, Lou. Get a good view of the Diamond Range from there, too. Find us some water as we move through the valley."

Foster nodded and rode out in front, leaving Louisa to ride with Corcoran. "Will we be okay, Terrence? Lou seems to think we might be short of food."

"If we don't find the sheriff or if we don't shoot something, we will be short of food and water. Lou will find us water. He had cattle up here often when he and his father were together, before the old man died. As far as the sheriff goes, we can only hope. I wouldn't worry your head too much about this."

"I'll try not to."

"When you think about it," Corcoran said, "Two days isn't very much. If nothing else, when we drop down into the Diamond Valley, we can stop at a ranch and see if we can get something to eat."

"That's interesting," she said. "My father would turn

away people if they stopped and were either hungry or thirsty."

I've known Jackson for some time, but never knew these things about him. Won't help a stranger in need? Won't clean or take care of game when hunting? And Louisa seems to be just the opposite, wanting to help. That man who wears buckskins must have a connection here somewhere. Business or personal?

"Those men who kidnapped you were working for someone who didn't take part in all the action," he said. "This unknown person may have had some kind of action with your father. Maybe looking for revenge, maybe just working hate out of his system. Did those men ever say anything about such a person?"

"Oh, my," Louisa said. She was watching the dust, now far off, as Lou Foster rode deep into the valley. Big, puffy, white clouds slowly drifted across a light blue sky, riding soft late spring breezes.

"Daddy isn't the kindest man in the world when it comes to his banking business, Terrence. Mama tries to get him to be a little more generous, but it's not in him. I'm sure there are people in the community who don't have good feelings for him. Is that what you're alluding to?"

Corcoran smiled. "You're going to do well in the law business, Louisa. That's exactly what I'm alluding to. The only description we have is of a young man who is thin and tall, and who wears buckskin shirts or jackets. Bring anyone to mind?"

"I don't think so, but let me think about it for a while." She let her gaze wrap itself all across the valley, noting that Foster was out of view. "Those men would have killed me, wouldn't they." It wasn't a question.

Corcoran spent some moments looking at the lovely Louisa Jackson, her face dirty from two days of hard living, her eyes so sad. *She's going to enjoy having a man as tough on the one hand and as soft as Lou Foster.*

"I'm afraid so," he said. "Your father would provide twenty thousand dollars, but they would not have given you up." It was quiet for the next several miles that morning.

————

LOU FOSTER TOPPED a small rise on the valley floor and saw a stand of cottonwood trees half a mile or so in front of him. *Well, now, there's a sight. Five animals in the shade of big trees. Sure hope that's the sheriff.*

He wiped the sweat from his face and rode toward the trees nice and slow. *Just because we're looking for the sheriff doesn't mean this is him,* Lou Foster thought. *Those outlaws might have been expecting to meet with someone, also.*

As he got closer, he could see smoke and thought he could smell coffee. "Hope that's Connor and hope they have food," he muttered. He tried to stay in gullies and behind brush as he moved closer. He was several hundred yards out when he recognized Ed Connor limping around a fire.

He picked up the pace and yelled out when he was close enough to be heard, "Hello, the camp. It's Lou Foster here."

CHAPTER FIFTEEN

"ABOUT TIME, DEPUTY," Connor answered. "Ride on in. Where's Corcoran?"

"I'll go get him. Be right back, Sheriff," Foster said, turned his horse, and put it in a good lope to bring Corcoran and Louisa to Connor's camp. The sun was climbing fast and the ride back was even hotter than earlier. "It's gonna be a scorcher today," he mumbled, keeping his horse at an easy lope.

"The sheriff is set up under a cottonwood canopy, Terrence. There's fresh water under those trees. Horses will be glad of that."

The ride to Sheriff Connor's camp was slow since the horses had little water overnight and little so far that morning. The ride into the shade of the trees was a welcome change from the blistering heat of the day.

They got the horses undressed and staked so they could get both fresh grass and fresh water. "Got them taken care of, let's see if we can find something for ourselves," Corcoran said. "Good to see you, Sheriff."

"Good to see you, too, Terrence." He had a smile on his face when he spotted Louisa. "Miss Jackson, it's very good to see you. Your father's been a worried man. Shorty's putting together a meal for you."

Corcoran and the sheriff sat on broken cottonwood limbs near the fire talking about the chase and capture of Chambers.

"That's an interesting thought, Corcoran. Another person involved but not with the gang. Go on."

"Chambers alluded to the fact, and I tried to press him on the matter. Badly wounded as he was, it was hard to get him to talk. He said there was a man who proposed the idea of kidnapping Louisa and holding her for ransom. Twenty thousand dollars to be split, ten to him and ten to the gang."

"But he wasn't to take part?" The sheriff asked.

"That's right. Chambers gave me the idea that the man was about the age of the gang members, was thin, and most often wore a buckskin shirt or light jacket." Corcorn looked at the sheriff and shook his head. "Can't seem to remember seeing anyone like that around Eureka. Older ones, yes, but not someone in their early twenties."

"A shame so many of the gang were killed. Always good to have more than one to question," the sheriff said. "I suppose Kemp is probably right in taking Chambers back to Lander County, but I wish you had more time with Chambers."

"Kemp was almost argumentative about it, Ed. He could very well have been with me when I talked with

Chambers. That entire gang was from Eureka. Shorty Duggan, Jake Hubbard,

Chambers, and young Jonas Johnson."

"And you're thinking that probably the man who wears buckskins is from Eureka, also?" Connor shook his head some.

"Not really sure of that. No, not necessarily. I do think, though, that he has had dealings with Jackson, at the bank or personally. As I said, Chambers gave me the impression that the man was young like the gang members. If our missing man has a gripe with Jackson, it's probably over some money matter rather than personal."

"You've got your work cut out, old man," Connors almost snickered. "Have you discussed any of this with Louisa? She might know something." He got to his feet and stretched. "Haven't ridden this much in a long time. This old, beat-up leg of mine is giving me hell, Terrence." He paced around, stretched again, and sat back down.

"We have more than enough food to get us back to town, so let's get it on, if you've had enough to eat. Gonna be a scorcher, I'm afraid." He looked at Shorty. "Make sure all those canteens are filled, Shorty. Lorenzo, get Heckman on his feet. Let's get those horses saddled and make some dust."

"Who is Heckman?" Corcoran asked.

"Works for Jackson. Instead of coming himself, he sent Heckman, a complete waste. Can't ride, won't help around camp, and complains constantly. Let's get it on, boys."

"Sounds like a trail boss moving cattle, doesn't he?"

Foster chuckled. He hadn't moved from sitting next to Louisa while they had their midday meal. "Pop used to talk that way and then laugh like all get-out."

"I always liked your father. You and he made a good team. Like you and Terrence now."

Foster thought about that for a moment or two. "I guess you're right. My dad was a hard worker, but was as kind as an old grandma making cookies. He babied them calves until they were weaned, and then they became beeves. Meat. Money in the bank."

He got pensive, stared into the deep sky, and smiled. "I miss that old man."

Louisa took his hand for a moment. "Best get saddled, Lou. Looks like the sheriff wants to get going. I haven't had a chance to tell you thank you." She leaned into him and gave him a soft kiss on his cheek.

"Thank you?" He reached up and touched his cheek.

"Yes, Lou, thank you for saving my life."

He rubbed his cheek, blushed, and looked around to see if anyone had been looking. Smoky gave him a nod, and Foster blushed even more.

"Let's ride. That sun ain't gonna be kind if we tarry much longer," Sheriff Ed Connor called out. "We'll make camp in the Diamond Valley about sunset."

———————

THE RIDE OUT of the high, rocky plain and down the mountainside into the Diamond Valley below went easy, along with a few stops so the horses could blow. "If I didn't know that it was still May, I'd be sure to tell anyone who asked that it was mid-August," Smoky said when they got off the trail and under some cottonwoods. He untied his bandanna and wrung it out to everyone's delight. "Sheriff, you and me been huntin' this country for many years. Ever seen it this hot this early?"

"Don't think I can remember a late spring being this hot," Ed Connor said, stepping down from his horse, bathed in sweat, both he and the horse. "Ten minutes, folks. We're just an hour or so from where we can camp. There's water and shade, but these horses need a rest."

"Horses?" Lou Foster almost sneered. "Me—need— rest." Connor had to laugh and shook his head.

Louisa stepped down from her horse, used her shirt sleeve to wipe sweat from her face, and walked a few paces off the trail. "Just look at all this beauty, will you," she said, stooping to pick a wildflower. She had a bouquet in hand in just minutes and handed a stem to Lou Foster. "For you, sir, for saving my life."

The smile that went with it was devastating, and Lou just stood, silent, embarrassed, and thrilled all at the same time.

"What's this? Ain't no girl ever give me flowers." Smoky cackled. "Best give that pretty little gal a big kiss, cowboy. Might never happen again."

Before anything else could be said, the trail boss, Sheriff Ed Connor, yelled out, "Saddle up. Got a lot a country to see. Let's go." Lou helped Louisa into the saddle, vaulted into his, and try as he might, could not wipe the grin off his face, nor ease away the deep blush that co-existed.

"Ride with me, you two," Corcoran said. "We need to

have a little talk." He lit a cigar as the horses began to walk along the pathway. "We're going to spend a lot of time searching for this missing person, Lou, and young lady, I'm hoping you'll be able to help us some."

"I'm not sure how I can help," she said. "But I'm sure willing to try. I've been gone for three years, you know. There have been a lot of changes in town."

"I'm going to have to ask you some questions about your father and the bank that might seem rather personal, but might prove essential to finding this fool who put your kidnapping scheme together. He seemed to know an awfully lot about your moves." Corcoran's attitude was gentle, quiet, giving Louisa time to answer.

She sat still for just a moment, glanced at Lou, and waited just a moment before speaking. "I hadn't thought about that. You're right, somebody must have known I was getting off the train in Battle Mountain, not Palisade."

"That's what I'm talking about," Corcoran said. "Did your father know? Or friends in Eureka? We'll probably have questions about the bank, too."

"I'll do my best, Terrence, but I don't know very much about my father's bank business. He's very careful talking about it." She leaned back in the saddle, ran her fingers through her snarled hair, and smiled at Lou Foster.

"You're thinking this man might be connected to the bank somehow? A disgruntled customer, angry about something?"

"Yup," Corcoran said. "Maybe seeking revenge.

Maybe personal business between him and your father went tipsy and he wants to get even."

Louisa closed her eyes, and all three, Corcoran, Foster, and Connor, saw that she was more than just upset at the conversation. Without opening her eyes, and with no smile at all, Louisa started talking, softly. "My father is a hard man, Terrence. He doesn't have much empathy in his veins, won't give, even friends, any quarter. Growing up, at school, I'd hear stories. I've never discussed any of this with anyone before."

Tears rolled down her dusty cheeks, and Lou reached out and took her hand. "This may not be the right time, Terrence." Was she going out of her way to talk with Corcoran and not the sheriff or Lou Foster? She let Foster continue holding her hand but was looking at Corcoran. "This is so strange. It's almost like you're asking me to tell stories about my father. Ugly stories. I'm not sure."

Foster squeezed her hand and gave her a warm smile as she brushed a tear away. "He's not always a good man, Lou, but he's my father, and I love him. Do we have to do this right now? I hurt everywhere, I'm filthy dirty, and I need to be alone for a few minutes."

Foster reached an arm around her shoulder and held her tight. The horses were bunched some, but she didn't care. She needed that hug.

"Just think about what we're asking," Connor said. "We don't need answers right away, but this man, whoever he is, did not have any intention of delivering you to your father. He needs to be found out, needs to pay for his crime, and you might have the answers we need."

Corcoran held back a smile, looking at his deputy, holding tight to a frightened little girl. *This young feller is going to make one fine lawman, but I'll bet this young lady will have that badge off of him before the year is out. I'm gonna lose him, and she's gonna hold him tight.*

"There is more than one person out there," Sheriff Ed Connor said, "who was hoping for a share of that money. Ten thousand to the mystery man and ten thousand for the gang, of whom, only one man is alive. Somebody, or some people, provided information about you to the mystery man and the gang." Connor looked at his two deputies. "I'm in favor of thinking there is more than just the one. That's just an awfully lot of money."

Connor took a deep breath and continued, "The worst part of all this? Louisa, you and us will know them. They may even have been friends for some time, and they passed on information that led to two stagecoach holdups and many deaths, and when they find out you are alive, that they won't be getting any blood money, they might just blame you."

"You're scaring me, Sheriff," she said. She looked over at Terrence, then to Lou Foster. "Is he right, Lou?"

"Count on it," Foster said, and saw a dark cloud cross her eyes.

CHAPTER SIXTEEN

"WE'LL RIDE into that copse of cottonwoods, yonder," Connor said, pointing at the trees. It was already near sunset, and the riders were burned to a crisp, the horses were worn out, and the thought of a spring full of cold water was the only thing keeping them moving. In Louisa's eyes, they were seeing a great pool of cool water, fires cooking thick steaks of beef, buffalo, and venison, and somebody to give her a two-hour massage.

Lou Foster rode up alongside the girl and did his best to hold back a chuckle. Her face was filthy with desert dust turned to mud by sweat, hair tangled in knots and parted by hot, dry winds, and eyes more tired than the young deputy had ever seen.

"I don't think I can get off this horse by myself," she said as Foster took the reins from her. "I'm just going to fall off."

Foster dropped the leads and grabbed her, eased her down, and held her close. "Don't ever let go, Lou. Ever." His arms tightened some, and he did as he was told. Just hang on. *To think this little girl could have ended up dead because of the gang, tears me apart,* Lou thought, squeezing Louisa gently.

What if Corcoran and I hadn't made that trip to Austin? She's been through hell and I ain't lettin' go for a long time. He had a broad smile on his face as he slowly eased her back some, looking deep into wide, lively eyes. Her smile equaled his.

They walked the horses into standing water for a long drink, and then brought them into the nearby green grass, and tied them off. "You need to be near where Shorty's getting that fire going, and I'll take care of brushing and caring for the horses," Foster said.

"Not yet," Louisa said. She walked out into the pool, bent over, and splashed cold spring water into her face and head, over and over, laughing the entire time. "Oh, Lou, that feels so good," and she splashed herself again. She was drenched within that short spell and stood next to him. "Now, the fire, then food, Mr. Foster. Lots of food."

He watched her walk toward the fire and wondered if any of this was real. "My lord almighty, but she is one hell of a woman." He pulled the saddles and bridals, had the horses tied good, and set the blanket down. Brushing the horses took a few more minutes, and the deputy kept looking at that pond of water, finally putting the brush rags away.

It was just three steps, and he kneeled down at the water's edge, doffed his hat, and splashed water into his face three or four times. "Lordy, that feels good." He got up and brought the bedrolls and saddle blankets into the camp area.

"We'll be in Eureka tomorrow," Ed Connor said. "Heckman, you and Smoky gather enough wood for supper and tomorrow's breakfast, Lou, you make sure Miss Jackson is well cared for, and Corcoran, let's take a walk."

Corcoran smiled, joining the sheriff, knowing the old man had been worrying himself on how to capture their elusive missing man. "This isn't going to be easy, Ed. Somehow, I've got the feeling that whoever is behind this hostage plot is a longtime acquaintance of the Jackson family. There's going to be more misery in that family."

"I'm afraid you're right, Terrence. That Louisa was coming to Austin on her way home is the tickler. A longtime and close friend of the family was looking for payback for something. To the point of willing to kill the girl. Is Foster man enough to handle what's going to be brought out?"

Corcoran chuckled softly. "I'm afraid so, Ed. When this is all over, that young man will be full grown, sir, and take my word, he won't be wearing a badge."

Connor stopped quickly and turned to his chief deputy. "I don't want to lose that boy. You've trained him into being a fine deputy." Connor slowed his pace, had his head bowed as he contemplated what was just said.

"Because of you," Connor said, "I had a good marriage, but that lovely lady I lost was always afraid that one evening I wouldn't be coming home. You, Corcoran, took the danger out of my job and put it on your shoulders.

And if my memory serves, you almost gave up the badge when you went to help friends in Humboldt County." He reached down and slowly massaged his bunged-up leg.

Getting shot in the leg was one of the few times Ed Connor had found himself facing danger. It was always Corcoran who walked in first, always Corcoran who challenged the killers. *I miss that lady so much. I was supposed to die first, not her.*

"Trying to find out who is behind this kidnapping is going to bring those two even closer together, and she's going to need all of his strength if we find out that whoever was willing to kill her off was what she thought to be a close friend." Corcoran kicked some dirt and scowled.

"Has to be done, Terrence. And you're the man to do it. Find whoever is responsible for all of this and arrest him or her or them. That's an order." Connor couldn't hide the smile and whacked Corcoran across his broad shoulder as they turned back toward camp and hot steaks.

They could smell the broiling meat from some way off and could hear Smoky yelling, "Come and get it while it's hot."

"He's definitely yelling at me," Connor said, picking up the pace.

———

NOBODY SAID a word during supper and cleaning up afterward. "I can't remember ever being this tired," Louisa said. "I've been a sweet little university girl for the last three years and all at once I'm expected to ride halfway across Nevada in a heat wave. Even if that bedroll is on top of sharp, pointed rocks, I'll sleep like a baby."

She, Lou, and Corcoran were sitting on the ground near the fire, enjoying a cup of coffee before bed. "Why is Heck Heckman here, Terrence?" The look she had was a combination of anger and fear. She had gone out of her way earlier to not let him get within ten feet of her.

"Your father said he wouldn't be able to make this ride and sent Heck in his place." Corcoran held back a scowl the best he could. Heckman had no business being on this kind of ride. Out of shape, physically, not particularly showing any great affection for the girl, and willing to complain about anything and everything. "Your question has been mine more than once, Miss Jackson. Why are you asking?"

Foster was looking at Louisa and saw a quick sadness work its way across her face. *This is something new,* he thought. *They never spoke when we met up this morning. Never spoke on our long ride today, and never spoke during supper, and yet, Jackson picked him to ride with the posse to bring her home.*

"How long a ride will it be tomorrow?" Louisa asked, and took a quick sip of hot coffee. "I won't be able to make a ride like today's, I'm afraid. I'll be belly-aching like old man Heck."

"I get the feeling you and he aren't particularly close," Terrence Corcoran said.

"Close?!" She flung the word out as if it tasted bad. "I've never liked the man. He's not a nice man, especially with children. Screams ugly words at kids, including me, years ago. Daddy used to say *it's just his way*. I don't like *his way*."

Corcoran and Foster took quick looks at each other before Foster said anything. "That's odd that your father would send him, then. Are you afraid of Heckman?"

"I was," she said. She smiled and finished her coffee. "Today? No. I can defend myself now. If he tries to touch me, I'll knock him a good one."

Foster chuckled at the picture he saw, but Corcoran had other thoughts. "He has tried to touch you before?"

"Only once, and when Mama found out, she forbid him to be in the house or to be alone with me. Daddy didn't believe me."

Corcoran's entire body visibly tightened up. Foster was sure he heard a growl from the man, and Eureka's chief deputy sheriff got up quickly. *He'll never touch another little girl. There are some things I'll tolerate, this is not one of them.* He walked off from the fire, checked on the stock, looked at the stars, and did what he could to let his mind come to a resting place. Corcoran had beaten men half to death for less when it came to how a man treats a woman.

He only had one rule, and a hard and fast rule it was —you will treat a woman as a lady unless she wishes otherwise. This went for girls, too. It took more than ten minutes for the big man to loosen up some and return to the fire.

"It's late," Louisa said. I'm going to wrap myself in that bedroll and not move until sunrise." She wrapped her arms around Foster, gave him a big kiss, right on the mouth, and walked to her bedroll. "At least I'm dried off," she whispered, pulling a wool blanket up to her chin. Like the buckaroos she used to watch, she used her saddle as a pillow.

Corcoran nodded to Foster to follow him, and the two walked down to the spring's edge. "Her own father was willing to let that man fondle his daughter? You had best keep a close eye on me, Mr. Foster. Both those men are in serious danger." Corcoran did not have a smile, nor did he follow up the statement with a good-natured chuckle.

"If I hadn't heard her say it, I would have a hard time believing it," Foster said. "If he's willing to treat his family this way, how does he treat customers of his bank? Working, as a boy, with my father, I learned how important it is to have feelings for those you work with, those you live with, those you care for. I'm glad I have not borrowed any money from Mr. Jackson's bank. I was ten years old when Dad came home from a trip to town more excited than I'd ever seen him."

Foster took a moment to clear his throat, and Corcoran took that moment to look at the stars through the dancing pines. "He held, as I found out later, the paid off mortgage to our little ranch, and was almost gleeful when he burned it at the fireplace. He and Mr. Jackson never spoke to each other again after that day."

"I'm afraid we're going to find more than a few horror stories about Jackson and that bank, and at least one of them will lead us to the man who wears buckskin shirts," Corcoran said, as they made their way back into camp and a good night's sleep.

CHAPTER SEVENTEEN

MORNING FOUND a bunch of people fighting to get out from under blankets with muscles as tight as the wings of a diving red-tailed hawk. "I'm gettin' old, Terrence," Ed Connor said.

"You don't know old, Sheriff," Smoky said. He was bent over, one boot on, dancing and fighting to get the other one on. "Somebody's gonna have to help old man Heckman, I think. He ain't budged since I kicked him awake."

Corcoran walked over and jerked the blanket off the man. He was in a fetal position, his arms wrapped around himself. "Get up, Heckman. Gonna miss breakfast if you don't."

"Ain't gettin' up. Ain't ridin' no horse, neither. Go away."

"Suit yourself," Corcoran said, and tossed the blankets aside. "Your horse is going with us," he said, and walked to where Smoky had a fire going and a coffee pot getting ready to boil. "That was a good supper, Smoky. Whatcha got for us this morning?"

"Sliced side meat and pancakes, Terrence. Even packed a jar of honey for the hot cakes. Jimmy Hendricks did us well, he did."

"I'll make sure to tell him so. Under normal circumstances, we could make it back to Eureka before sunset, old man, but I don't think Louisa is up to another long day in the saddle. How you doing?"

"Me? Hell's bells, boy, I was born in the saddle." Smoky cackled some as he fed the fire. "I guided for the Army if you remember, when we fought off old Thunder Cloud back in the sixties. You don't have to worry about me. Sheriff's leg is giving him trouble, but he's as tough as you are. Heckman will hold us up."

"Best bet then, is to make this a two-day ride back to Eureka. Heckman's on his own, Smoky. He rides with us or walks. Don't much care which." Corcoran's mouth was drawn down in a snarl, but he quickly let it pass. "Got enough food for that?"

"Henderson gave us more than enough. Something going on I might need to know about?"

Corcoran shook his head as he grabbed up some rags, picked up the coffee pot, and poured the two of them their first cups of the day.

Sheriff Ed Connor walked up, not limping, smiled, and poured himself a cup. "Best sleep I've had in a long time. We'll be riding in half an hour, so get those hot cakes a cooking, Smoky. It's time to get home." He saw Louisa and Foster, who were standing with Corcoran and Smoky, and shook his head.

"Where's Heckman?"

"Wouldn't get up. Said he wouldn't be riding. I told him his horse is going with us, him on it or not," Corcoran growled. "Think we need to make it a two-day ride, Ed."

"I agree. Louisa's safe, nobody needs a doctor, yet," he said, looking over to where Heckman's bedroll might be. "Make it a nice slow ride, spend another night under the stars, and ride into town nice and fresh." He smiled and found a log to sit on. "Get to cooking, Smoky."

———————

IT WAS the smell of the sliced side meat that got Heck Heckman out of his bedroll, and he showed up at the fire almost bleary-eyed and limping. No one said a word to him as he filled his plate with hotcakes and side meat. There was just a dab of honey left in the jar, and he smeared it over his pancakes. No one said a word to the man.

"Riding in ten," Connor said. "Let's get saddled. Me and Smoky leading, Foster and Louisa next, and Heckman, you ride with Corcoran. This will be a nice, easy ride today, and we'll camp within ten to fifteen miles of Eureka. Heckman, help Smoky clean up the breakfast mess."

Heckman whimpered as he got to his feet but when Corcoran told him they would ride off and leave him, it caught his attention. He had heard enough stories about Terrence Corcoran over the years that he knew the man would ride off and leave him.

"I don't feel good, Smoky. You got anything to help?

My back, my legs, my head. Maybe a quick snort of something?" Heckman wasn't talking, he was whimpering, wringing his hands, pleading for help.

Smoky had a hard time with this, shook his head, and turned his back on the man. "We've only been out two days." Smoky was ten or more years older than Heckman and couldn't imagine ever acting like this. *I wonder what kind of work this fool does for old man Jackson? I pick up ten or twelve sticks for the fire, and he grabs two. He can't lift his saddle onto his horse, almost needs help mounting the animal. What kind of man is he?*

"Nothing, Heck. Sheriff don't want no drinking on a ride like this. Help me pack the mule and then stomp out the fire, and do a good job of it. Ain't gonna burn up this fine country. You and Corcoran riding behind me and the sheriff leading this outfit, so get to moving. Ain't got time to be complaining."

It was closer to twenty minutes before the posse was ready to pull out, but Corcoran noticed a change in Connor as he stepped into the saddle. "You're looking mighty spry, Sheriff. You all right?"

"Just fine, Terrence. Just fine." Ed Connor reached down and gently rubbed his bad leg. "Must be the long two days in the saddle. Leg's either numb,"—and he laughed—"or the hard ride had helped it along." *I've been babying this old leg for more than a year now and won't be able to get away with that anymore.* He chuckled at the thought. *Got myself caught.*

———

LOU FOSTER HADN'T BEEN able to put aside what Louisa said about Heckman trying to take advantage of her, even trying to touch her, and her father's less-than-a-father's reaction. He rode up alongside Corcoran late in the morning. "I want to talk about Mr. Jackson's reaction to what Heckman tried to do with Louisa. I can't fathom a father ignoring such an encounter."

"Jackson doesn't give the impression that he cares for anything but his bank and its money, Mr. Foster. I won't tolerate Heckman's behavior in a man, and you might want to keep an eye on me when Heckman is nearby. I've whipped on men for less. As far as Jackson, the fact that he isn't here with us tells me too much about the man."

Hour after hour, they made their way south along the main north–south road between Eureka and Carlin. The mighty Diamond Range was on their left, peaks soaring well over eight thousand feet, some still carrying snow. The sights were captivating, and Foster was aware he wasn't enjoying the sights.

What kind of a man is it who would allow an older man to get fresh with his young daughter? And then send that man to help escort the girl back home? I don't know who I want to kick ass the most, Heckman or Jackson. Foster looked over at Louisa, sitting comfortably on her horse, enjoying the splendid sights.

"You're feeling much better this morning, aren't you?" he asked.

"I am, Lou. I am. A good night's sleep, a good breakfast, and I feel fine." Her smile would have lit up the Diamond Valley if the sun hadn't already done so. "Those mountains are beautiful, aren't they? The sunlight is so soft. A velvet mist, almost," she said, her eyes as bright as Foster had ever seen them.

"As a girl, I was riding in those rocky spires as often as I could. My friends and I had a secret cowboy's line camp shack that we used as ours. It's where we played cowboys and Indians."

She had the softest tinkle of a laugh. "Got caught once when a couple of buckaroos showed up with supplies. Never rode a horse that fast before."

Foster was lost in her story, smiling at what must have gone through those buckaroos' minds, chasing off a few teenage girls. "Probably scared those boys as much, too," he said. They rode close for another several minutes.

"Is this a good time to talk some about your father?" Alone together on the trail would be easier on both of them than around the fire at camp, or in some other situation where people could hear.

"It will never be a good time, Lou, but I know you have to. You're sure that someone close to our family has to be involved, aren't you?"

"I'm afraid so," he said. "Too much money. Too much personal stuff about you had to be known. We'll take it nice and slow, Louisa. To start, who besides your immediate family knew you would be stopping in Austin instead of coming straight through?"

"My friend in Austin knew, of course, and Dad. I sent wires to both of them."

"Interesting," Foster said. "So, that creates a problem, I'm afraid. It could mean that one or both of the telegraph employees is involved, or said something to someone." He gave her a weak kind of smile.

"You're sure that's all?"

"I can't imagine telling anyone else, Lou."

Foster let that run around in his mind. Did her father mention it to someone? Did her friend in Austin? Did one of the telegraph operators blab the information? Somehow, he thought, the man who wears buckskin found out that she would be spending time in Austin instead of coming straight through.

So many possibilities, he thought. One simple comment overheard by the wrong person and two stage coaches were stopped, many people were dead, and the banker's daughter was kidnapped.

"Would your father have had to change plans? For instance, having to stop a grocery order or some such?"

Louisa laughed. "He wouldn't know how to make a grocery order. No, but he might have said something at the bank. I get along with most of the employees even better than he does. They may have been planning some kind of welcome home for me."

"That's the kind of information I need," Foster said. "Now I've got something to look into." *I wonder if one of the telegraph operators or one of the bank employees happens to be friends with a man who wears buckskins.*

"You've been in the Bay Area for three years, and I don't remember you coming home during the summer breaks."

"No, I didn't. This is the first time I've been home. I've been staying with my mother's sister's family near Menlo Park. They have a general merchandise store and since I've been studying bookkeeping and business, I've worked for them to pay my school tuition and my board."

Foster thought that was interesting. Her father didn't pay for her education or for her board? The banker made his daughter work for that? "Was that your idea, to pay your own tuition and pay for board with your mother's sister?"

Louisa's eyes narrowed some, her open smiling face fell into a grim look, and she didn't answer for several moments. "Daddy doesn't believe in women going to university or holding a position in business. He thinks I would be a happier woman cooking and washing for my husband."

She was scowling, and he could see her shoulders tighten up, and watched her begin to sit taller in the saddle. "He tried to forbid me going to university and we had a big argument over it. I'm sure we'll have another when I get home."

Foster couldn't believe that would lead to the stagecoach affair, but did it lead Jackson to talk about her coming home, and then looking to spend a few days in Austin first? "Did your friends in Eureka know you were coming home?"

"One or two. Seems, Mr. Foster, that my three years in San Francisco, and my studies, have combined to create a bit of a wedge between me and my old school friends. I'm afraid I've outgrown many of them."

She smiled at him, thinking how her advanced education separated her from those who didn't have one. *Will we renew our friendships?* she thought, as she looked at Lou Foster, reached out, and took his hand. "But not you. I'm so glad we're making this ride, learning about each other."

CHAPTER EIGHTEEN

"LET'S ride off under those trees and have our dinner break," Sheriff Connor hollered out to the riders. "Need a quick rest, give the horses a break. There's water and grass." He'd been watching the sun and looking for a site off the main road where they could have a fire for a hot meal. Connor had to chuckle to himself, wondering what kind of fool would want a fire in this heat.

"I'll take a guess that we're probably twenty, maybe twenty-five miles from town," Smoky said. "I'm sure we can make that after dinner. Might not have to spend another night under the stars."

"You're right, Smoky," Connor said. "Take a mid-afternoon break for the horses, and ride in before sundown. Have you forgotten somebody, Smoky?"

"Nope." The longtime Army scout and night jailer for Eureka County snuffed once or twice as they rode in under the cooling limbs of the cottonwood trees. "Damn fool wouldn't keep up, and I'm not a nursemaid. Can't get lost riding a road like this, but he sure as hell might miss a meal." The wonderful cackle of his laugh spread across the little hills and dips of the valley.

"You want me to go get him?"

"No, Smoky. He's a grown man on a fair horse, and we ain't payin' him." Connor stepped down and led his horse into good grass and near a bubbling spring. "Let's get a fire going and get some meat fryin', eh?"

Corcoran, Foster, and Louisa had their horses pegged and were busy taking saddles and bridles off. "You'll be in your own bed tonight," Foster said to Louisa. "Home safe and sound." He couldn't help but think how it could have been so much worse if they hadn't busted up that gang.

He quickly wiped away horrible pictures of Louisa being troubled by the gang, being wounded, or worse. The worst picture? All of them riding back without her. All because so many people wanted money from Jackson's bank. *Money*, he thought. *It's always about money, gold, or riches isn't it. Almost all crime, almost all problems can be traced back to a desire for money, or more money.*

Or, was it deeper than that? Lou Foster found himself back on a horse, driving his father's cattle, doing mind tricks to keep him from dropping off to sleep. Did they want to hurt Emil Jackson? Were they sure he would pay handsomely for his daughter's release? And why did they feel that way? He joined Corcoran at the fire Smoky was building.

"Learned a lot on the ride this morning," Foster said. "Just not quite enough to know who to arrest," he said, and chuckled. "Glad we're riding on in."

"Yup. I've been thinkin' that this stage-robbing and kidnapping is very close to Jackson's family. More his family than the bank. Can't get it out of my head why he sent Heckman with us instead of coming himself. He's a cold man, but this is more than that, I think."

"I don't know a thing about his family. His wife has a sister near San Francisco, and she and her husband own a mercantile business. Louisa has been boarding with them for the last three years, paying her own way."

"If Jackson has a family somewhere, I don't know about it," Corcoran said. "With her new education, why is Louisa moving to Pennsylvania instead of working at the bank?" Corcoran cocked his head to the side. "She has a degree in bookkeeping and management."

Foster just shook his head. "Jackson doesn't believe a woman should be out of the kitchen or bed, Terrence. Wouldn't contribute a dime for her education. There's going to be one hell of an explosion around that home in the next few days."

"Do you think he's behind all this?" Corcoran looked around quickly to make sure no one was listening. "My god, man. Do you?"

"No, I don't, but it sure is something we need to think about."

Corcoran sat down on a broken limb near the fire and let his mind run wild for a few minutes. By the time the coffee was boiling and smelling wonderful, he decided that he was going to spend a great deal of time with Emil Jackson when they got back to town. *This thought is more than worrisome. Could a man hate his daughter enough to try to have her killed? Horrible thought.*

———

"WE GOING to just ride off and leave Heckman to his own devices?" Corcoran was looking at Sheriff Ed Connor. "I'm not in favor of that." The men had their horses saddled and were waiting for Smoky and Louisa.

"No, Corcoran, neither am I." He turned to Smoky, who was making sure the cinch was tight on his saddle. "Go find him, Smoky, and bring him back. Whup on that fool if you have to, but bring him back." He looked at Corcoran and Foster. "This might make for a change in plans, again."

"Hold up, Smoky," Corcoran yelled out. He looked at Connor. "Great time for me to question that gentleman. When you've got everyone ready, go ahead and ride on. We'll catch up." He mounted and set off at a good trot on the back trail. The heat had been building, and leaving the shade and cool of the cottonwood trees let Corcoran know it was going to be an uncomfortable ride to find Heckman.

It was a long ten-mile ride when Corcoran spotted Heckman's horse standing near some stunted spruce along the rim of a runoff ditch. He rode up slowly to the horse, picked up the reins, and stood up in the stirrups for a good look around.

"What the hell did that fool do?" He couldn't see him anywhere and wondered if he'd gotten down in the ditch. Summer thunderstorms dropped considerable amounts of rain in these parts, and those ditches are deep and dangerous during the storms.

Corcoran stepped off Dude and tied the two horses to some sage. He hadn't taken three steps when he heard what sounded like someone crying. He followed the sound to the rim of the ditch and saw Heckman, flat on his face at the bottom of the arroyo. It was muddy, but there was no standing or running water. *What is that fool doing?*

Corcoran walked back, untied the horses, mounted, and found where livestock found their way down into the ditch and used their trail. The ground was loose sand and dirt, and at the bottom just a little bit muddy. Corcoran tied Heckman's horse to Dude's saddle and stepped down and left Dude ground-tied.

"What happened, Heck? What are you doing down here? Are you hurt?"

There was no response from the man. "You were crying just minutes ago. What happened?" He stooped down and rolled the man onto his back. Heckman's face was scratched and his shirt was torn, but there didn't seem to be any other injuries. Arms and legs were okay, no heavy bleeding, and Heckman's eyes were open, looking all around.

"What the hell happened, Heckman? You fall off the edge? What, damn it?"

"Thought there would be water down here. Tripped and rolled down. Can't get up. Help me."

"Pitiful," Corcoran said. "Smoky left you with two canteens full. You drank both canteens? Both of them?" Corcoran's anger was building fast at the ignorance of the man. "You had enough water for the entire day. More than enough. Get up." He snarled and prodded the man with his boot toe.

What kind of person is this Heckman fellow? Left on his own, he promptly drank up a day's worth of water, then fell in a ditch looking for more? I'm guessing that he's somewhere around thirty, soft as a ripe plum, and ignorant as a rock. Or, the thought flashed across his mind, *is this a game?* "Get up," he snarled, and used his boot toe again.

Heckman cried out, but Corcoran knew he was faking it and grabbed the man by an arm and jerked him to his feet, despite Heckman's overweight. "Fall down and I'll jerk you back up. Fall down again, and I'll drag you to your horse and tie you across the saddle. Let's go, Heckman," he ordered, and pushed him off toward the horses.

Smoky might have had the right answer: Just ride off and leave the fool. And then, there's that problem I have about taking care of people. Even fools and outlaws.

Heckman must have believed the big deputy and stumbled his way to the horses. Corcoran untied Heckman's mount and growled at him to climb aboard. Down in the ditch, there was no breeze, the sun was beating down on them, and sweat was running freely. "Get on that damn horse or I'll fling you across the saddle and tie you down."

Corcoran mounted Dude, almost laughed at the fear that crossed Heckman's face, and again, as the man wasn't able to get in the saddle until the third try. "We're riding up and out of this ditch, and at the first wrong move, I'll tie you down, Heckman. Follow me."

Corcoran rode to where he had come down, a not very difficult ride up through loose sand and dirt that any horse could make with ease. Dude lunged twice and was up and out, and Corcoran turned to watch Heckman. "Just let the horse make its way," he hollered down at the man. "Take hold of the saddle horn and lean forward. Keep your weight in the stirrups."

Heckman started to say something like, "I can't," when the horse did. Three lunges and he was up and out. Heckman's feet were out of the stirrups, he was sitting cock-eyed in the saddle, and Corcoran rode over quickly and pushed the man back in place.

"Let's go," Corcoran said, and whacked Heckman's horse on the rump. They rode off on the well-used road at a fair trot. "We've got some catching up to do, so ride as soft as you can on your horse."

Heckman simply was not a horseman—he sat heavy in the saddle, taking every step of the trot with a heavy bounce. "Horse isn't gonna take much more of your weight, Heckman. Surely you know how to post. Do it, or so help me, I will tie you across that saddle."

Heckman's attempt at a post was poor at best, but Corcoran was sure the horse appreciated it. At a good trot, one can ride for miles, taking a break back into a walk every half hour or so. "Listen, Heckman, on the open range, a cowboy can make a sixty-mile circle in a day, so toughen up and give me ten miles." He chuckled. "Or else."

Heckman quit fighting it after a few minutes, and Corcoran watched him come into a much better rhythm. *Now might be the time to see if I can get him to open up.* "How long you been with Jackson?"

"Probably ten years." He moaned and whimpered, trying to answer.

"That's quite a long time. What exactly do you do for him? Work at the bank?"

"Hell no," he almost shouted it out. "Except to do cleaning and stuff," he said, much calmer. "I take care of the plants and bushes at the house. Rake leaves. Take the garbage to the dump. Do some painting and fix things when they break."

"Keep the place looking good for visitors, eh?" Corcoran said, keeping it as light as he could.

"Jackson don't get many visitors. His wife, Beatrice, don't get along with the local ladies. They aren't welcome."

"She hard to work for?" Corcoran asked. As friendly as Louisa was, this information about Mrs. Jackson surprised Corcoran. "Make life hard on you?"

"She ain't never happy with the way I do things. The old man's the same way. Always complaining about something."

"Why do you stay?"

Heckman was quiet for what seemed like several minutes before answering. "Got nowhere else to go. Why you asking me all this?"

"Just interested," Corcoran said. "Interested," he repeated. "Why did Jackson send you on this ride instead of coming himself? Doesn't that seem strange to you? I mean, if you had a daughter whose life was in danger, wouldn't you want to be on the ride to save her?"

"Ain't got no daughter," was Heckman's answer.

The ride was quiet for some time, neither man speaking. *That was not the answer I was expecting,* Corcoran thought. *Something strange about Heckman's relationship with the Jacksons.*

The sun was boiling hot as they rode into the afternoon and Corcoran brought them back to a walk. "We should be catching up to the sheriff soon. Don't you think that Jackson should be on this ride instead of you?"

"He don't much care for that gal. He don't much care for nothing but that bank. That gal's a looker, ain't she? Jackson don't like it when I talk to her."

"Then why did he send you? Obviously you'd be talking to her."

"Don't know and don't care. We gotta stop real soon. I'm gonna fall right off this horse."

"You do, and I'll lay you across that saddle and tie you off. We got a few miles to go." He watched to make sure the man wasn't going to fall off his horse, and tried to get some kind of answers from the man.

"What kind of friends does Jackson have? People he has drinks with, or goes fishing with?"

Heckman snorted. "He wouldn't know how to fish. He ain't got no friends. Neither him nor Beatrice have any friends. They talk to each other, say nasty things about people in town. She calls them ignorant, he calls them stupid. He laughs when somebody can't pay their debt to the bank."

"And they talk this way in front of you?"

"They don't know when I'm listening," he replied and chuckled. "It's my secret."

Corcoran wanted to keep going but he could see dust a mile or so in front of them. "Let's pick it up, Heckman. That's probably the sheriff in front of us."

"I don't like him. You'd think he was my boss the way he talks to me. You ain't my boss either. You wear a badge and carry a gun but that don't make you my boss."

"Jackson's your boss, Heckman, and he told you to ride with the sheriff's posse to save Louisa, so that makes the sheriff your boss. Do you have any idea what kind of trouble Louisa was in? She was kidnapped and that gang was going to kill her."

"Wouldn't be no skin off my nose. Mr. Jackson's neither," he said, almost defiantly. "None of them likes each other, don't like people in town. Only thing they like is that bank and the money inside its vault."

Corcoran was almost smiling as they neared the dust raised by the sheriff's posse. *Learned a whole bunch about that family, except for one thing. Is our man in buckskins an outsider? Is he someone who owes money to the bank? Those answers won't be coming from Mr. Heckman.*

CHAPTER NINETEEN

"HE DRANK both canteens of water and went looking for more?" Smoky just stood in the dust, shaking his head. "I know he ain't smart, Corcoran, but that's just plain stupid."

"I don't think our man has ever been on any kind of trail ride. Certainly not one on which he had to make critical decisions. If I hadn't gone back to find him, he'd be dead by morning."

The sheriff moved the group off the roadway when Corcoran and Heckman came into sight and walked up to where the big lawman was talking with Smoky.

"Learn anything?" Sheriff Connor asked. "I heard part of what you were talking about. I've been nursing the situation with Heckman. I've got this idea that maybe he's just a big act. That he's playing the part of a loser."

"The Jackson family is not what might be considered normal, Ed, so you might just be right. I've had that same thought. They don't like each other or anyone else. Don't seem to have any friends." He looked over at Lou Foster. "Something you might follow up on, Lou."

"We were talking about that while you were gone. Louisa has many friends from her school years. We talked about them, but her folks don't seem to have any that she could pinpoint. This almost means the man behind her kidnapping must be a customer of the bank."

Both Corcoran and the sheriff nodded in agreement. "Or a complete outsider seeing potential money," Foster said. "We still going to try for town?"

"I don't think so," Connor said. He was looking at a late afternoon sun falling into those western mountains rapidly. "Babysitting Heckman and now stopping here has changed our timetable. We'll run out of light miles before we reach town. Might just as well set up camp here and ride in in the morning."

"It's the heat that's slowed us down," Foster said. "Between the extreme fear during the kidnapping, then that long, hard run on the horses, and our saving her, Louisa is wrung out. Another night out will do her wonders."

"I'll get Heckman and we'll gather wood," Smoky said. "There's plenty of grass and water. This has been a good spring."

"Too hot for my blood," Ed Connor said. "A couple of good thunderstorms would please me no end right about now."

"Not tonight, Boss," Smoky said. His cackle led him off to find wood for the fire, and Lou Foster moved quickly to help Louisa with her horse.

"Strange to me," Connor said, jerking the saddle from

his horse, "that not a single name has come up from either Heckman or Louisa. Here we have a gang of outlaws dead with one exception, hired by an unknown to extort money from a banker by kidnapping his daughter, and there isn't one single name that might seem out of line."

The old law dog stood straight, shook his head, and finally just kicked some dust. "I've dealt with bank robbers, murderers, and the filth of mankind for all these years, Corcoran, and there has always been that one piece that doesn't belong. We need that piece right now."

Corcoran moved some dust around with the toe of his boot, listening to the sheriff. "That could mean that whoever is behind this mess might very well be awfully close to the Jackson family," he said. "We haven't looked at those bank customers who might have a grudge, but still, it's odd that we haven't heard a single name of someone who might be upset with old man Jackson."

"We haven't looked at those that work for the family, either. Don't know a thing about Heckman. Who else works for the family? How about those that work for the bank?"

Connor looked at Corcoran. "You got a lot of work to do, Terrence, when we get back."

The two men were frustrated, banging their heads so to speak, at a lack of information. "We're trying too hard," Connor said. "A good swig of whiskey and a hot supper, and we'll think better."

"I wonder why it is that we only think that this plan to extort money from old man Jackson has something to do with either him or the bank? Why might it not have something to do with Mrs. Jackson? Or, even Louisa?" Corcoran reached out for the bottle that Sheriff Connor produced, took a drink, and handed it back. "Mighty fine, Ed. Clearing my head already."

Connor laughed, took a swig himself, and they walked over to where Smoky and Heckman had a fire going and sat down on a log to wait for the coffee to boil. "Hey, Heckman," Sheriff Connor yelled out. "Come on over here for a minute. Do the Jacksons have groceries delivered? What, once a week or so?"

"I guess," the overweight and tired man said, flopping down on the ground, back some from the fire. He'd had enough heat for the day.

"You said you were at the house most of the day. I'd think you would know," Corcoran said.

"I don't pay much attention to things like that," Heckman said. "I think I've seen a boy from Malone's Grocery come by once in a while. In a wagon. Never paid much attention."

Corcoran rocked back on his log and looked up at the clear blue sky, wanting to smash in Heckman's face. *He ain't smart enough to be messing with me, he's just a lump of dirt. Doesn't see delivery people?*

"Tell me, Mr. Heckman, who cooks the meals at the Jackson house? Do you eat with the family or do you have to cook your own?" Sheriff Connor showed that he was as upset as his chief deputy.

"I have a shack and do my own meals when I feel like it," Heckman said. "I suppose Mrs. Jackson does the cooking. Wouldn't know for sure. Why would I?"

"Thank you, Heckman," Connor said. "Why don't

you help Smoky with camp chores, eh?" He looked at Corcoran as Heckman made a great effort to get to his feet, groaning and griping the whole time.

"I think we'll get farther along asking that tree there, than Heckman." Connor chuckled and reached out for the coffee pot. "Let's see what Louisa might have to say about it."

"I know Molly Malone has a kid who delivers for her. You were thinking maybe whoever delivers might put together a plan to kidnap Louisa? Considering his answer, I think that's out."

"Yup," the sheriff said. "Good thought, though. Who else would have access to the house? Who might learn something about Louisa?"

"The Jacksons don't seem to have much contact with people in the town, Ed." Corcoran sat still for a minute. "We're going to have to go on a customer with a grudge plan, I think."

Lou Foster and Louisa walked over, and she sat on a log slightly away from the fire. "You two look mighty serious," she said. "Smoky says we're staying here for the night. I've given up on ever seeing a bed again," she joshed, laughing softly.

Foster looked at her soft eyes, wondering how she could even begin to smile after what's happened over the last two days. *Amazing,* he thought, *that she can even walk, more or less act as if things like kidnapping and threats of death happen every week or so.* He poured coffee for the two of them and sat next to her.

"We were talking with Heckman about how your

folks get their groceries and who does the cooking, and he didn't seem to know."

"My mom is a wonderful cook, Terrence. He should have known that." She looked over at the man laying in some wood for the fire. "She has standing orders with Molly Malone for fresh vegetables and domestic and wild meats. Heck should have known that. Why would you ask?"

Corcoran poured another cup of coffee before answering. "Somebody knew your plans, Louisa. We need to know those people who had access to your mother and father. I think we can cancel out the delivery kid. Somebody is close enough that that kind of information might just be a part of a conversation."

"It's that kind of conversation that might have gotten you killed, little lady," Connor said. "We'll find that person. Count on it."

Louisa felt the shudder start at the nape of her neck and shiver all the way down her spine. *Somebody did want me dead. Somebody wanted my father to pay a ransom and then they would have killed me. I'll never get that out of my mind. What kind of terrible person is that? Terrence will find out. I hope it's not somebody I've known forever.*

Her face gave away those horrible thoughts, and Lou Foster tried to ease the fear. "You're safe now," he said. "Whoever was behind this is frustrated, not getting all that money, but you can bet that with the three of us looking for him, he won't try anything else."

"Buffalo jerky and hard tack on the menu, folks." Smoky was all smiles, standing near the fire. "Soak 'em both in hot coffee and you'll dine in elegance."

"Eat well, folks," Sheriff Connor said. "We'll be pulling out early tomorrow."

————

IT WAS WELL after noon when Sheriff Ed Connor led his little trail-worn train into Eureka. Smoky, Heck Heckman, and the pack mule headed for the county stables. "I don't care if you're hurt, Heckman. You are helping me take care of these animals and our equipment. When we get through, you can head for home, but not until everythin' is taken care of." Heckman was still moaning less than half an hour later as he headed to his cabin. Smoky headed for a saloon.

Foster escorted Louisa to her home, and the sheriff and Terrence Corcoran headed for the Bonanza Club and a cold beer. "Didn't expect to see you for another day or two," Jimmy Henderson called out from behind the bar. "Everybody safe?"

"For the time being," Connor said. "Depends on how long it takes you to get a couple of cold beers lined up in front of me."

Henderson laughed and poured quickly. "You'll find wires from Austin on your desk saying that Pete Chambers died on the trail back. I left several on your desk. A couple are for you, too, Corcoran. Before you get all pushy, no, I did not read them." Corcoran chuckled but didn't say anything, like, *then how do you know Chambers is dead?*

"Thank you, Jimmy, and thank you for the provisions," Connor said. "Does Emil Jackson come in here much?"

"Very seldom, Sheriff. He isn't a drinking or gambling man. Got the personality of a pine board. I doubt he'd even know anyone here unless they owed him money."

"That was going to be one of my next questions. Does he have any friends in the community?"

"That man doesn't trust anyone, more or less call someone a friend," Henderson said. "How is Louisa? She's got more friends than both the Jacksons combined. She still as cute as a little doll?"

"No," Corcoran answered. "She's as beautiful a lady as you've ever seen. All growed up, Jimmy, and ready to challenge the world."

"She just went through something that very few live through," Corcoran said. "Tough little lady, in my opinion. Ripped from a stagecoach by armed men who were shooting and killing others on board. Held by those men until we interrupted their play. It'll be a long time before that terror leaves her mind."

"Ah, to be young again," Henderson said, thinking more of what the sheriff said, than Corcoran. He stared up at the ceiling, sighed, and poured two more tankards of beer for the lawman. "She's got spunk, Terrence. It'll take time, but she'll not feel wounded for long."

"You sound like a man who took on the world at one time, Henderson," Connor said. "Did the world win, or you?"

"It was chasing the gold that made me a life-long bachelor."

"You never chased the gold, you built a business to

take the gold from those that did the chasing," Corcoran said. "You never married because you'd have to give up her share of your gold."

The three men laughed long and loud and continued, the deeper the red on Henderson's face and head. "Got me there, Corcoran. I do have a deep love of gold."

"So does the man at the top of my suspect's list," Ed Connor said. "The gang that robbed the two stages and kidnapped Miss Jackson is dead, Jimmy, all of them with one exception."

"Who is that?"

"Wish we knew," Corcoran said. "Someone other than the dead ones put this all together and won't be happy knowing Louisa is home safe and sound. The only thing we know about that person is, he's probably in his mid-twenties and wears buckskins. Bring anyone to mind?"

"A couple of old gentlemen who live in the mountains north of here, but no young ones. Think he's from here? I can't place anyone," Henderson said.

"Ain't spent this much time in the saddle for a long time, Terrence. I'm going home, fill a tub with hot water, and sit there until it's frozen cold."

Corcoran chuckled. "I'll see how the office has stood up to being empty for several days. Keep us posted if you think of anything, Jimmy."

CHAPTER TWENTY

"YOUR FOLKS WILL BE glad to see you," Lou Foster said as they rode up to the Jackson house, which sat on a large plot behind the bank. Built in the Victorian style popular in mining communities of the west, its three stories were filled with vast amounts of filigree, newel posts guarded the stairways and deck, and the roof was steep.

"I'll walk you to the door." He helped Louisa from the horse, tied the two animals to a tethering post, and took her hand. "I've wanted to do this for many years, Louisa. Many years."

"Me, too," she whispered.

"That's not proper behavior in public, young lady," Emil Jackson said as he walked out on the high porch. He was scowling, shaking a finger at the two coming up the walk. "You take your hand off my daughter's right now," Jackson barked.

Foster was stunned and let go of Louisa's hand immediately. He looked back and forth at Louisa and her father.

"Hello, Daddy," she said. It was not the excited squeal that Lou Foster had expected. "Is this how you welcome me home? Deputy Foster saved my life. The least you can do is say something nice to the man."

She turned and looked deep into Lou's eyes. He saw the beginnings of a tear well up and retook hold of her hand. He turned to Jackson. "Sir, I'm Deputy Sheriff Lou Foster, Eureka County, returning your daughter, safe and sound. I'll see to it that you have a full report on the situation within the day." He bowed to Louisa, turned and nodded to Jackson, spun on his boot, and walked to the horses.

Certainly didn't expect that. Man never even smiled at his daughter, only chastised me. What kind of a family is this? Foster's face was filled with anger on the one hand and questions on the other as he mounted his horse and rode quickly to the office. *I haven't had a bath or a change of clothes for damn near a week.* He chuckled, stepping down in front of the sheriff's office. *My stench must have offended the gentleman. I've arrested murderers with more manners than Mr. Jackson.*

———

"HELLO, Smoky. Everything where it's supposed to be?"

"Looks like it. Wires on the desk there, some for Corcoran, some for the sheriff. Sure glad to get rid of Heckman. What a sad example of manhood. He never learned nothing growing up." Sweat was running down his forehead, and he motioned for Foster to leave the door open.

"Maybe get a breeze through here. Get that sweet little lady returned to her family?"

Foster just stood there for a moment, trying to figure out how to answer. "I did, but if you think Heckman's a strange man, you haven't met Louisa's father. Both she and Terrence have tried to let me know that Jackson wasn't your normal person, but I wasn't ready for him."

Smoky saw the look on Foster's face and decided it might be best to not continue the conversation. "I was going to make coffee, but it's just too hot in here to light a fire. I'll just go home and get put back together. You've been on the road even longer than I have."

"Don't I know it," Foster said. "Sure that I smell like it, too." He sat down at the desk and pulled paper, quill, and ink from the top drawer. "Gotta get all this written down before it gets forgotten. Want one from you, too. Everything as best you can remember. When we catch this unknown, buckskin-wearing fool, I want the judge to know everything."

"I've always kept a journal, Lou. Learned that scouting for the Army. Yup, you'll have my report."

The older man headed out the open door, his shoulders straight, his head held up. Tough old geezer. Several days on the trail and you'd never know it

————

"This is the condensed version of your report?" Terrence Corcoran held several sheets of paper filled with Foster's report for Emil Jackson. "Jackson might have a different view of things after reading this. Hard to believe how he acted toward you." He handed the sheaf back. "Tell you what, Mr. Foster. Let's the two of us deliver that report to the banker tomorrow morning, at the bank."

Foster started to say something, but Corcoran waved him off. "Go home, take a nice long bath, eat well, sleep well, and we'll be dressed clean, smell pretty, and invade Jackson's territory in the morning." There was a glint in the Irishman's eyes and an evil grin on his face.

"You make me laugh, Terrence, even when I'm bone tired. You, too, get a good night's sleep," the young deputy said, and walked out of the office. It was hot and dry but his little house was just a block or two away, and he had a good well with cold water waiting to be splashed over his filthy body.

The only thoughts in his quick mind were, *we saved her*, and *gotta find the man who wears buckskins*.

———

"WHY WERE you so mean to him?" Louisa stood in the entryway to the Jackson mansion, her hands flared on her hips, glaring at her father. Mud from several days on the trail mixed by sweat, only went to show her anger. "He saved my life!" she scowled. "He killed the men who kidnapped me," Louisa cried out at him. She was sobbing, actually blubbering, for the first time since being saved. She fell to her knees in front of her father, who sat, rather regally in a stiff armchair. "You remember Lou and his father, you said you liked the young man. Why did you treat him that way?"

"You're filthy, young lady, and he was worse. You need to bathe and change into something appropriate. You can tell me all about your little adventure later. I'll be at the bank," Jackson said. He stood up, wiped a hand down his front as if the dust and dirt from his daughter had gotten onto him, and walked from the rather elegant parlor.

Louisa remained on her knees for another moment or two, wiped away her tears, smudging the mud about, and stared at the empty chair. *I questioned going to Pennsylvania, but I have my answer now.*

As she got to her feet, thoughts of a business life in Pennsylvania got all mixed up with holding hands with Lou Foster, and seeing him with that rifle up in the rocks, lighting up like a bonfire upon seeing her.

"I'll need work if I stay here. I'll have work in Pennsylvania. I'll be warm and happy with Lou Foster. I don't know anyone in Pennsylvania." She talked to herself all the way to the kitchen, where she began preparing the water for her bath.

"I can't imagine where Mother is," she murmured. "Why isn't she here?"

CHAPTER TWENTY-ONE

CORCORAN SAT down at the kitchen table in his little cabin. Dude was put up after a long rub-down session, chomping on fresh grass hay that Corcoran sprinkled with oats. The long, tall deputy was bathed and dressed in fresh clothes. "Just one thing missing," he said, walking toward the cabin's door.

At the well, he took up a second line, not connected to the pulley, and snaked a net bag containing a large, dark bottle from deep in the cold water. "Some people keep their butter this way," he murmured, walking back into the cabin. "I keep my beer."

He poured a mug and sat back down to read through the wires that were sent while he was on the trail. "So, Dirk Mallory, what have you got for me?" Someone standing by would have seen an angry cloud come to work its way across Corcoran's face as he read the missive. "Damn that sheriff."

Mallory spelled out how, instead of questioning Pete

Chambers before riding off, the sheriff wanted to wait until they were back in Austin. Chambers died within three hours of leaving their rocky campsite, never being questioned. *So we know nothing more. Our unknown man remains our unknown man.*

He let the information go and tried to think on things he knew to be true. He had the names of all the Eureka men making up the gang. *Problem with that is, not one of them was smart enough to put together such a plan. How would they have known Louisa wasn't coming all the way home, was stopping off in Austin for a day or two?*

He poured a second mug of beer and sat back in his chair. "Shorty Duggan got his head caved in at Justin Flint's saloon after showing off a twenty-dollar gold piece and gets gunned down while part of the gang holding Miss Jackson. Time to visit the Justin Brothers," he said right out loud. "Dude ain't gonna like this," he scoffed, grabbing his hat.

———

It was late in the day, still hot and dry, as he rode into town. The Justin Brothers Saloon was less than two blocks from Molly Malone's grocery store, and he stopped there first. Many years ago, before she married the late Mr. Malone, she and Corcoran were the talk of the town, and the spark was still there in Corcoran's mind.

He couldn't shoo away his thoughts. Two times in his long lawman career, he had been willing to think about giving up the badge. Crazy Hair, the first, had already won out before she was viciously killed. It was because of that that he balked at tying the knot with Molly. He shook his head a couple of times, hoping the memories would slip away as he walked into her grocery store.

The aroma of fresh vegetables and fruit, some brought by rail all the way from California, filled the large, one-room building. "Well, won't miracles never end. Terrence Corcoran gracing my place again. So nice to see you," she said from behind the counter. "You've been in the sun, sir," she said. After so many days in the saddle, Corcoran was as dark red as the finest Paiute in the Diamond Valley.

"You're even lovelier than the last time I saw you," he said. Her smile was devastating as she offered a nice blush. Molly Malone was in her late twenties, and while never having the pleasure of seeing the green hills of Ireland, she was Irish in every atom of her soul. Molly was close to five feet nine, might have weighed about one forty, and had long, shapely legs, seldom seen by others.

Her long, dark red hair, a match with Corcoran's, hung in long curls, often covering the delightful patches of freckles across her broad shoulders. "I need a little help, sweet lady."

"I'm always ready to help the law, Terrence. Tell me about it. Have anything to do with the Jackson girl? What a terrible thing, to kidnap such a lovely person. If those men had gone off with the banker instead, there would be cheering."

Corcoran chuckled at the comment and followed Molly to some chairs spaced around a pot-bellied stove, which in the winter would be cherry red at this time of day. "We found her and brought her home to her family. The men involved are all from around here. Shorty Duggan, Pete Chambers, Jake Hubbard, and Jonas Johnson."

"I know all of them. Drunks, bums, thieves." She looked at Corcoran and saw the smile work its way in. "What are you smiling at? None of those men are smart enough to do what was done. You aren't telling me who their leader was, Terrence."

"I'm not. You're right, because I don't know." He scowled and looked around the store for a moment. "And my charming lady, that's why I'm here. All I know about their leader is, he was about their age and wears buckskin shirts."

"That's it?"

"Afraid so," Corcoran said. "So, I've come to you, since you know everyone in the county and will give that man away, and I can go to the saloon and make a fool of myself."

"You can make a fool of yourself with me anytime, bucko, but as for a young man wearing buckskins? You've got me." She smiled and reached out for his hand. "What are your ideas?"

"That he's not from here, and he has had dealings with Emil Jackson in the past. Yours?"

"Bad dealings with that nasty banker," she said. "Probably fifty or more people here in town would fit that description. Including me, Terrence. He tried to foreclose on this place while Mr. Malone's body wasn't even cold."

"Well, you're out of the picture, although I would love to see you in buckskins," Corcoran said. He squeezed her hand and slowly got to his feet. "If you think of anything, let me know," he said, kissing her hand.

She felt the spark of electricity spread from her hand to her head and down her spine as she took her hand back. *Do that again, Mr. Corcoran, and I'll wrap my arms around you so tight you'll never get loose.* "You'll be the first to know my every thought," she said. She grabbed him by the shoulders and pulled him in close. "My every thought."

He kissed her gently on the forehead, remembering all the wonderful times they had together. It was because of that damned badge that he and she aren't one. She wouldn't marry him unless he gave up the badge. She had heard too many stories about lawmen not coming home for dinner.

"I still make the best lamb stew you've ever had, Terrence Corcoran."

"Name the day and time," he said, ever so softly. And she did.

———

"So, Eureka's finest comes to call, is it." Justin Flint was behind the bar and his brother Todd was standing at the end of it. "The rules about fighting still are posted, Terrence. Behave yourself, tin badge or no."

"Oh, Justin, you're breaking my heart, you are. Here to talk about Shorty Duggan."

"Haven't seen him since he got his head cracked. What do you want to know?"

"He was killed along with the others who held up the last stage to Eureka and kidnapped Emil Jackson's daughter. She's safe. Duggan is dead. What do you know about him? Who does he hang out with?. And while you're conjuring an answer, I'll have a cold beer."

"Show me some gold and I'll get your beer. As to Shorty, he's a punk who won't work, plays big shot outlaw, and hangs around with people like him. Pete Chambers and that bunch."

Corcoran flipped a cartwheel onto the bar, and Flint handed him a beer. "Well, Chambers and that bunch are dead, too. Somebody a whole lot smarter than any of them put the kidnapping idea together, and I'll see to it he hangs. Anybody come to mind, Flint?"

Flint laughed. "Why would I tell you?"

"Because you're a good law-abiding citizen," Corcoran said. "The gang is from here, the victim is from here, so it stands to reason the man behind it all is from here." He quaffed the cool beer and nodded for another. "Duggan came here with a twenty-dollar gold piece, probably from the first stage robbery. Did the gang drink here regular?"

"Those who drink here are none of your business, Corcoran. You suggesting I might be a part of this? You might want to do your drinking somewhere else."

"Ain't suggestin' nothing, Flint. Just looking for answers. Did they drink here regular, and was there someone else with them from time to time?"

"Time for you to leave, Corcoran," Flint said, taking away the empty mug. Corcoran smiled at the big man and knew that the gang did drink there, and there was someone who drank with them.

"Adios," Corcoran said, picking up his change before walking out the door. He mounted Dude and rode down to the main street and tied the big stud off in front of the Bonanza Club.

"How-do, Deputy Corcoran," Jimmy Henderson said from behind the bar. Got yourself cleaned up some, eh? What'll you have?"

"Some friendly talk and a hefty shot of good whiskey. Did Duggan and Chambers hang out here?"

"No, we prefer paying customers, Terrence. Chambers and Jake Hubbard at least had part-time jobs. Duggan was broke more often than not. That feller from the old candle and lamp shop would buy them a drink once in a while, but they never came in without him."

Henderson pulled a bottle down from behind the bar and worked the cork loose before placing it and a glass in front of Corcoran. "He was a bit of a dandy, I think. Never got his hands dirty."

"I remember him," Corcoran said. "Good at making fancy candles but couldn't make decent lamps at all. Glass would break at the slightest bump." Both men snickered some. "Nobody would buy them after they caused several fires around town."

"He's been gone for several months after closing shop. He and Chambers seemed to get along. Chambers worked part-time for him and at the livery." Henderson pulled a glass from under the bar and poured himself a drink from Corcoran's bottle.

"Other than drinking with the candle maker, those bums didn't come in here."

"Thanks, Jimmy. Have another if you want," Corcoran said, and chuckled softly. "What was that man's name? Can't remember."

"Jason something, I think," Henderson said. "Max Spivey bought the shop and changed the name and the product. Jason...Matlock," Henderson said. *"Jason Matlock's Fine Candles and Lamps."*

That's it. Is he still in town?" Corcoran poured a hefty second shot and offered one to Henderson.

"Last I heard, he was talking with old man Williams about his undertaking business. Jordan Williams has been wanting to retire for years now," Henderson said.

"One business I would not want," Corcoran said.

"What's this all about, anyway?"

"Well, you heard me and the sheriff talking about someone much smarter than that gang of fools who abducted Louisa Jackson. That person, about their age, probably lives here or near here, may have had a bad experience with the banker or his daughter, and may be looking for a big payday."

"Well, having a bad experience with Jackson's bank includes a lot of people, Corcoran. I have no idea if Jason Matlock owed the bank any money when he closed shop. Not even sure if he's still in town."

Corcoran slipped the cork back in the bottle and shoved it across the bar. "I'll finish this tomorrow." He put a five-dollar gold piece on the bar and turned to leave just as Lou Foster walked in.

"Looking for you," Foster said. "Got some trouble at the Panda Bear. Julie asked that you handle it."

"Oh, she did, eh? What kind of trouble?"

Foster cocked his head to the side, smiled a bit before answering, "One of her guests doesn't want to pay. The usual. Julie gets 'em all worked up and then presents the bill. Too dumb to ask how much before the game starts."

Corcoran chuckled. "Let's take a walk. See you later, Jimmy."

CHAPTER TWENTY-TWO

"THAT ENDED WELL," Lou Foster said as they stepped out the door of Julie's Panda Bear House of Pleasure.

"Pay the girl or go home with a knot on your head usually makes a man smarten right up," Corcoran said. It was well after sunset, and it was still stifling hot as the two men walked to their horses. "It's even too hot to eat," Corcoran said.

"Me and Smoky had some of the grub left over from the ride when we unpacked the mule. Henderson threw in some mighty tasty sliced buffalo hump." Foster stepped into the saddle, chuckling. "That Smoky's sure got some tall tales to tell about his days scouting for the Army."

"You can bet they're true, too. That old man's tougher than anyone I know." Corcoran rode with a gentle smile on his face, thinking about standing back to back with Smoky, not that many years ago, putting down fights at saloons. "Yup, most of those stories are for sure real. Well, young'un, it's been one long day. I'm heading for the barn. You and me have some people to visit tomorrow, so get a good night's sleep."

"I'm not sure Mr. Jackson will even let me in the bank after the way he carried on today," Foster said. "He doesn't seem to care what he says to people."

"He thinks because he has a lot of money that he's better than the rest of us, Lou. I'll take good manners from someone before bowing to dollars. He showed me his real self by not taking part in the rescue of Louisa. How does he treat his customers after showing us the way he feels about his own family?

"Remember that, Lou. It will help us find the man behind the abduction attempt. Jackson does not have good manners or good customer relations. See you in the morning." He turned Dude for home and put the big horse in a good trot.

I'll ride with Corcoran for as long as he'll let me, Foster thought, riding off the other way. *Interesting, there's such a difference between Louisa and her father. I know I'm not looking forward to that meeting in the morning.*

———

"JUST LOOK AT THIS," Sheriff Ed Connor said, pouring a cup of coffee. It was early morning and the office was already hot and stuffy, and Connor made it worse by lighting a fire in the wood stove for his coffee. He walked behind his desk and sat down, a smile on his face. "The entire Eureka County Sheriff's office is on duty and it's not quite eight o'clock."

"Stiff, sore, and looking for trouble, Sheriff," Corcoran

growled. He walked over and opened the door. "Do you remember Jason Matlock?"

"The candlemaker? Damn near burned my barn down with one of his lamps. Lit it and less than five minutes later it broke up into a hunert pieces. Yeah, Corcoran, I remember Jason Matlock. What about him?"

"Understand that he's studying undertaking with Jordan Williams since his shop closed."

Sheriff Connor looked at Corcoran, Smoky, and Foster. "I assume that somewhere in all this there's a point?"

"He had a loan with the bank and there's bad feelings. First name on my list of people to talk to. Matlock is a bit of a dandy and has a nasty temper, you might remember. Don't remember him wearing buckskins, though."

"I'll have a talk with him," Connor said. "You and Foster seeing the banker this morning?"

"In about an hour," Foster answered.

"Remember that note he brought me, about the twenty thousand dollars. It was sent to him by way of the Austin telegraph office, not just a note written here in town and delivered. Might have been from one of the now dead gang members, might not."

"Molly Malone was threatened with foreclosure when old man Malone died, and she's sure there are many like her," Corcoran said. "She's going to scout about a bit for us." He walked to the open door and stood out on the board sidewalk, looking at the Diamond Range stretched out to the north. "Went from winter to summer this year. I'd like to be in a camp high up in those mountains right now. Breaking ice to make coffee," he said, slipping back inside the office.

"How's that leg of yours?"

"That long ride did it more good than all the crap old Doc Whidby has had me take. Don't feel bad at all this morning." Connor walked to the coffee pot and poured another cup full. "You think Heckman might be involved in any of this?"

"Not smart enough to get out of his own way, Sheriff," Smoky said. "Although he might have known that Louisa wouldn't be coming straight home and casually passed it along to one of the gang. Or someone who did."

"I'm more inclined to believe the brains behind the plot is a customer of the bank who feels mistreated somehow," Corcoran said. "Someone close enough to the family to know about Louisa being in Austin."

Corcoran looked over at Lou Foster and nodded. "About time, Lou. Let's head for the bank."

———

The sheriff's office was across the street from the Bonanza Club on the main street of Eureka, and the Bank of Eureka was two blocks east. The two deputies, both large men with big chests and wide shoulders, took up most of the walkway and doffed their hats and moved aside for many as they made the short walk.

Most of the conversations they heard had to do with the blistering heat and lack of a breeze. More than one person said they were praying for thunderstorms. "I think we're about to create a bit of a storm ourselves," Corcoran said, but with a smile.

"Simply don't like that man," Foster said. "Suggested I was not a gentleman. Me, Lou Foster, not a gentleman? Humph."

Corcoran chuckled as they walked up two stone steps to the open doors of the bank. It was as hot inside as outside, and they walked up to the clerk. They were the only ones there, which surprised Corcoran. "Good morning, Childers. We have an appointment with Emil Jackson. Would you be kind enough to let him know we're here?"

Elmer Childers was in his fifties, single, and always appeared to be in some kind of pain. His walk was stiff, and he was bent slightly to the right. He had been a clerk at Jackson's bank since the day it opened.

"Nice to see you, Deputy. Always nice to have the law close at hand. Mr. Jackson said you would be coming in. Go right on around. You know where his office is."

Corcoran and Foster nodded and smiled at Mr. Childers, and walked around the little picket fence separating the public and private sections of the bank. Walnut woodwork, granite stonework, and ornate lamps made up the decor, but the heat dominated the environment.

Corcoran knocked lightly on Jackson's office door, waited a couple of seconds, didn't get an answer, opened the door, and walked in. Jackson was slumped across his desk, half his head missing.

"Whew," Foster said. "Shot from behind, Terrence. Right through that window."

"Close the door, Lou." The window was shattered, and Corcoran looked at the wall across from the desk. "Had to be a rifle for the bullet to break the glass, blow through the old man's head, and still wedge in the wall there."

He stood at the wall looking at the bullet, wedged deeply into the hardwood paneling. "Have Childers close the bank and come in here, then you head for Doc Whidby's. After you send Whidby down here, you better head for the Jackson's house and gently pass on the information to Mrs. Jackson and Louisa."

"Ain't gonna be easy, Corcoran."

"Nothing's easy in this business. Take it as another hard lesson." Corcoran walked to the broken window behind the desk and tried to line up where the bullet came through and where it ended up, then followed the trajectory back the other way. *Probably right over there behind that tree. Less than fifty yards. I'm thinking, probably just one man. Would be a good shot, slightly uphill, and Jackson inside, shaded.*

Corcoran looked out the window again, thinking that whoever did the shooting had probably been at that location more than once, practicing, so to speak, in order to know what Jackson's moves would be once he sat down at the desk.

He walked back to the wall across from Jackson's desk, pulled his belt knife, and dug the bullet out of the walnut wood panel. He pulled a bullet from his gun belt and matched them. *Forty-five. Winchester? Henry? Damn fine shooter.*

Corcoran was walking back toward the bloody desk

when Elmer Childers walked in and gasped at the sight. "Oh, no," he cried out. His knees failed him, and Corcoran caught the elderly and frail bank clerk.

"Easy now, Mr. Childers." Corcoran helped him to one of the chairs near the desk. Here," he said. "Sit down and catch your breath." He eased the man into the finely upholstered bent wood chair. "I need to ask you a few questions, all right?"

"My god, Corcoran. How...? Why...?" And Elmer Childers almost passed out.

"Was Jackson here when you got here?"

"He arrived ten minutes or so after me. That's when he told me you would be coming in. Then he went straight to his office."

"It looks like someone was across the street over there and probably used a rifle. Didn't you hear the shot? There was just one."

Childers sat still for a minute, looking around the ornate office before answering, "I did hear what might have been a shot but didn't pay it any attention. I don't hear that well anymore," he said, pointing at his ears. "With these thick walls and that heavy door," he said, again pointing, "I didn't hear any breaking glass or anything. Who would do this?"

Maybe the same person who planned the Louisa Jackson kidnapping, Corcoran thought, but didn't say anything right out loud. "You can bet I'll find out. Doc Whidby will be arriving shortly, Childers. Make sure he can get in. Better make up a sign that the bank will be closed for a while. The family is going to be depending on you."

"Louisa," Chiders said quickly, as if something crossed

his mind. "Is she okay? I almost forgot. Oh, my god, this is terrible." Childers stood up and brushed himself off. "She's just out of college, and Jackson refused to let her come to work in the bank. Looks like that education of hers is about to pay off. The bank's hers, now," he said, his eyes wide. Corcoran noted the slightest smile on the old man's face.

"How's that?"

"Jackson made out his will some time ago and has never changed it. He left the bank, their home, and all the properties to Louisa. He always hoped that he would have a son but his wife was unable to get pregnant. He never changed the will."

Childers slowly walked out of the office and made his way to the big doors to wait for Dr. Whidby. Corcoran walked behind the desk again and tried to see what papers might have been on the desk. The bullet did more than serious damage to Jackson's head, and blood, brains, skin, and bone were splashed across everything.

Can't tell what he might have been looking at. Have to wait until Whidby is finished and the body is moved before I can get into any of it. Interesting that Louisa's been studying economics and law and now might be the owner of this business after she was kidnapped, probably because her father was a cruel banker. He stood looking over the scene, slowly shaking his head.

Whidby knocked once and stepped into the office. "So, the tough man gets his head blown off, eh, Corcoran?"

Tough man, you say?"

"Should have said mean," the doctor said. "You'll find you might have a hundred or more suspects, Terrence.

Man was despised." Whidby looked at the window, the body, and even the far wall. "You dug the bullet out? Let's take a look." Corcoran handed it to him. "Forty-five, eh? Must be a hundred or more guns this could have come from. Rifle or pistol. Glad you're doing the investigation."

He chuckled, moving back to the body. "Glad you were able to save Louisa. She'll have a hard time cleaning up this bank's reputation. You think her kidnapping and Jackson's death are the same crime?"

"The idea's bouncing around, Doc. The more I hear about Jackson and his way with people, the more sure I am. Unfortunately, we managed to kill all of the gang that abducted the girl. Only whoever planned it all is still alive, and we don't know much about him."

"I've brought two men and my wagon, so let me get my work done, and we can talk later, Terrence. I may have some stories to tell you about this man."

"I want to hear 'em, Doc. Deputy Foster will be bringing the family down at any minute. Tell him to meet me at the Bonanza." Corcoran walked out of the office, told Childers that he would have more questions later, and walked down the stone steps and onto the street toward the Bonanza.

CHAPTER TWENTY-THREE

"GOOD MORNING, LOUISA," Foster said. "I have horrible news. May I come in?"

"Of course," she said, stepping back. She looked closely at the big man and saw grief and sadness in his eyes, and no hint of a smile on his rugged face. After several days together, after he and the others saved her from that monstrous kidnapping, what could bring this on? *His eyes, always bright, almost dancing, so sad.*

"Mama and I are having coffee in the kitchen. Please join us. Horrible news? Daddy?"

She grasped his arm with both hands, tight, as she led him toward the kitchen at the far back of the large house. "I'm afraid so," Foster said. The kitchen was all but utilitarian, no built-in warmth as Foster would expect in a ranch house, like he was raised in. Pots and pans hung on the walls, there was a small, rough wood table that must have doubled as a cutting block in the center of the room, and only three chairs.

The kitchen was the center of activity in a ranch

house, but in Victorian architecture, it was the dining room or the parlor. "Good morning, Mrs. Jackson. I'm Eureka County Deputy Sheriff Lou Foster," he said, and was interrupted by the woman.

"I know who you are. Take your hands off him, young lady. Remember who you are."

"This is the man who saved me from those men who abducted me, Mother. You remember Lou from my school days," Louisa said.

"Hmmm," Mrs. Jackson said. "Well, young man, what do you want at this ungodly hour?"

Foster stood, almost stunned by this reaction to his visit. *She's looking down her nose at me, as if I'm some reprobate. What a strange family, and how did Louisa grow into such an outstanding young lady?*

"I'm afraid I have some terrible news. There was a shooting at the bank this morning, and I'm afraid your husband was killed." He couldn't think of any other way to spill the news and felt Louisa's fingers dig deep into his arm.

"You'd best sit, Louisa," he said. He pulled the chair she had been in and helped her down. "I'm terribly sorry to have to bring this to you." He said most of it to Louisa and watched her face crumble into sobs. Her eyes locked onto his, and she continued to hold tight to his arm.

"Oh, Mother, this is terrible. What will we do?"

"The first thing we'll do is make some changes around this place." She glared at Foster, then Louisa. "Take your hands off that man this instance. As you know, Louisa, in the event of Enid's death, the bank is yours. Young ladies who own banks do not hold onto young men of no means. Now let go."

Lou Foster was dumbfounded by Mrs. Jackson's reaction to her husband's death. There was no reaction. He had been a deputy sheriff long enough to have had to bring bad news of this sort to more than one family and had not been privy to anything like this.

Foster took in a deep breath and looked at Louisa. She smiled back at him and did not let go of his arm. "What must we do, Lou? I've never been in this position. Did Daddy suffer? Oh, dear." He saw the tears rolling down her cheeks again and used a napkin from the table to wipe them. He wanted to reach out, lift this lovely creature from the chair, and wrap his arms around her, protect her from what's happened.

"I'll help," he said. "Dr. Whidby should be at the bank now. When he's through with his examination, I'll ask him to move Mr. Jackson to the Jordan Williams Parlor. You can then make arrangements with Mr. Williams."

"Thank you, Lou. Thank you. I'm so sore and tired. Daddy never wanted me to work at the bank, and now, it appears, I own it. That won't go well with many of the men in the community. A woman controlling their assets?"

"You'll do fine, dear lady," he said. *But she's right,* he thought. "I'd best get back down there. I'll keep you advised as to how our investigation goes. Probably have a million more questions for you. Do you have help?"

"Just Mr. Heckman. I'll have to hire someone to help with the house. I have the wonderful Mr. Childers at the bank." She looked right at him, took his hand, and kissed it lightly. "Please stay close. Please."

Foster looked over at Mrs. Jackson, thought to hell with it, and kissed the lovely girl on the forehead. He heard the gasp, and Louisa walked him to the door. "Just ask, I'll be there for you," he said, and headed downtown and the grisly work at the bank.

How did she end up being the wonderful girl she is with a mother and father like that? It was a short walk to the bank, but Foster's mind was hard at work with every step. *Was our missing man the shooter? Logical. He lost ten thousand dollars when we saved Louisa. Could make a man a little upset.*

He was chuckling softly when he walked into the bank. "Dr. Whidby, glad you're still here. I just left the Jackson ladies. Would you be kind enough to deliver Mr. Jackson to the Jordan Williams Parlor? They'll get in contact with him."

"Be glad to, Lou. How are they taking this?"

"Louisa is a strong woman, Doc, but I don't think what's happened has registered with Mrs. Jackson. She was far more worried about Louisa holding my hand."

Whidby chortled some as he hailed the two men who came with him. "She may never get over something like that. After all, my dear Mr. Foster, you're not born of the elite, you know."

Foster started to go into the office when Whidby remembered: *Corcoran said he'd be at the Bonanza and to meet him.*

"Thank you, Doctor. Mr. Childers? Better lock this up tight. The ladies might not be down for a while. Please don't try to clean up the mess in the office until

Corcoran says it's all right." He looked around, shook his head in disgust, and left the bank.

A lot of people are dead, a lot of lives turned upside down, more grief than I want to think about, and all for a few lousy dollars. Is the possession of those few dollars worth all this? He nursed the question for a moment. *Maybe that's where Mrs. Jackson is coming from. The almighty dollar rules and is far more important than character. Well, not with me.*

———

"Do you have any ideas on all of this?" Corcoran asked, as he, the sheriff, and Foster were sitting at a table in the Bonanza Club restaurant, destroying large steaks and mounds of french fries. "I'm going on the assumption that the kidnapping of Louisa and the killing of Jackson are part of the same crime."

"It looks that way to me," Sheriff Connor said. "You've been a deputy for just a short time, Mr. Foster, but you've been in on more than one serious crime. How do you see this?"

Lou Foster sat stock still for just a moment. *The sheriff is asking his opinion? Corcoran was smiling at him, suggesting that he, too, wanted that opinion?* He took a deep breath before putting together an answer.

"Someone is not getting the ten thousand dollars he was expecting because we killed the gang and saved Louisa. That person was already angry enough at Jackson to arrange the kidnapping, so I would say the killing of Jackson is that man's anger fulfilled."

"Well said, Lou," Connor said. "How do we find that angry man? Corcoran?"

"I stopped at that tree the shooter stood behind and saw boot prints but nothing outstanding about them. He didn't eject the cartridge, didn't leave anything that I could see. The shooting does seem to answer one question, though. Our man is most likely a Eureka local."

"There aren't any homes right around there, either," Foster said. "But there are several businesses and they were either open or being opened at that time of the morning."

"There's your next job, Lou. Visit each of those businesses and see what you can learn." The sheriff looked at Corcoran. "I'm going to the undertaker's and talk with Mr. Matlock. What are your plans?"

Foster noted that the sheriff didn't tell Corcoran what to do, but rather let his chief deputy run the investigation. *Trust*, the young deputy almost said to himself. Connor must have tremendous trust in the man. *Just sitting with these two old law-dogs, I learn something every minute it seems.*

"For some reason I can't explain, I want to have another chat with Heckman." Corcoran drained his coffee cup and looked around the table. "Something in the way he talked about Jackson tells me he wanted out of their relationship but seemed to be afraid to just leave. He's a loser, timid, but where did the fear come from?"

"We still need to go over what might be available to us at the bank," Connor said. "I'm not sure they can actually give us the records, but we might be able to find out what properties have been foreclosed on and which might have been threatened."

"I can start that after talking with businesses," Foster said.

"No," Connor said. "It's best if that's done with all three of us present. Either later today or first thing in the morning."

"We might get more information from the newspaper than trying to get the bank to release it," Corcoran said. "After I brace Heckman, I'll swing by their offices and see what I can learn. They're not under any obligation not to talk about such things."

Sheriff Connor harrumphed, folded his napkin, and stood up. "Let's plan on meeting back at the office later this afternoon and put all of what we learn together. I gotta walk off that steak or go home and take a nap," he said, laughing as he walked from the table.

The plates were empty and the three men walked off in three different directions at the beginning of a hot, late spring afternoon.

CHAPTER TWENTY-FOUR

ED CONNOR WALKED to the undertaker's, stopping to say hello to various people he met on the street. He had been sheriff of Eureka County for almost eight years now, and many were wondering if he was going to stand for re-election, what with a bunged-up leg and his age of nearly fifty.

"Well, Mr. Schwartz, to tell you the truth, I haven't made up my mind yet. My leg is fine, now, and I'm healthy as a horse, but those rivers and streams out there are filled with dancing rainbow trout needing to be caught."

The two men laughed loud. "If you decide to run I'll vote for you, Ed. And if you decide to challenge those trout, I'll go with you, rod in hand."

Connor had a grand smile on his face as he reached for the doorknob at Jordan William's undertaking parlor. The aroma of chemicals used in the process was strong, almost overpowering.

"Sheriff," Jordan Williams said, as Connor walked in.

"A good morning to you. I understand you were successful in saving young Miss Jackson from those horrible men. Good job. That family now has another grief to get over. Dr. Whidby delivered our banker here."

"Yes, Mr. Williams, I know. I've been led to believe that you have hired an assistant. One Jason Matlock. Is that so?"

"Well, yes, I did hire him and was going to train him in the business, but I believe he may have quit. He didn't show up this morning and there's been nothing from him. He wasn't complaining of being ill or anything like that, yesterday."

Sheriff Connor tried to not show any reaction and simply humphed some. "Not ill. Injured, maybe?"

"He's a bit of a morose person, Sheriff. Upset at losing his business, not particularly excited about becoming an undertaker despite the economic benefits."

"I wanted to talk with him. Do you know where he lives? He did have an apartment behind his store, but I guess that's out."

"I believe he's staying in the stables behind Mr. Heck-man's cabin. Interesting that, since Mr. Jackson owns that property and Mr. Matlock has such a deep anger with Jackson."

"Indeed," Connor said. "Well, thank you, Mr. Williams. I won't take up any more of your time. Have a good day," he said, and slipped out the door, taking a deep breath of the fresh, but hot air outside.

What an interesting situation, Connor thought, walking toward the sheriff's office. *Rooming with Heckman who may have known that Louisa would not be coming straight to*

Eureka. Matlock driven out of business by Jackson's bank, and he's living with a man who works for but doesn't like Mr. Jackson.

The sheriff turned from heading to the office to walking toward where Heckman runs the Jackson stables and ran into Terrence Corcoran. "Matlock didn't show up for work today, but even more interesting, he rooms with Heckman. Want some company?"

Corcoran chuckled as the two walked toward the Jackson stables. "Williams say much of anything about Matlock?"

"Only that the man is more than angry about losing his business to Jackson's bank, and probably holds a grudge. Not showing up for work on the same morning the banker is gunned down might make this a bit of a dangerous house call, Terrence."

"The killer has a high-power rifle and is a good shot, Ed. Let's work this out, not just barge in, eh?" Corcoran chuckled, and the two men slowed down. "The stables is made up of three buildings, as I recall. One of them is the cabin Heckman lives in, another holds the horses and feed. I think the Jacksons have a team they use for their carriages, and two saddle horses.

"The third building holds the carriages, all the tack, and equipment. And tools for building maintenance. That cabin isn't big enough for two men to live in it, Sheriff."

"It's not," Connor said. "Williams said that Matlock might be housing with the horses. In a stall with the horses."

"We're about a block away," Corcoran said. "Let's hold

up for a minute. How about you take the long way around and come up on the carriage house, and I'll wait until you're close and walk right up to Heckman's little cabin. That way we can cover each other."

"Works for me," Connor said. "Of course, we're both assuming that Matlock is our shooter. He might not be, you know."

"Either way, Ed, we're safe."

Corcoran watched the sheriff take a side street in order to come around from the other side of the Jackson stables, and when he saw him, he walked to Heckman's cabin and knocked on the door. The sheriff held back, standing behind a small tool shed.

Heckman called out, "Who is it? I'm sick. Go away."

Corcoran eased the loop away from his gun's hammer and called back. "It's Sheriff's Deputy, Corcoran, Heckman. Need to have a little talk. Coming in."

He slowly turned the knob and pulled the door open, holding back for a moment or two before stepping into the darkened cabin. Heckman was on his cot, under a heavy wool blanket, groaning as he turned over to face the visitor. His hands were visible, and there were no weapons to be seen.

The shack was just one room with Heckman's cot along one wall, a table with two bent wood chairs sitting slightly off center, and hooks holding clothing along one wall with the single window. It was that other wall where the door was that caught his attention. Half of it was door and window, but the other half was lined with shelves filled with books.

Corcoran's quick glance told him that Heckman

wasn't the same man that he was making himself out to be. *Shakespeare, Cicero, Homer. Volume after volume of classics. For three days, he wanted us to believe he was a dolt, a fool, one who couldn't take care of himself, and I'm looking at the personal library of an intellectual. Was he a teacher before whatever led him to what we see today?*

"What's the problem, Heck?" Corcoran turned as he asked. He pulled a chair away from the table and sat down, just a couple of feet from the cot. "That little ride of ours got you down, some?"

"Little ride? Bah! I need a doctor. I have broken bones, Corcoran. You and the sheriff went out of your way to hurt me. Mr. Jackson will hear about this."

Corcoran cocked his head at the statement. *He doesn't know Enid Jackson is dead? Or is this a part of the ruse?* Looking around the single room, Corcoran looked at the one wall lined with books of all kinds. Greek philosophers, European history, literature, poetry. A library, such as a highly educated man might have. *And here he is complaining about some bumps and bruises, most of which he brought on himself.*

"I understand that Jason Matlock is staying at the stables as well. You and him friends, are you?"

"He's in with the horses. Jackson don't know that."

"Why are you still with Jackson? He doesn't treat you well."

"Got nowhere else to go," Heckman said. "Besides," and the man let the word drift off into the hot air.

"Besides what? Are you afraid of the man?"

Heckman turned aside with a groan and didn't

answer. "What has Jackson got on you, Heck? What are you afraid of?"

"Don't need to talk about it. Ain't none of your business anyway."

"Maybe it is, Heckman, if he's got you living here almost as a slave. What threat does he use? What keeps you here, afraid, not living a decent life?"

"Damn it, Corcoran," the man said, groaning loudly as he turned back to face his tormentor. "Jackson will kill me if I say anything. Go away. Leave me be." The man was whimpering, groaning, and his face was red with anger. "I can't talk about it." The change from illiterate street talk to a gentleman's speech caught Corcoran by surprise.

There's an awfully lot about this man that we don't know. On the trail, he acted like a fool, a bumpkin, a man who doesn't know how to take care of himself, and yet, look at those books, listen to his change in speech. Corcoran remembered what Louisa had said about the man. "Is it because of something you did? Maybe years ago? To Louisa?"

"What do you know about that?" Heckman snapped, realized immediately what he'd done, and rolled over to face the wall. Not groaning, not whimpering. He pulled the wool blanket up tight around his head, hiding, as Corcoran thought.

"I know many things about you, Mr. Heckman. Many things about Enid Jackson. Many things about Louisa Jackson. Tell me what Jackson has on you and what he's been doing about it." His approach had changed from demanding to asking, and Heckman slowly rolled over, eyes red from crying, but also angry. About being found out?

"I'm afraid, Corcoran. He'll kill me if I say anything." Heckman collapsed into his wool blanket, burying his head, but no longer sobbing like a baby. "I did something a man shouldn't do. I was a drunk, Corcoran. A horrible man. I took advantage of young girls."

"Including Louisa Jackson," Corcoran said, not asked.

"I tried, but she's strong. Fought me off, and Jackson found out. Forced me to tell about others. Whipped me with a leather harness strap and made me go to work for him. Said if I ever said anything about any of this, or about him, he would kill me. He uses me, Corcoran, horribly." He was sobbing again, hitting his blanket, hitting himself in the head, beating his fists into the wall.

"Sexually, Heckman?"

"Don't tell him I said anything. Yes, in every way," Heckman sobbed, trying to hide, using the blanket.

Corcoran sat still for a moment and finally got up and grabbed the man's hands and arms. "That's enough, Heck. That's enough." Heckman slowly calmed down, breathing heavy from the workout, and lay still on the cot.

He uses me? Horribly? Am I hearing this right? If I am, I might also be hearing a motive for Jackson's death. Is Heckman smart enough to throw me off, pretending he doesn't know about the death?

Do you hunt, Heckman?"

"Hunt? You mean, like kill animals?" His eyes were wide, his mouth hanging open. "No. No. I don't even have a gun," he said. He looked almost questionably at

Corcoran. "Jackson hates to hunt, too, but he does once in a while. Why?"

Corcoran went out of his way not to look at the empty rifle saddle scabbard hanging on the wall and also changed the subject. "Tell me about Mr. Matlock. Did you invite him here?"

"He lost his business and all his property to Jackson. Had no place to live. Thrown out like a cur dog by that bastard. I know what that's like, Corcoran. To be thrown out, to beg for food, to be laughed at, spit at. Jackson doesn't know Matlock is here. Please don't tell him."

"I won't," Corcoran said. "Is he around? I'd like to talk to him."

"Probably in with the horses. That's where he stays. All day. Doesn't want to talk or see anyone."

"I'll take a walk over. Thank you for talking with me."

CHAPTER TWENTY-FIVE

CORCORAN STEPPED out of the rundown cabin and saw the sheriff slowly making his way into the complex and waved to him to join him. The two stood off from Heckman's cabin, looking toward the stables where they might find Matlock.

"Heckman has a horrible story to tell, but I can't tell you that he's not the killer. He says he doesn't even own a gun, but he has a rifle scabbard hanging empty. Most importantly, Ed, the man has a fantastic library," Corcoran said. "Matlock's been living in the stables there," he said, nodding toward the large building that houses the Jackson horses.

"Library?" Connor asked, standing with his mouth open.

"Heckman is well read, well educated, Sheriff, and somewhere along the years, he also has a terrible story to tell. His attempt to fondle or worse, Louisa, might only be a small part of his background. The man may have had relations with young girls before, and I think Enid Jackson found out about it.

"He's holding Heckman almost as a slave. Possibly worse. Has whipped him with a horse harness, beat him with axe handles, and held food from him. His becoming unable to take care of himself is his way of self-protection. Act, be stupid, ignorant, helpless, and you might not get hurt again."

"Amazing," Connor said. "You said there was an empty rifle saddle scabbard in the cabin? Did it look well-used?"

"Tried to stay away from it, but yes, it did. It recently was filled with a repeating rifle. The indentation of the lever was plainly visible. That's a small cabin, and I did not see a rifle or pistol."

"Interesting," Connor said. "Where's the rifle? Well, let's see if Jason Matlock is home, eh?" He made sure Corcoran was off to the side and had a clear shot through the door if need be, and knocked loudly.

"Go away," Matlock answered.

"Eureka County Sheriff here, Matlock. Need to talk. Open the door." Connor's voice was strong and forceful. Almost a threat, Corcoran thought. He couldn't hold back the smile. *The old man talks about retiring, having a life of fishing, but he's never going to give up that badge, that power.*

Connor heard rustling from inside the stables, but couldn't tell if it was horses moving about or Matlock doing something. Finally, the door was pushed open, and Matlock stood off to the side, mostly in the shadows.

"What do you want, Sheriff?" The man was tall, thin, and dressed in a housecoat over long pants. His hair hung long and stringy, hadn't been brushed in some time, and it looked as though he hadn't shaved in a day or two, either.

"Me and my chief deputy would like a few words with you, Matlock. Can we come in?"

"Come on, then. I suppose you plan on telling Jackson I'm here."

"Not at all," Corcoran said, following Connor into the dark stable. *So, he might not know Jackson's dead? Heckman and Matlock don't know? Nonsense.* Corcoran took a quick look around the stall Matlock called home, hoping to see a rifle.

Matlock had a bedroll spread out in an open stall, a chair, a hanging oil lamp, and a book or two on undertaking, borrowed from Jordan Williams. There was one spindly chair and a milking stool outside the stall, along with a put-together tabletop made from sawhorses.

"You'll have to stand or sit on the ground," Matlock said, sitting down in the one chair. Corcoran squatted on his heels, leaning his back against the rough wood wall, and Connor remained standing. "Mr. Williams asked us to check on you, Matlock, since you didn't come to work and didn't send a message," Connor said.

"Everything all right? You need a doctor or anything?"

The look of surprise on the candlemaker's face almost brought a chuckle from Corcoran. He looked around the stall but didn't see any firearms or ammunition. "You afraid of the banker?"

"Who isn't?" Matlock said. "One wrong word in public, one late mortgage payment, and the man comes down on you like a rock slide."

"Which one got you?" Corcoran asked.

Matlock couldn't hide an ugly, snide look and commented, "Both, Corcoran. A little whiskey talk at Flint's saloon, and a day late with my loan payment. Enid Jackson is an evil man with ears everywhere. He'd have me beaten if he knew I was here."

"You been here all morning?" Connor asked right out.

Matlock cocked his head, looked back and forth at the two lawmen, and said, "All night and all morning. Why?"

"Any way you can prove that?" Corcoran stood up and brushed the dirt from his pants. "Something happened early this morning."

"I hope that means Jackson fell off his high horse and broke his neck. Heckman and I had breakfast in his cabin, and we talked for an hour or so. You can ask him."

"I will," Connor said, and he and Corcoran nodded to the man and started to walk out. "Oh, one more thing," Connor said. "Do you have a hunting rifle?"

"Never have gotten much into hunting or fishing. Too easy to just go to the store and buy what you need. I don't own any firearms, Sheriff. Never have." Corcoran caught himself looking hard into Matlock's face and turned away. Did he see something in those eyes? Was the man telling the truth?

"Thank you for your time," Connor said, and he and Corcoran left the stables.

"Believe him?"

"Not for a minute," Corcoran said. "No dirty dishes at Heckman's. An empty rifle scabbard hanging in plain sight. We got us a pickle, Sheriff."

"Something about him, though," Connor said. "If he shot Jackson this morning, he would have been a little more uptight from my questions, don't you think? He wasn't the least bit testy on the one hand, nor did he try to evade the questions."

CHAPTER TWENTY-SIX

LOU FOSTER WAS STANDING NEXT to the tree the
shooter used in Jackson's killing, looking across the
street, picking out the businesses he would be visiting,
the ones in which someone may have heard or seen the
action. He noted that there wasn't very much walking
traffic, but there were horses and riders and buggies,
shays, and delivery wagons aplenty.

*Jackson opens his bank at nine and he and Mr. Childers were
there but hadn't opened yet when he was killed. Why didn't
Childers hear the shot?* Foster pulled some paper and a
pencil from his shirt pocket and wrote that question
down.

The closest business was that of Ernie Thompson's
apothecary, and Foster walked across the dusty street and
into the shop. A little bell tinkled as he opened the door.
"Well, young Mr. Foster," Thompson said. "You not
feeling well?"

"It's been several years, Mr. Thompson. You're
looking well." Foster was sent to town often for medi-

cines as his father's illness grew worse and worse. "I'm a deputy sheriff now, sir, and here on business, I'm afraid."

"Well, good for you. I was so sorry to hear about your father's passing. Is this visit because of that shooting this morning?"

"Exactly, sir." Foster pulled the papers and pencil from his shirt pocket. "We believe the shooter was standing behind that tree right over there," he said, and pointed across the busy street. Did you hear or see anything? It is important to our investigation."

"Well, I'm sure it is. As you know, I live behind my little shop here, and as a matter of fact, I did hear what I thought was a gunshot this morning. Just one single shot." He walked to the doorway and looked across at the tree, and then over toward the bank. "I was in my apartment fixing my breakfast and didn't come out front. Pancakes, Deputy, I do love my pancakes. They came before being nosey," he chortled.

Foster had to chuckle as well, looking at the very thin man worrying more about his pancakes than whether somebody was being shot at.

"I did see Sheriff Connor and Corcoran out by the tree, but that was later. Guess old man Jackson won't be harassing people over their mortgages any longer, eh? You got any ideas on who the shooter might have been? Some will think the killer a hero, you know."

"We're working on it, Mr. Thompson. Mr. Jackson wasn't well-liked, we know that. Are you one he's harassed?"

"No. This old place has been paid for for years. Don't know why some people feel they have to treat others so badly. I wish you well on your investigation, young friend."

Foster shook hands with the apothecary and walked out onto the sidewalk. The building next door was empty, and the one next to it housed a small and tidy café. He slipped in and took a table by the front window. The swinging doors opened from the kitchen as Maud Fuller came out.

"Lou Foster," she said. "What a pleasure. That big old badge looks good on you. What brings you into my little shop?" The woman, probably near fifty, a bit rotund from sampling her wares, was always full of joy, the first to offer help to anyone in need.

Maud was a widow, and it still pained her that she and Turki were never able to have children. Many is the child in Eureka who calls her Auntie Maud.

"Do you still bake the best apple pies in the county?"

"No, it's now the best in Nevada," she said, and laughter rolled across the hardwood floor. "Want some coffee with that?"

Foster nodded. "And a little talk about this morning's shooting, if you have a few minutes."

"Oh, my. That was horrible. Just horrible. Let me set you up, and I'll have some coffee with you."

Foster looked at his notes as she set up his pie and coffee and brought her cup to the table. "What a terrible homecoming for Louisa," Maud said. "That girl has really grown into a striking young woman, hasn't she. She used to come in here, all legs and arms, skinny as a rail. She never walked anywhere, Lou. She ran and skipped. Oh, to have that kind of energy today."

Foster wanted to talk and dream about Louisa and jerked himself back to business. "Were you in the shop early enough to possibly hear the shot, or see anyone out there around that big tree?"

"I was in the kitchen fixing breakfast for three men sitting over there," she said. "They were laughing about something when I came out."

"Laughing about a gunshot?" Foster asked. "That's not right. Who were they? I might want to talk to them."

"No, Lou. I heard the shot, they didn't. They were joking and laughing and didn't even hear it. When I asked them, they looked at me like I'd lost my mind. You know them, woodcutter Jeff Riley and his workers. Always joking, teasing, laughing. Good regular customers, though."

"Did you happen to see anything near that tree?"

"Not a thing, Lou, sorry. It was hours before I learned about Jackson being killed." She took a sip of her coffee. "How's that pie?"

"Best I've ever had, Maud." He folded his papers and tucked them away. He paid for the pie and coffee, kissed Maud's hand, and slipped out the door. *People hear a gunshot early in the morning and just ignore it?* Deputy Foster was shaking his head as he turned back toward town and the office. *Won't much enjoy telling the sheriff I didn't learn a thing.*

Actually, he did learn something. Never expect anything from those who should be observers.

———

"WHY WOULD Matlock lie about having breakfast with Heckman? He answered every other question straightforward," Corcoran said. "We need to have another chat with the man. What are you writing?"

The sheriff lifted his head, smiling. "Making a list of those we know for sure would have reason to shoot the banker. Heckman has a past that is dark and evil, probably illegal if we knew more about it. Matlock lost his property and his business, has no money, and is squatting on Jackson's property. These two we know about for sure. Any others?"

"Only from other people. Molly Malone said she was threatened, but not foreclosed on. Do you think we're missing someone? I know I do and the only way we'll find out who, is to see those bank records."

"Why don't you and Lou take a walk over to the bank and see what their response might be. I'll find the district attorney and see what the legal answer might be." Connor sat back in his chair and wiped sweat from his brow. "We need a good old-fashioned thunderstorm, Corcoran. Get on that, would you?"

"It's on my list," the big deputy said. Both men were laughing when Foster walked in.

"Glad you two are in a good humor." He hung his hat on a hook and wiped sweat from his face. "Nobody around the bank saw anything. The gunshot was heard, but nobody bothered to see what that was about."

"Typical," Connor said. "Need you to do one more thing, Mr. Foster. We need to know who Jackson has foreclosed on in the most recent months. The bank might not be willing to release that information, but we need you to ask.

"Mr. Corcoran and I are going to see the district attorney to find out the legalities." Connor switched his plans, probably thinking that Foster's relationship with Miss Jackson might prove beneficial. "It might take a court order to get that info, or it might simply be illegal. If the bank refuses, don't push it."

"Maybe I'll take Louisa to lunch and do it that way."

Corcoran and Connor looked at each other and smiled. "That just might work," Connor said.

CHAPTER TWENTY-SEVEN

"THERE ARE all kinds of problems, Lou." Louisa and her mother were in the bank's office. It had been cleaned, blood wiped up, broken glass removed. "It seems that neither Mother nor I can own property, at least that's what an attorney told us. I'm going to have a talk with the district attorney about that."

He saw the grim look on her face and knew she would definitely find out just how far she would be able to go. Would that hold true in his search for answers?

"You'd best do that as soon as possible," Lou said. "It appears as though the vultures are flocking about." He smiled at her. "We, that is, the sheriff and Terrence Corcoran, believe that the gunman may be someone who has a grudge against the bank or your father."

"Mother and I feel the same way. Father was often rather rude and hard on people," Louisa said. She looked at her mother and got the slightest nod. "I hope you're not asking to see some of the bank's records. We couldn't allow that."

"I understand that," Lou said. "Would it be possible to just offer a name or two?"

"I don't think so," Mrs. Jackson said. "I'm furious with our attorney for insisting that we can't own property. I know he's wrong, and Louisa and I will fight that battle right to the end, but as far as divulging information about our clients? That's out. No one would ever trust the bank again. Ever."

Louisa got up and walked to Foster, taking his hand. "I know you understand. Everything is in such an uproar right now. Will you keep us informed?"

"Absolutely," Lou said. "Have there been any threats made, that you know of? Did your father ever talk of such?"

"None that I've heard of," Louisa said. "I just got back in town so wouldn't know of any." She looked at her mother. " Did Daddy ever talk about threats, about personal problems?"

Mrs. Jackson seemed to pull back and did not answer right away. "This might be most important, Mother."

"We rarely talked about the bank, its business, its clients. I wouldn't know of anything like a threat," Mrs. Jackson said.

"That's a shame," Louisa said. "Can I walk you out, Lou?"

"I'd like that," the deputy said and squeezed her hand. He noticed that Mrs. Jackson was not complaining about the two holding hands this time.

At the bank's large doors, Louisa slowed to a stop. "I'll find out about threats, Lou, and let you know. That would be something about a crime, not something about the bank's business."

"You're one bright lady. I'm not very good at this, but would you have supper with me? At the Bonanza Club restaurant?"

"Mother will throw a fit, sir, but I would like that very much."

"About seven, then?" Louisa smiled and nodded, and did not want to let go of his hand as he turned. He bent and kissed her on the forehead and eased his hand away. "I still have some of our things from the ranch, including a very nice little buggy for us."

————

FOSTER WAS STILL WALKING on air when he returned to the office but that left him when he started to make his report. "There is no way we'll be able to sift through the bank's records, but Louisa is going to see if any threats had been made, which might give us a name."

"We didn't do any better with the attorney, either," Corcoran said. "But one good thing came out of our visit. Heckman may not be the fool he pretends to be. He almost gave himself away when I talked with him, but Petri, the DA has a list of grievances against him, including complaints about his behavior around young girls from back east."

"Isn't that what Heckman said Jackson was holding over his head?" Foster asked.

"I believe so," Corcoran said. The big deputy looked first at the sheriff, then at Foster. "I asked Tony Petri specifically if Enid Jackson had ever filed a complaint against the man, and the DA said no complaint has ever been filed locally. I need to have another talk with that guy."

"Want company?" Sheriff Connor asked.

"No," Corcoran said. There was no smile as he continued. "I might need to use a little force to get some answers, and you don't need to know about that."

———————

HE WALKED RIGHT UP to the shack and pounded on the door. "Heckman, it's Eureka County Deputy Sheriff Corcoran. Open up, we need to talk."

He heard rustling around from inside and pounded on the door again. "Open up, Heckman. Let's not turn this into something."

It was just moments, and the door was opened. Heckman was out of his cot, fully dressed, and Corcoran could see sweat on the man's forehead and fresh sweat stains on his shirt. "Looks like you've been busy. May I come in?"

Heckman stood aside, and Corcoran stepped into the one-room shack. The first thing he noticed was the missing rifle scabbard from its hook on the wall. "Sit down, Heckman. This won't take long. Just had a talk with Tony Petri up at the courthouse. Why didn't you tell me about those complaints he has about you?"

"That was a long time ago, Deputy, and far, far away. The district attorney also tell you there are no local complaints?"

Corcoran wasn't talking to the same Heck Heckman he had spent three days with on the trail. This was an educated man speaking in his defense, not a crawling, sobbing man who was afraid of his own shadow.

"Yes, he did. Is it those held by Petri that Jackson was holding over your head?" Corcoran got a nod back. "Why hasn't Petri acted on them?"

"I paid the price. I served three years. It was over. I was being looked at to get my teaching certificate back, and be able to return to the school room when Jackson found out about them and threatened to go to the school board if I didn't take care of him."

"That's the second time you've used that phrase, Heckman. What exactly does it mean, to *take care of him*?" Corcoran watched as Heckman almost returned to the sobbing crybaby he first met. "Tell me," he said.

"He beat me physically, with rope, with whips, even with lengths of willow limbs. It was the only way he could be a man, and I endured it so he wouldn't tell what he knew. His physical whipping did less damage than the emotional damage he's done." His look was imploring, almost demanding.

"He had me in his power, Corcoran. Do what he demanded, or the entire community knows my background."

"You're telling me that you committed crimes against young girls when you taught school back east, got caught and went to prison, and had a chance to return to teaching when Jackson found out?"

Heckman straightened up, wiped sweat from his forehead, and nodded. "That's right. Now, there will never be a chance of returning to teaching. All I have is my education, my reading, and what little writing I've been able to do."

"What will you do now, now that Jackson is dead? Will you stay on and work for Mrs. Jackson?"

"No, I'll not let myself be treated this way again, Corcoran. I've embarrassed myself enough." He had a crooked smile on his face. "I've been invited by a religious group to open a school for them on their private reservation far from Eureka County."

"Do you have a timeline of that?"

"Within the next month is what they want. I've already started packing some of my books. I want to be ready when they come to get me."

"Thank you for talking with me, Heckman. Good luck." Corcoran stood up and walked to the door. His mind was churning on the walk back to the office. *Certainly can't let him leave town, now, can we? Mr. Heckman just moved from being a potential suspect in Jackson's murder to the number one suspect. Another session with Jason Matlock is in order, and then, find the rifle that fits in the scabbard, the one that's now not on the wall.*

CHAPTER TWENTY-EIGHT

TERRENCE CORCORAN and Sheriff Ed Connor held an option on a table at the Bonanza Club barroom, a bottle of whiskey, two glasses, and a pair of cigars ready to be attacked. They looked on these meetings like they were at camp after a nice ride across part of the Great Nevada range. The sheriff and his chief deputy were working out a problem. "Did you get that second meeting with Matlock?" the sheriff asked. He was pouring some excellent bourbon into the glasses.

"Interestingly, no, Sheriff, I did not. Do you remember being told by the man he didn't even bother getting dressed anymore? That he never left the little Jackson livery compound? Well, so we are now both aware, he dressed and left. The stall filled with his stuff was empty. And when I went back and faced Heckman with that news, the man denied knowing any of it."

"Any ideas where he might go? He doesn't have anything worth selling. Does he have any money at all?"

"If he does, it wouldn't be much. I checked both the

stage office and the train depot, and he didn't buy tickets out of town. He's around, someplace. Probably being put up by others who had been taken advantage of by Jackson. Where does all this leave us?" Connor and Corcoran had taken that first drink of bourbon down quickly, and Connor poured another.

Corcoran chuckled. "Heckman went to number one suspect after my talk with him, and Matlock is number one because I can't talk with him. When we're through here, I'm going to see Molly Malone. She seemed to know at least something about the man."

"He didn't have many friends because of those lamps he made. Caused too much damage when they fell apart while burning," Connor said with an ugly look on his face. "Just between us, I put Matlock as the number one suspect. Heckman has a lot of reason to take out the banker, but Matlock seems the more likely of the two." He chuckled, looked up at the pressed tin ceiling, and took a quick sip of bourbon. "Think about it, Terrence. Heckman emptied his canteen by drinking it straight down and then rode into a coulee because of the heat, and he had no water.

"Does this sound like a man who could plan and carry out the murder of a banker?" He took another sip before continuing. "I'm not sure Matlock's that much smarter. Are we zeroing in on those two because we haven't had a chance to look at the bank's records?"

Corcoran shook his head and smiled at his boss. "Probably fifty suspects when we do."

"Look what I found, Mama?" Louisa said, holding up a sheet of paper. "It was in Daddy's top desk drawer with a couple of others."

Beatrice Jackson took the letter and read it quickly. "My heavens," she almost cried out. "Oh, dear. Why didn't Enid tell me? Why doesn't the sheriff know about this?" She looked at the missive again, and handed it back to Louisa. "What should we do?"

"I'm taking this to Lou Foster, and the others that I found, as well?"

"Do they all say the same thing?"

"Yes," Louisa said. "I think they are all from the same person. Father has been living under this threat for some time. He should have given these to Sheriff Connor. Oh, Daddy, just too proud to ask for help."

There were three letters, all calling for Jackson's death, appearing to have been written by the same person, and Louisa slipped them into an envelope and walked out the door. *My own father not willing to ask for help and look what it got him. I hope Lou or Corcoran can let these lead him to the killer.*

———

Despite the heat, it was a quick walk to the sheriff's office, and hopefully, she thought, some answers. "They were in your father's desk? Interesting that he would keep them," Sheriff Connor said, handing the notes to Corcoran.

The chief deputy scanned the notes quickly and handed them to Lou Foster. "Looks like they were written by the same person. Shame they aren't dated. They must have been dropped off, not mailed in an envelope. Nothing there to follow up on."

"To the point, for sure," Foster said. *You will die, Banker, for your wicked ways.* Foster wagged his head. "I can't imagine getting something like this and not letting someone know. He should have brought the first one straight here."

Foster looked at Louisa, and she nodded in agreement. He wanted her by his side, and that's where she wanted to be, but neither one moved. "I haven't seen that many hand-written notes from people around town, so I don't recognize the writing," Foster said.

"I have several notes from Jason Matlock after one of his lamps almost burned me out," Sheriff Connor said. He started digging through a file he kept in one of the side drawers on his desk. "Here we go," he said, pulling out several sheets of paper. "All hand-written."

He shook his head at the first one and handed it to Corcoran. "Damn it. Just Damn it," he said, caught himself. "I'm so sorry, Louisa. You didn't need to hear that."

"I just spent one day with a gang of murderers and two days with roughneck lawmen, Sheriff. I think I can handle it."

"No match, I take it," Corcoran said. Instead of answering, Connor just handed him the note. "Not even close," Corcoran handed it to Foster. "Right back to where we were, which is nowhere," Corcoran said. "No dates and no specifics. An angry and hurt man willing to kill who he believes is responsible for doing something that brought physical pain as well as economic loss."

Corcoran stretched, grabbed his hat, and headed for the door. "Going to see Molly Malone and then the Bonanza Club. Still want to know why Matlock moved out of his stall," he said.

Lou Foster looked over to Louisa. "Would you or your mother have any notes or anything from Heck Heckman?"

"No, I don't think so. He's almost illiterate, I think. I better get back. Do you think whoever wrote those threats is the one who killed my father?"

"I'm pretty sure, Miss Jackson," Ed Connor said. He looked at Foster. "Didn't Corcoran say that Heckman had been a teacher before his problems with young girls?"

"That's right, Sheriff." Foster turned to Louisa. "Why do you and your mother think the man's illiterate?"

She cocked her head to one side. "I'm not sure. I guess it's just the way he acts. Like someone who has never learned to read or write. You say he taught school? I find that far-fetched, Lou."

"According to Corcoran, the man has one wall of that shack he lives in, filled with books," Connor said. "Literary classics, Greek mythology, the stuff a teacher might read. Heckman was not illiterate. But here we go again, there's nothing in this note that would indicate it was written by a well-educated man, either."

"Mr. Matlock is a candlemaker of good note and a rather poor maker of glass lanterns," Foster said. "Sheriff, I don't think either man wrote those notes. Somebody who did business with the bank and ran head-on into Jackson wrote them and is probably the killer."

Sheriff Connor sat back in his chair and looked at the two young people. "There is also the possibility that whoever wrote those notes never followed through. As much as either Heckman or Matlock may have their own reasons for wanting Mr. Jackson dead, neither one was involved."

"I'll walk you home," Foster said, leaving the sheriff sitting at his desk, chuckling softly.

CHAPTER TWENTY-NINE

"Terrence," Molly called out as Corcoran walked into the grocer's. "I'm glad to see you, big boy. I have an elk's haunch that needs your ability to cut it up properly." She looked up at the ceiling for just a moment. "Remember those steaks you cut on a camping trip we took?" She pretended to swoon, and Corcoran had to chuckle. "And if you do it for me, you can join me for supper later on."

"A man would be most foolish to turn down an invitation like that. I know you have some fine knives, dear lady. Show me the way." *Oh, yes, Molly Malone, I remember carving the steaks and a lot more about our camping trips. So much more.* Whether Molly saw the smile on his face or not, he couldn't hide it or his thoughts.

She came around the counter, took his hand, gripped it tightly, and walked him into the back room where a cutting table held the meat. An array of knives, cleavers, and saws were spread near the haunch. "Let me have your hat," she said.

"You've had these knives a long time. Where did they come from? They're excellent."

"My father had them made. He was an excellent butcher, meat cutter," she said. "He's the one who taught me the proper way to sharpen and keep an edge."

Corcoran moved the haunch onto where he could work but also wanted some answers if he could get them. "Jason Matlock has moved from Jackson's livery. Do you have any idea where he might have gone?"

"My goodness," she said, slightly taken aback by the question. "I wondered why he was staying in that stall in the first place. He lost his home, business, and cash in the foreclosure, so if he's left the livery, I wouldn't know where he might go."

"That means he hasn't been in for groceries?" Corcoran had cut away a large muscle group and was about to slice some steaks from it.

She never took her eyes from his work, and the look on her face said if he asked, she'd light a fire and they could grill a steak or two right then. She shook her head and tried to get back into the conversation.

"I guess you're right. I don't think he's been in for a day or two. Other than Heckman, he doesn't have any friends." She was watching the large elk haunch become steaks, a roast or two, and stew meat. "Won't take long to sell that. Beautiful," she said.

"There is one lady, Susan Clymer," Molly went on. "She has a little shop of kitchenware and home items not far from the Flint Brothers Saloon. Just up the hill a little. She sells his candles but never his lamps. She might have some idea of where he is."

"I know the place. That's where I'm heading, then. As soon as I'm through here. About seven?" She had a big question written across her pretty face, and Corcoran chuckled. "For supper?"

"Of course. Seven would be fine." She ran her fingers across his strong shoulders, turned so he wouldn't see the smile and walked back toward the front of the store. *I wish that man had as much love for me as he has for that damn badge he wears.* She blushed at the thought.

———————

"HELLO," Susan Clymer said when Corcoran entered the little shop. "And what brings the Eureka County Sheriff into my place?"

"I'm Chief Deputy Corcoran, Terrence Corcoran," he said. He looked around and saw pots and pans hanging, cooking utensils displayed, and a nice arrangement of candles near the checkout counter.

"Nice to see you again, Miss Clymer. Are those candles from Jason Matlock?"

"Why, yes, indeed they are. I'm sorry Enid Jackson was killed, but the man treated so many people terribly. Including Mr. Matlock."

"Did he treat you poorly as well?"

"No. I never gave him the chance." She fluffed up her apron, worked to regain her smile, and asked how she could help the deputy.

"I'm trying to locate Mr. Matlock. He's left where he's been staying, and I need to have a little chat with the gentleman. Do you know where I might find him?"

"I do know, Deputy, but I'm worried about what you'll do to him."

"Just talk," Corcoran said. He cocked his head and wondered what brought on a comment like that. "He might know enough about Mr. Jackson that he could lead me to his killer."

"Well, then follow me." She walked to the far back of her store and through a door that led into a small apartment. Jason Matlock was seated at what might have been the kitchen table. "You have company, Jason," she said. Susan Clymer turned and left immediately, closing the door behind her.

"Hello, Jason," Corcoran said. "May I sit at the table with you? I have some questions that need answers." He noticed the big window that the table sat in front of, and a small rocking chair near a wood stove that could also be a cook stove. He also saw the large bed by the far wall. *Most interesting. Are they a couple?*

"What brought you here? Why did you leave the livery?"

"Heckman told me I had to leave. Said you were too interested in my being there. How did you find me?"

"That's not important. How much about Heckman are you aware of, Mr. Matlock?"

"What do you mean? Aware of what?"

"His personal life. His background. What he's done before going to work for Jackson."

"He reads a lot. Sure more than I would. He has a hatred for Jackson almost as much as I do. Whoever killed that man did this community a favor. Miss Clymer is going to help me try to get my place, my tools, and my business back."

"Seems as though you two are rather tight." Corcoran noticed Matlock's clothing was hung alongside the lady's in an open closet, too.

Matlock ignored the comment. Corcoran's eyes never stopped searching the small apartment, and he spotted what looked like a rifle scabbard hidden under the bed. Just enough of it could be seen for him to know what he was looking at.

"I thought you said you didn't own any guns, Jason. Isn't that a rifle scabbard under the bed?"

Matlock smiled and walked over to pick it out from under the bed. It was more than a scabbard, it also held a fine-looking fowling piece. "Susan loves hunting quail, ducks, and geese. As I told you, I don't have any firearms, nor do I hunt."

Corcoran tightened up as Matlock took the scabbard and pulled a ten-gauge shotgun out and handed it to him. "Rather heavy for quail," he said.

"She has a smaller gun for them and rabbits," Matlock said. Corcoran couldn't help but notice that the man's eyes had softened when he was discussing Miss Clymer. *These two have been together for some time, I think. If I'm right, why did he move into Jackson's horse stall?* He answered his own question. *Propriety. The man's a gentleman. Doesn't give me the impression he could simply walk behind a tree and blow another man away.*

"Heckman has a scabbard similar to this one," Corcoran said. "But he doesn't hunt, does he?"

"He had to hide the gun away so Jackson didn't take it. That bastard treated Heck badly. Beat on him with heavy clubs, whipped him with lengths of leather strapping. Even ripped up a few of the man's books."

"Do you know what kind of rifle it is that Heck has? Did Jackson take it? Are there others?" Corcoran was amazed that Matlock was answering these questions. Heckman denied having any weapons, never mentioned one or more having been taken.

"I don't know much about guns, Corcoran. If Heckman had others, I don't know."

"And you don't have any?" Corcoran said. Matlock nodded, put the shotgun back in the scabbard, and slipped it under the bed. Corcoran was quick to notice that Matlock handled the gun as one who is familiar with firearms.

I wonder what else is under that bed? I wonder why Heckman had an empty scabbard hanging on his wall and now doesn't? I wonder who might be telling the truth? Corcoran took a deep breath, realizing just how many unanswered questions there were, floating around this case of the dead banker.

"Well, Matlock, thank you for your time. I might find more questions."

Jason Matlock just shook his head and opened the door for the big lawman. "Have no idea why you would have questions, but I'll be right here."

Corcoran nodded and walked back into the tidy little shop. "Thank you, Miss Clymer," he said and walked out the door. *Now, I have more questions than I had walking in.*

He chuckled, heading down the street and made a beeline for the Bonanza Club. *If I thought that Heckman made my head spin, Matlock is a fair match. Both he and Heckman have access to guns, but does either one of them have the kind of rifle that killed the banker?*

CHAPTER THIRTY

"You look whipped, Terrence."

"Hot, Jimmy Henderson, and as dried out as a ten-year-old corpse. The man needs a fresh barrel of cold beer." He leaned against the bar and pulled a cigar, lit it, and took a deep drag. "There are times, old friend, that the world wins and Corcoran loses." He looked around the friendly confines of the Bonanza Club.

The fireplace with the chairs wrapped around wasn't lit, of course, but was inviting. Oil lamps hung about, only a few adding their light to the large barroom. One gaming table was operating, the other three waiting for a shift change at the mines. "You have a most comfortable operation, my friend."

It wasn't that many years ago that Jimmy Henderson arrived in the new mining camp of Eureka, put up a tent and called it the Bonanza Club, the first saloon in the county. The tent soon had wooden walls, and then became a full-fledged building. Within just a year, the site held a two-story hotel, full-service restaurant, and a warm and welcoming saloon. Henderson laughed at Corcoran's comment as he poured a glass of Jimmy's own brew. "The town's abuzz over Enid Jackson's killing. Some wondering why you haven't arrested anyone."

"That include you, Jimmy?" Corcoran wiped the foam from his massive mustache and eased the glass Henderson's way. "Fill'er up, Pard, and we'll talk about that."

"You first," Henderson said, filling the glass.

"Things we know," Corcoran said. "Jackson was shot dead from outside his office. Jackson was difficult to deal with, as a banker, and as a human being. Many people seem to have reason to see the banker dead, even to the point of writing threatening notes." Corcoran paused to take another long swig of cooling beer.

"There's more?"

"Oh, yes," Corcoran said. "Someone put together a gang of local men to kidnap and hold for ransom, Louisa, Jackson's daughter. That person was to receive ten thousand dollars, and the gang was to split another ten thousand dollars. It's my opinion that that person is also Jackson's killer." Corcoran took half the beer down and re-lit his cigar.

"What's your opinion, Jimmy?" He ran his hand back a forth, wiping foam from his deep red mustache, smiled, and finished his second beer. "After you fill this up."

Henderson had been through this little drama more times than once with Terrence Corcoran. The deputy used Henderson to bounce ideas off, and asked the right questions, most of the time. Henderson thought this might be one of the times that wasn't right.

"You have one hell of a lot more questions than you

have answers, my friend," Henderson said, sliding another mug of beer down the bar. "From what you've told me, I'd say you have somewhere around fifty or more possible suspects. That bank holds a lot of mortgages, Terrence, and Jackson was a cruel banker."

"The threatening notes were hand-written and I don't recognize the handwriting." Corcoran turned from drinking his beer to sipping the delightful suds. "Heckman or Matlock drink here?"

"Matlock's been in a time or two, but Heckman doesn't drink, as far as I know. Never seen him in here. You seem to be lining your sights up on one or the other of those two."

"Yeah," Corcoran said. "I guess I am." He drained the beer and slid away from the bar. "Thanks, Jimmy. You've only enlarged my field of operations." Corcoran chuckled. "Tell the town talkers you'll have more information for them, later."

————

THE MIDDAY SUN was blistering hot as Corcoran walked out onto the main street. It was a two-block walk to the Flint Brothers Saloon, and he could have made the walk in ten minutes or less if he hadn't had to walk past so many businesses. He was stopped at almost every one of them to enlighten the shopkeepers of the current Jackson situation.

"You here to start trouble, Corcoran? If so, turn right around and leave. Don't want no more of your trouble."

Corcoran smiled and walked right up to the bar. "You

got a lot of room to talk about trouble, Justin. Tell me about your relationship with Shorty Duggan."

"Duggan? Relationship? What the hell's wrong with you? Been out in the sun too long?"

"Might be, but Duggan was here when he got his head banged up. He a regular?"

Justin Flint gave Corcoran a long look before he answered. "Who comes in here," he said, thumping the bar, "isn't any of your business, Corcoran."

"Doing business with a known outlaw could get your license jerked off the wall, Justin. Give that a little thought before you cross me. Duggan a regular?"

Justin Flint's eyes narrowed down, his grim mouth closed even tighter, and he stood behind the bar, seething. Corcoran kept a close eye on the man, knowing there was a shotgun under the bar, within easy reach.

"I don't much care for threats, Corcoran. Get out before I throw you out."

"No, Justin, not until I get some answers. Shorty Duggan was a customer here. Got his head caved in by another of your customers. A few days later, that same Shorty Duggan kidnapped Louisa Jackson and was killed as she was being saved. You see where I'm heading, Flint? Answer me, or I'm shutting this place down, after I arrest you for possibly being involved in that kidnapping."

Did he have that right? Flint asked himself, anger boiling up. *Can he really do that?* "You bastard," Flint said. "Yeah, he and his cronies drank here. Henderson cut them off at the Bonanza. So what?"

"The so what, Flint, is this. Duggan was spending more money than you had ever seen him with. Where did he get that Double Eagle? Even you questioned it at the time. Other than the men who died with him, who else did he hang around with? Heck Heckman? Jason Matlock? Enid Jackson?"

"Jackson? Ha! That skinflint wasn't welcome here. Don't know anyone named Matlock, but Heckman came in from time to time. He and Pete Chambers were long-time friends, the way they put it." He scowled at Corcoran. *This guy is trying to tie me into Jackson's killing. Damn you, Corcoran, I ain't gonna let that happen.*

"That's it, Deputy, get out. No more questions, no more answers. Out." Justin Flint tried to make himself look as big and menacing as he could, which would frighten most any man you know, but Corcoran just snickered, turned, and walked toward the door.

"By the way, Flint," he said, turning back, "what kind of rifles do you own?"

"Get out!"

CHAPTER THIRTY-ONE

CORCORAN WAS STILL CHUCKLING as he walked into the sheriff's office. He left the door open as he found it, hoping there might be a breeze. He hung his hat on the rack and pulled a chair near the door. "Be glad when summer gets here. Be cooler, I believe. I just left Justin Flint, Sheriff, and found out that Heckman and Shorty Duggan knew each other and drank together from time to time. He and Pete Chambers have been friends for a time as well."

Sheriff Connor gave a little *harrumph* as he sat up in his chair. "I thought you or Jimmy Henderson said Heckman didn't drink," Connor said.

"That's what I was told. Told also that he didn't hunt, but he has a rifle tucked away somewhere. I need to find that."

"Yeah, you do," the Sheriff said. "Any ideas? Can't just go searching around."

"Well, now, Sheriff, if you send Lou Foster to bring Heckman here for a little talk, and I go to Heckman's shack to have a talk, and go looking for him, well, you never know what might be found."

Connor tried to stifle a chuckle, turning his head some. "Don't ever let a judge know that, Terrence. Don't never." The sheriff turned toward the door that led into the cell area and hollered for Foster to come out. Corcoran looked out the open door, letting his smile spread across his ruddy face. *That feisty old guy says he might not run for re-election, but he loves this kind of stuff too much.*

"Sheriff?"

"Want you to get over to Heckman's place and bring him into the office. I have some questions for him. Don't arrest him or anything like that, just need to ask him some questions."

Foster grabbed his hat and scurried out the door. "Only the two of us know this, Corcoran. Let's keep it that way," the sheriff said. "For Pete's sake, don't be seen."

Corcoran let Foster get well ahead of him, stood in the shadows of a building, waiting to watch the young deputy and Heckman head for the office before walking into the Jackson's livery. The door to the shack wasn't locked, and Corcoran slipped in.

Such a small little building. Where would I hide a rifle? His gaze settled on the cot Heckman slept in, took a quick glance around the room, and got down on hands and knees at the cot.

It almost has to be here or in that open closet near the back window. He threw the bed covers up and lifted the cot. There were two heavy cardboard boxes that he pulled out, neither one large enough to hold a rifle. Untying the cord holding the first one closed, he found a gentleman's set of clothing, clean, and nicely folded.

"He said he was leaving. These must be the clothes he will wear as a teacher," Corcoran muttered. The other box was heavier than most men could lift, and when the deputy fought it open, he found it filled with books. Corcoran found nothing else under the cot and set it back in place, got back on his feet, and walked around the room.

Corcoran's own cabin was small, but compared to this little shack, it was large. "He has one room for a cot, a table, and two chairs." He shook his head, looking around. The shelves that held the books were empty, and there was only the closet to look into. "I couldn't live like this," he murmured.

At the closet, he pushed aside what was hanging on a thin rope tied somewhat tight and found nothing. *Jason Matlock said he hid the gun. In the cabin? Where else? Was Matlock lying?* Corcoran stood back from the closet, and using just his eyes, started an inch-by-inch search all the way around the little cabin. About halfway around, it dawned on him that the cabin had a peaked roof, and there was a flat ceiling in the room.

How would one get into the attic? The search resumed but at ceiling level, and Corcoran spotted an almost hidden trapdoor right over the top of the cot. He shoved the cot aside, moved a chair under the attic entrance, and climbed up. The trapdoor easily lifted up, and he set it aside, and pulled himself up and inside the attic. The first thing he saw was an oil lamp.

Hope this isn't one of Matlock's, he murmured, getting it

lit. The dust was thick, but Corcoran saw where someone had been up there recently. He followed a trail of disturbed dust, using the ceiling joists across the attic, and there it was, a rifle, wrapped in oilcloth, sitting on ceiling joists.

He's hiding this from Enid Jackson, not from me or Matlock. I wonder what else he might have hidden up here? At some point, I'll have to give this little attic a full look-see. I gotta get out of here. How long can the sheriff keep him in the office?

It didn't take a lot to climb back down into the cabin. Fitting the trapdoor back in place was easy, too. Corcoran dusted himself off and took a seat at the table. *Let's see what we have, eh? There's a lot more to this Heck Heckman fellow than the bumbling, cry-baby, worthless trail-mate that we rode with. A most complicated man. Is he a murderer as well?*

Corcoran pulled the oiled wrapper away and found a lever-action Henry repeating rifle, and when he opened the action, the gun was loaded as well. He ejected the loads and slipped them in his pocket and closed the action. He pulled one bullet from his pocket and looked at it.

I'd bet a lot of money that this matches the spent cartridge I've got at the office. Corcoran tried to make it look like no one had been in the room, knowing Heckman would probably know anyway, and walked out. For someone walking along the streets of Eureka, seeing Chief Deputy Terrence Corcoran patrolling with a large caliber rifle would not raise an eyebrow, and he made for the office.

He saw Heckman coming back from his visit with the sheriff and stepped into Tommy Lane's Saddles, Harness, and Leather Works. "Terrence. What a pleasure," Tommy Lane said. He was sitting at his work table, lacing a tooled head stall. The fragrance of freshly tanned, well-oiled leather filled the air and seemed to change Corcoran's attitude immediately. That aroma was everything Corcoran loved the most. His horse. Riding a mountain path toward his camp. Getting a fire started and brewing coffee.

He could smell every minute of that. "How can you work in this atmosphere. I'd saddle my old brute and head for the mountains." Corcoran shoved his hand out to the businessman.

"Nice to see you, Tommy. Don't know what it is about the smell of leather that warms my heart. How are things?" He tried to get next to a display of harnesses so as not to be seen from outside.

"You looking for somebody, Terrence? I was hoping you were looking for a new saddle."

Corcoran chuckled as he watched Heckman walk right on by. "Dude wouldn't know what to do with a fancy new Tommy Lane saddle. Hoped you had a breeze flowing through. We need some thunderstorms."

"You getting close to whoever killed Enid Jackson? Glad I never did business with that old man. Good job, by the way, saving little Louisa. Saw her yesterday for the first time in years. Has that little girl grown up or what?"

Corcoran smiled and turned to leave. "Thanks for the chance to cool off a bit. Jimmy Henderson will let you know when we catch the killer," he said. His attempt at humor was lost on the man. He was still a block or two from the office and went out of his way not to get too close to the Bonanza Club and a cold beer.

"You found it," Ed Connor said when Corcoran walked into the office. "I found something, too." The sheriff picked up a sheet of paper. "Just take a look at this."

Corcoran set the rifle in the rack and sat across the desk from Connor. "What have we?" he said, picking up the paper and reading it. "It's Heckman's report on our ride out to save Louisa?" The sheriff sat back in his chair.

"Give the sheet another look."

Corcoran took his time and read the report, all at once realizing what he was reading. "Oh, boy. How did you get him to do that? "

"Said I needed it for my report. Look familiar?" Connor reached into the top drawer of his desk and handed him two other pieces of paper.

"My lord almighty," Corcoran said, looking at one, then another of the sheets. "You are a bit of a devil, Sheriff. The handwriting is a match, for sure. This," he said, waving the report, "and the rifle, might just send Mr. Heckman to the gallows."

"There's a lot missing," Connor said.

"I know." Corcoran put the rifle bullets on the desk. "Pull out that empty cartridge you have in the desk. Let's see if this is a match, too."

Connor handed him the empty brass and watched Corcoran match them up. "Yup, Terrence, my friend, Mr. Heckman is in trouble."

"Let's give that a little thought, Sheriff," Corcoran said. "Getting Heckman to write his report will get by the judge with no problem, but I don't think the rifle will. How did it come into our possession? The judge will ask for sure."

"You have another problem," Lou Foster said. "Heckman told me he was leaving tonight to take the new job with that church group."

"Tonight? Damn," Corcoran said. He started to get to his feet when Sylvia Clymer came through the open door, almost wheezing from the effort she put in getting to the office.

"Miss Clymer, here," Corcoran said, offering her his seat. "Lou, get the lady some water, please." He turned to her. "What's happened? You and Matlock have a problem?"

Foster handed her a mug of water, which she drank right down. "It's awful, Terrence," she cried out. "Jason's been shot. I went to the doctor's first, but you must find that horrible man."

"Who, Miss Clymer? Slow down now, catch your breath, and tell us what happened. Right from the start." Corcoran took a quick look at the sheriff and Foster. *This has been one hell of a morning, so far,* he thought. *Why would Matlock be shot?*

Sylvia used a hanky to wipe the sweat from her face, let her breathing come back to normal, and made herself comfortable in the wooden chair. "It was about half an hour after you left, Terrence, that Mr. Heckman burst into my store, pushed me aside, and shot Jason."

"Shot him?" Corcoran asked, looking at the Henry repeater in the rack. "With a rifle, a pistol?"

"He had a pistol. Oh, Terrence, this is terrible. Poor

Jason was just sitting there, bleeding. Dr. Whidby is with him now."

"Did Heckman say anything?" Lou Foster offered another cup of water as he asked.

"He said something, but it wasn't easy to hear. Something about, 'You took it,' I think. Heckman shot him and ran out of the store."

"Do you know which way, Miss Clymer? Back toward town, maybe?" Corcoran was on his feet, getting his hat off the rack.

"He ran out the door and turned south, Terrence. My street only goes another two blocks. I don't know where he would be going that way."

Corcoran nodded to Foster and looked at the sheriff. "Get what more you can, Ed. Foster, get our horses saddled and meet me where that street ends. I'll see what I can find in the meantime."

CHAPTER THIRTY-TWO

CORCORAN DIDN'T WAIT for an answer, just walked out of the office. Terrence Corcoran is a tall man, and he put those long legs of his to the test as he walked fast to Sylvia's shop first, made sure he would be able to talk with Matlock when he came back, which Doc. Whidby assured him he would, and he took the two-block walk to the end of the street.

The street, filled on both sides with small shops and private homes, simply changed from a wide village street to a narrow, two-track trail that led south into mountainous country. The southern end of the Diamond Range. Rough, rocky country that sloped down into a broad open prairie. It was Western Shoshone and Southern Paiute country, and they didn't always enjoy visitors. On the other hand, many local hunters enjoyed herds of mule deer and antelope.

This would be strange, he thought. *Whether he was game-playing with us on our ride to save Louisa or not, the man is not an outdoorsman. On his feet, carrying only a pistol,*

*Heckman is not the man to run off into the wilderness without
food or other provisions. I don't think I'll find anything, but I
have to look.*

Corcoran walked a hundred yards or so up the rocky
trail before he stopped to look for sign. "If Heckman ran
to this trail, I should be able to see his prints in the dust,"
he murmured. Walking in a zig-zag from side to side for
about ten yards or so, he stopped and turned around. He
walked to the west side of the trail and walked back,
slowly, to where he had started.

"This ain't right," he said right out and crossed to the
west side, and walked again to where he had stopped.
"Not one footprint anywhere, except mine. Not one
overturned rock, not one busted dead branch. Heckman
did not run up this trail."

Corcoran walked slowly back to where the street
ended and looked around in all directions. The street
headed north back into the heart of Eureka, and the
closest cross street was a block south of Sylvia's shop.
That cross street went both east and west.

"She must not have seen him turn," he said to no one.
He turned when he heard Lou Foster riding up. "Glad
you're here."

Foster stepped down, handed Dude's reins to Corcoran, and waited for the big deputy to say something.

"I'm not really sure what to do right now," Corcoran
said and explained what he had found, or in this case, not
found. "Where we are is several blocks from that shack
of his, Lou. Did you say he was leaving on the Eureka and
Palisade tonight?"

"That's what he said. He must have found out you

had the rifle and thought that it was Matlock who broke in. Where did he get the pistol?"

"It was probably buried in that box of clothes. I didn't go through them, damn it. I was looking for a rifle that wouldn't have fit. No one has ever even mentioned that Heckman might have a pistol. This man is like a lizard who changes color with everything he's near."

He mounted Dude and just sat for a moment. "He's on foot, Lou, looking to be out of town tonight. Train leaves at six. He would need a horse and wagon to move his books and clothing to the depot, and now, he's shot a man. What would you do? Where would you go?"

Corcoran wheeled Dude around and nudged him into a walk back to town, and Foster rode up alongside. "I think I would head back to Jackson's livery and saddle one of those horses, Terrence. But he's a terrible rider, hates horses, and doesn't even own a camp coffee pot."

Corcoran laughed at the picture Foster drew. "You're probably right about the horse, though. He's scared and probably not thinking straight. Let's start at his shack."

The two lawmen rode to the Jacksons' stables, dismounted, and tied their mounts. "Nice and easy, Lou. The man has a gun, has already shot someone, and is scared. You come up on the shack from the right. There's no window on the left or right. Only in front and back sides."

He pointed off to the right and moved toward the left side of the cabin. "Door's ajar, Lou. Watch out." Corcoran moved slowly up to the side of the porch and tried to see if he could see into the cabin, but it was in deep shadow.

Lou Foster came up on the other side, and Corcoran waved him around to the back side of the shack, indicating he wanted him to try to look through the window. The young deputy made the move quickly and stayed as close to the side of the shack as possible as he sidled up to the window.

The sun was overhead in the clear air, and Foster was sweating profusely as he tried to get a look inside without being seen. It didn't work. He found himself looking into the eyes of Heck Heckman, trying to look out the same window.

Foster jumped back, dove to the ground, and Heckman put two bullets through the cabin wall, missing Foster by just inches. Corcoran heard the shots, burst through the door, took two steps across the small cabin, and slammed his pistol into Heckman's head, knocking the man to the floor.

Heckman tried to move, and a second smash of cold steel knocked him out. "You okay?" Corcoran yelled out, and Foster grumbled, "Yes," as he scampered around the building to come in the door.

"He was looking out as I looked in, Terrence. Damn near lost it," Foster said, shaking his head. "Ain't never had that happen."

Corcoran had to chuckle as he wrestled Heckman over to the cot. "Better go get Dr. Whidby, Lou. I hit him hard, twice." He got the man on the cot and quickly searched him. *No pistol on him.* He looked over to the window and saw it on the floor and moved to gather it up.

"This school teacher likes big guns," he muttered,

looking at a fine Colt. There were four empty casings, two from his shots at Matlock, and two at Deputy Foster. He pulled up a chair and sat next to the unconscious Heckman. "Well, if nothing more, you'll spend time for shooting Matlock and shooting at Foster."

Corcoran looked around the room quickly, saw the two boxes that had been under the cot, and a few more pieces of clothing, ready to be moved to the train station. "How did you plan to get them there, Heck?" he asked the man who couldn't reply. "How much of your actions on the trail were play-acting, eh?"

He untied the box holding the clothing and used the rope to tie Heckman to the cot and walked out toward the stables. "Well, will you look at that?" he said, opening the wide doors. One of the Jackson horses, fully-harnessed, was hitched to a buggy.

"You were ready to move out, eh, Mr. Heckman. Looks like we got here just in time." He walked out of the stables and checked the sun. "That train leaves out at six. You weren't going to the station, were you?" Corcoran muttered. "It's early afternoon, mister." Corcoran was almost back to the shack when Foster arrived with the doctor.

"I'm going to send you a bill, Corcoran. I'm too old to be kept this busy. No more," Dr. Whidby snorted.

"Well, Doc, at least this one isn't a gunshot," Corcoran said. "Busted his head some, is all."

"Humph," Whidby said, and walked into the cabin, not hearing the chuckles from Corcoran and Foster.

"Step into the stables and check out the buggy, Lou.

I'm not sure Heckman was planning on taking the train at all."

"The doctor said we should talk with Jason Matlock. Something about double-cross," Foster said.

"You stay here with Heckman, place him under arrest, and get him back to a cell. I'll go see Matlock." He walked back to where they had the horses and mounted his big stud. "Double-cross? The two of them were working something together?" The muttering continued most of the way to Sylvia Clymer's shop.

CHAPTER THIRTY-THREE

"HELLO, JASON. HOW'RE YOU FEELING?" Corcoran stood at the man's bedside in the little apartment behind Miss Clymer's shop. The candlemaker was pale, probably from loss of blood, and in pain. "Want to tell me about you and Heckman? And what the two of you were planning?"

"Don't know what you're talking about," Matlock wheezed. He had his eyes closed tight, as if in pain, and held his hands close to his chest.

"Like hell you don't," Corcoran said. "He shot you, Jason, because he accused you of a double-cross. Best if you tell me all about this little problem. He shot you with a pistol you told me he didn't have. He accused you of a double-cross of something you told me you didn't have. A business deal? Unless you want to recuperate from those holes in your body in a jail cell, talk to me now."

Corcoran stood over the wounded man, an angry and grim look on his face. He carried centuries of Irish

LAST STAGE TO EUREKA 237

empathy toward the wounded, but also had trouble with his temper when lied to. "You and Heckman had something planned. Don't lie to me."

Jason Matlock groaned as he tried to make himself a little more comfortable, and looked at Corcoran. "It was his idea, not mine. I didn't want to be involved. I wasn't involved. He lied to me." Each little phrase was separated by groans and wheezing, and Corcoran was sure the man was playing a game with him.

"You're about as good a liar as you are a lamp maker, Matlock." Corcoran shoved the wounded man aside and sat on the edge of the bed, glaring into Matlock's face. Matlock howled with pain and Corcoran gave him a little nudge. "Heckman sent threatening notes to Enid Jackson. Did you know that? Or is that part of what you're talking about? Best start talking straight with me, or I might forget you're hurt and rough you up some. Got it?"

He was snarling in the man's face by the time he was through talking, and Matlock was crying like a baby, trying to back away from this most dangerous man. "What was the plan that you double-crossed Heckman?" He bumped the bandage-covered wound just enough to get Matlock to cry out. "Sorry, about that," Corcoran said, patting the wound not very gently, again getting Matlock to cry out in pain.

"Time to talk to me, nice and truthful, honest as the hot day is long, Mr. Matlock. I'm a busy man, have things to do. Don't waste any more of my time." He moved to bump the wound, and Matlock cringed, waiting for the pain, and when it didn't come, let out his breath.

"I thought it was a good idea to send those notes," Matlock groaned. "It was all his idea."

Corcoran listened and wondered what was all his idea. The notes? Was there something else that was all his idea? *Mr. Matlock seems to think I already know what the two of them were planning. Interesting.*

"There was more to it than just sending notes, wasn't there? Keep talking."

"Heckman wanted to do something to put the fear of death in the man, not just scare him with notes."

"What would that have been?" Corcoran was being played with, he was sure. "Tell me, Matlock or suffer the consequences of messing with the law." Corcoran's big right had turned into a fist and was brought up near Matlock's face.

"He wanted to hurt Louisa when she got back to town, but I told him that was wrong, that she didn't have anything to do with our problem with the bank, but he wouldn't listen."

Corcoran sat up straight at the comment and stared at the man, his eyes narrowed, his fist still cocked. Was this how the kidnapping plan came about? Was he getting close to answers about that? Was one of these men the man in buckskins?

"Go on, Matlock. You're doing fine."

"We talked about hurting her, but it scared me too much. I wanted to hurt Jackson, not the girl. That's when we quit talking about it. I quit talking to him."

"What about this double-cross he accused you of?" Corcoran was getting frustrated with the man. "I don't see any double-cross."

"He said that me not wanting to help was a double-cross," Matlock said. "He's not right in the head, Deputy."

"So, did Heckman continue with his plan to hurt Louisa?" Corcoran was almost afraid of what Matlock might say, but continued, "Was he behind the girl being kidnapped?"

"I never talked to him again," Matlock said.

"That's a damn lie!" Corcoran exploded. "You were living in the stables. Saw him every day. Had breakfast with the man. You hated Jackson as much as Heckman. Were you in on the planning for the kidnapping? Were the two of you going to split the ransom money?"

The questions came rapidly, each one a little louder than the one before, and Matlock was trying to edge away from this most dangerous lawman, groaning from the pain of moving, crying out in fear.

"No," he finally called out. "No, Corcoran, that's not what I did."

"Then tell me what you did, and I'll not take another lie from you. You'll spend the rest of your life in jail, Matlock. I'll see to it. No more lies."

Matlock saw the anger in the man, felt the fear of making that anger grow, and took in a deep breath. "I think Heckman may have had something to do with it, but I was not involved. He wanted me to be, but he scared me, the idea scared me. I'm telling the truth." He groaned, pulled the blanket up around his neck, and cowered from the big lawman.

"That's better," Corcoran said. "Did he talk anymore about his plans?"

"Not to me," Matlock said.

Corcoran stood up and straightened the covers over Matlock. "We're going to have a lot more to talk about, Matlock. Just remember, I hate liars. Don't even think about leaving town." He turned and walked out of the apartment and shop, stepped in the stirrup and rode off, back to the office.

"YOU NEED SOME HAY, and I need a cold beer, Dude. Somehow, I am doubting what I think I just learned. Matlock all but told me that Heckman is behind Louisa's kidnapping. I'm going to need a lot more than his talk. Heckman doesn't seem smart enough to get out of the rain, more or less plan what we just lived through." He shook his head, thinking about that.

"On the other hand, the man is well-read and was a schoolteacher. Can a man be a teacher, a bumbling fool, and plan a kidnapping like what happened? Seems a bit far-fetched to me." He casually waved to people walking down the street, thinking about this conundrum. "He's been faking it. He's smart as a whip, acting like a fool to keep me off his trail. You lose, Heckman."

SHERIFF CONNOR and Deputy Foster sat almost in awe as Corcoran told them about his talk with Jason Matlock. They were sitting around a table in the Bonanza Club

Saloon. "It all fits, Terrence," Connor said. "Why don't you believe him?"

"You're right, Ed. It all fits so nicely. But you spent all those days on the trail with the man. Heckman gave us the opinion that he simply can't be the man behind that kidnapping plot. I want to think that Matlock is lying, but it's more and more likely that Heckman has been playing the part of the fool."

"We haven't tried to talk to him. Dr. Whidby left just a short time ago. Said something about you being overly aggressive."

"He just took a shot at Foster, Sheriff. Want me to be nice to the guy?"

"No, Corcoran, you did fine. Doctors don't like to see men get whipped, that's all." Connor whopped his chief deputy on the shoulder. "Seems to me it's about time for a cold beer. We can put together a plan on how we'll question Heckman. The part about him being all cozy with Shorty Duggan and Pete Chambers would be a good starting point."

———

"EUREKA'S WOMEN and children must be safe if all three of you are in my saloon," Jimmy Henderson said. "What'll it be, gents?"

Corcoran was wiping sweat with his bandana, muttering, "Beer, Jimmy, cold beer." They took a table near the front window of the saloon. "And just keep bringing them."

Sheriff Connor walked up to the window and looked

out at the thermometer that hung over the covered walk-way. "Ninety-three degrees," he said. "Last week in May, not July, not August. Wish I had a garden, though."

Mugs filled with golden beer were brought to the table, and Henderson stood just to the side. "You waiting for something?" Corcoran asked, knowing that Henderson wanted an update on the banker's killing. "Something on your mind?"

"The saddle-maker said he thought you might be closing in on an arrest," Henderson said. "I saw Dr. Whidby bring Heck Heckman to the jail, bloody as hell. He the one?"

"He's under arrest for shooting at Deputy Foster," the sheriff said. "We're talking to several about Jackson's death." He took a long drink, wiped some foam from his lips, and smiled. "We need to be several thousand feet up in those Diamond Mountains with this beer. Cool mountain air would feel good right about now."

Corcoran gave the impression that he was enjoying the conversation, but his mind was not inside the Bonanza Club's walls. *Jimmy said that several people came to him asking about our progress on the case, but the one that he keeps mentioning is the saddle-maker. Is it because he sees him more often, or...* and he let his mind come back to the present.

"Give us some space, will you, Jimmy. We need to do some official talking for a few minutes," Corcoran said. "We'll wave when it's time for seconds."

It was obvious that Henderson didn't want to, but he moved back behind the bar, keeping watch and being as close as he dared get. "He'd make a good reporter for the

Eureka Sentinel," Foster quipped. "Do you think that Matlock was lying about not helping Heckman with the plot to get money from Jackson?"

"I'm not sure," Corcoran said. "Heckman's relationship with Duggan and Chambers is my main thought right now."

"Let's not forget that missing man," Sheriff Connor said. "Remember, half the ransom goes to the gang and half to that man. Would that be Heckman? Or Matlock? Or someone we don't know?"

"And not one member of that gang is alive," Corcoran said. "Never got a chance to talk to any of them. What we have is Justin Flint, Heck Heckman, and Jason Matlock, all three of whom might be involved."

"Why Flint?" Foster asked.

"He was there when Heckman met with the gang members. Might have gotten himself involved. He isn't exactly the best citizen we have in our little community," Corcoran said. Connor laughed right out, spilling some of his beer.

"I'm thinking first of how to talk to Heckman," the sheriff said. "I'm sure you're right, Terrence, about him shedding personalities at will. I'm going to treat him as a very smart man who put this plan together. They almost carried it off, you know."

"Somebody let them down. Planted their food and material too far from the stage holdup. Too long a ride to get to it. Would that person also be the missing person? Is that why Heckman acted like such a fool when you brought him along to meet us?" Corcoran sat back in his chair, took a long drink of beer, and waved at Henderson to bring more.

"We might be getting somewhere," Connor said. "Matlock's double-cross. Is he our missing man? The only thing missing would be the buckskin shirt. He's the right age, tall and thin, smart."

They stopped talking as Jimmy Henderson brought fresh mugs of beer. "You boys have a serious pow-wow going on here. Want some smoked elk, sliced cheese? Need to keep your strength up."

Corcoran laughed. "That's a damn good idea. Bring it on, Jimmy, and we might even let you know some of what we're talking about."

Connor chuckled, gave his nod of approval, and Henderson scurried toward the kitchen. "He's a good man," Corcoran said. "Mighty interested is all." He stood up and stretched, took a walk around the table, and sat back down.

"If Matlock is that missing man, we might have a hard time proving it," Foster said.

"We're having a hard enough time proving anything that Heckman might have done. Whose gun is that Henry repeater? Heckman's? Or Matlock's? Heckman drank with Shorty Duggan and the gang. Planning the kidnapping?

"Somebody was supposed to make sure the gang had food and water near the ridge line but left it miles from where it should have been dropped. Matlock? Is that the double-cross?"

Henderson brought out a tray of meat and cheese, and fresh-baked rolls, replenished their beer, and the three men talked for another half hour, finally calling it quits and headed back to the office.

"Been one hell of a day, boys," Connor said. "Get a good night's sleep, and we'll start with questioning Heckman in the morning. We have a good idea of what we think happened. Let's stay on course unless one or the other of those men leads us off in a different direction."

CHAPTER THIRTY-FOUR

CORCORAN SAT STRAIGHT in the saddle as he rode Dude out of town. Coming out of the Eureka

canyon, he let the big stud horse slip from a trot to faster and faster speeds, loving the power he felt from Dude.

"What would it feel like if I could run like this?" He shouted it out and eased the horse back into a nice walk as he neared his cabin. "You are something, Big Man," he said, as they walked up to the corral. He stepped down and undressed the horse, spending some time wiping him down and giving him a good brushing.

"Best friend I've got," he murmured, throwing some hay into the corral. He slipped into the cabin, pulled clean clothes from his closet. "Supper with Molly Malone," he almost whispered. "Nice end to a long day."

It was a cold water clean up and a quick time getting dressed. Dude stood quiet as Corcoran re-saddled him, and he was off to see the charming and very attractive lady. *I'm about to have supper with a wonderful woman, and I*

can't get my mind off the fact that several men tried to kidnap
and probably kill the banker's daughter because of how he treated
his customers. Such a contrast.

One man treats his customers terribly, hurting them, while
these other men treat a girl terribly, not because they hate her, but
because they hate her father. Two wrongs don't make a right, the
old proverb says, and so many now are dead.

He let the thoughts linger for a few more minutes,
riding up to Molly Malone's cabin, behind her grocery
store. The cool of the evening felt good, and his mind
was filled with thoughts of the pretty lady as he stepped
down from Dude.

"You're in a good mood, Terrence," Molly said as she
opened the door for him. He smiled and gave her a little
kiss on the cheek as he came through. "We're a few
minutes from supper. Let's sit on the couch."

He put his hat on the rack and settled into the
comfortable couch, watching her walk to the stove. It
brought back so many memories, mostly of the good
kind. Their long nights together, their three and four-day
camping trips into the Diamond Mountains, enjoying
days and nights just being with each other.

She joined him on the couch, bringing a glass of Irish
whiskey, and as she said, a splash, meaning mixed with a
little water. "You have a good memory." Corcoran smiled.

"I think of you often." She reached out and touched
his hand with her fingertips. "We were good for each
other. I was too young, Terrence. Too young to understand just what you meant to me."

"Well, Molly-girl, I think I was far too much in love
with this old badge I wear." He couldn't stop it, but

thoughts of Crazy Hair flooded his memory, and then thoughts of so many fun times with Molly.

"I suppose both of us needed a little growing-up time," he said.

"Does that badge still make the rules?" Molly took a little sip of the white wine she had sitting on the side table. "I want us to be friends, Terrence."

Corcoran was smiling at the thought, trying to figure out how to answer. *As friends, we would be safe,* he thought, *but safe isn't my style. As we had been before would be best, but she wants to go to that next step. A finalized couple. Marriage.*

"Let's be friends, Molly. That's why we got along so well. We like being with each other. I like you, Molly-girl."

Molly was about to say something when there came a loud pounding on the front door. She started to get up, and Corcoran kept her back, jumping to his feet. She watched him pull his revolver as he took two steps to the door and yanked it open, shoving whoever was there well back off the porch.

"Corcoran, no!" the voice exploded.

It ended fast as Corcoran pulled the man to his feet, tucked his gun back in its holster, and brought the man into the house. "Molly, I think you know Smiley, our night jailer." She nodded her hello and welcome, and Corcoran demanded, "What's this all about?"

"Sheriff wants you at the jail. Trouble, Terrence, big trouble. Heckman might be dead by now. Gotta hurry. Nice seeing you, ma'am," and Smiley turned to lead the way out.

"Damn. Well, all right, Smiley." He turned to Molly. "I'm sorry," he muttered, and followed Smiley.

Molly Malone watched them walk out the door, heard it click closed, and slowly got to her feet. The tears were running down her cheeks as she pulled a leg of lamb from the stove. "Friends. Damn you, Corcoran. I can't fight that badge."

————

"WHAT HAPPENED?" Corcoran asked coming through the door.

Sheriff Ed Connor and Dr. Whidby were sitting across from each other at the desk.

"Smiley went to get supper for he and Heckman, and while he was gone, someone broke in and beat the hell out of our prisoner," Connor said.

"What do you mean, Smiley left to get their supper. It's always been delivered. That's our contract with Henderson."

"Not tonight," Smiley said. He handed a note to Corcoran who read it twice before putting it down on the desk.

"The delivery boy is sick? Pick it up yourself?" Corcoran looked back and forth between Smiley and the sheriff. "You were set up, Smiley. Dollar to a dime, Henderson doesn't know anything about this." *I wonder if our missing man is behind this? Getting worried that we might be getting close to him?*

"What's your thoughts on Heckman, Doctor? Is he going to live?" Corcoran pulled up a chair and sat down.

"We haven't had a chance to talk to him, Ed. I'm thinking this is our missing man." He waved the note.

"Me, too, Terrence. Smiley, see if you can find Lou Foster. Might be at the Jacksons having supper with Louisa."

"That's where I'd be," he said, laughing loud as he left the office.

"Whoever got to him used a length of hardwood, Sheriff. A club, and it did a lot of damage to an already damaged head and body." Dr. Whidby was looking at Corcoran as he talked. "I can't tell you that he will last the night."

"I'm just not satisfied with any of this," Corcoran said. "Smiley gets a note from Henderson? Nonsense. But then again, when he got there, the food was waiting for him. So what happened in between there? How was it the delivery boy didn't show up? Does that boy or his parents have any connection here?"

"You've got all the right questions, Terrence," Ed Connor said.

"And none of the answers. Yet. Let's start with that boy who didn't show up." He stopped talking suddenly. "Whoa up there, Pard. If Henderson had someone available to deliver that note, why didn't he just use that person to deliver the food?"

"I'll hold things down here," the sheriff said, "until Smiley and Foster get back. Go talk to Henderson."

"First Jimmy, and then Flint's place." Corcoran reached for his hat. "If Heckman and Chambers talked often, was there a third man at the table? I think we are getting close, Ed. Tell Foster to catch up. I like his quick mind."

Corcoran smiled at the doctor. "Try to keep Heckman alive, Doc. He's still my number one suspect in the banker's murder."

Corcoran never got to see Whidby's frown as he walked out the door.

CHAPTER THIRTY-FIVE

"You're spending a lot of time around here, Corcoran. Something wrong?" Jimmy Henderson was standing at the end of the bar, as owner of the establishment, not barkeep. He had a night shift barman on duty.

"Need a quick couple of questions answered, Jimmy. Let's sit at a table for a few minutes. Bring a bottle, if you please."

Settled, drinks poured, the two men looked at each other. "I don't know what the problem is, Terrence, but I don't think you've ever looked at me like this."

"I'm strung tighter than any banjo you're ever heard, Jimmy." He pulled the note out and handed it to him. "Tell me about this."

"Good lord," he said. "Where did you get this?"

"Is it from you? This is more than important, Jimmy."

"Oh, well, yes. It's from me but at least a year old. It's from when we had the flu problems last year. Kept it in the kitchen in case we couldn't deliver. How'd you get it?"

Corcoran sat as still as he ever could, looking into

Henderson's eyes. *He's telling the truth. I've known this man for years, trusted him with my life more than once. He's not lying, and now I'm stuck in some deep mud.*

"What I'm about to say, Jimmy, I'd like it to be just between us. Not to be spread about." Corcoran watched Henderson look about and shook his head in agreement. "Good. That note was brought to Smiley at the jail tonight. And while he was coming to get the food, someone broke into the jail and beat the hell out of Heckman, who might not live."

Henderson's eyes narrowed, his mouth turned grim, and his anger could be seen from across the street. "The delivery boy was called home, but after Smiley picked up the food. He was about to make the delivery when Smiley showed up."

"How do you know this, Jimmy? You seldom go into the kitchen. I hate to have to ask these questions, old man, but this is a murder investigation. Please."

"I understand, Terrence, and you know I'm not involved. Cindy came out and told me. I found it more than strange and planned on talking to you about what happened."

"You're right, you are not involved. Whose boy does your deliveries?" He took a moment and added, "And who delivered the note to Smiley?"

"No one from here delivered that note, Terrence. Hell, man, if there was someone to deliver the note, there would have been someone to deliver the food." Henderson was getting upset because so many fingers were being pointed right at him.

"Larry Simpson, I think he's twelve or close to it,

does most of our deliveries. He's always shown up and on time. He got a note saying he was needed at home, but after Smiley picked up the food. Cindy said that Smiley showing up was confusing to everyone."

"Thank you, Jimmy. You've done well here. Have you ever had any trouble with the Simpson boy?"

"Never, Terrence. I don't understand any of this."

Corcoran wanted to say that he, too, didn't understand, but he knew he did. "Somebody has to keep Heckman from telling us everything he knows. This was well planned out and designed to make you look involved. I'm more than satisfied that you're not. You're just too damned honest, Jimmy."

Both men laughed, and Corcoran drained his glass. "Lou Foster may come in looking for me. Tell him to meet me at the Flint Brothers Saloon in about an hour."

"It isn't going to take you an hour to get past those three little blocks, Corcoran."

Corcoran laughed. "No, it won't, but I have a stop in between." Henderson looked for more, and Corcoran just smiled and headed for the door.

"TERRENCE? My goodness. What can I do for you? It's rather late, you know."

"I do, Mrs. Simpson, and I apologize for that. May I come in?"

"Certainly," she said, holding the screen door open for the big man. "I hope this doesn't concern Larry. He's most upset already."

"I'm afraid it does. Can he join us?"

Alice Simpson took in a great breath and walked down the hallway to Larry's bedroom and brought him out. He was long-legged and tall for twelve years, but was light as a feather. His growth spurt was in arms and legs, not body weight.

"Larry, I'm Chief Deputy Terrence Corcoran, and I have a few questions for you."

"About what happened tonight?"

"Sit down and tell me what happened tonight, will you? I want your mother to hear everything as well, okay?"

The boy had bright eyes, strong shoulders, and a big smile most of the time. That smile couldn't be seen as he took a seat at the dining room table. "I work part-time at the Bonanza

Club to help Mama. Since Papa died, things are a little thin around here, and I make some money, and Mr. Henderson also lets me bring food home once in a while."

"It's been a godsend, Terrence. A real godsend for us. I can only do a few things for others, like cleaning or washing. It's been hard for us," the widow Simpson said.

"I'm sure it has," Corcoran said, and nodded to Larry to continue.

"I went to work this evening, and one of my chores is to deliver the evening meal to the jail, but Deputy Smiley showed up to pick it up, which surprised everyone. Then I got the note from Mama that she needed me at home. When I got here, she told me she hadn't sent the note. I lost twenty-five cents by not getting to work tonight, and somebody thinks it's a joke."

Simpson showed a touch of anger, which Corcoran liked. "Do you have that note?"

"I do," Mrs. Simpson said. She walked to a small table by the front window and handed it to him. "I most certainly did not write that," she said, showing the same anger as her son. "This isn't funny, Deputy."

Corcoran read the short note while looking at the two: *Come home, Larry, I need help*. Corcoran read it out loud. "And you didn't write this?"

"Not a word of it," she snapped. "Oh, Larry, someone played a joke on you. A bad joke."

"No, ma'am," Corcoran said. "This isn't a joke. It has a lot to do with banker Jackson's murder, I'm afraid." Corcoran looked at Larry's horrified face. "It was supposed to be delivered well before you got it. Make a little sense now?"

Larry nodded, looking back and forth between Corcoran and his mother. "That's why Smiley was there. I wasn't supposed to be. Why?"

"Somebody needed to break into the jail and harm Heck Heckman. It worked, I'm afraid." Corcoran looked at the note and handed it to Larry. "Do you recognize the writing?"

Larry read it again and handed it to his mother. "I've never seen it before, I'm sure."

His mother said the same thing, and Corcoran stood up. "Afraid I have to keep it. Thank you for your time. Other than getting you out of the kitchen, you're not involved in this investigation, so let that worry go," he said with a smile. Larry jumped up and stretched out his thin arm for a man-to-man handshake.

"Thank you, Deputy Corcoran. I'll see you to the door."

Corcoran caught the nod and smile from his mother, and followed the boy to the front door. "You have a very lucky mother, son. Take good care of her," he said, and gave the boy's shoulder a good, solid grip. "Good night."

_____

IT WAS a quick ride to the Flint Brothers Saloon, and he found Lou Foster standing at the bar with the younger Flint brother as barman. "Glad Smiley found you," Corcoran said. "Evening, Jake. Got a couple of questions for you."

"You and this little kid with a badge are nothing but trouble, Corcoran. Ask and I may or may not answer."

Corcoran noticed there was no drink in front of Deputy Foster. *He called Lou a little kid with a badge? That little kid with a badge might just wipe the floor with Jake's face if he's not careful.*

Like his older brother, Justin Flint, Jake was about average in height but heavy and strong. He had a deep chest, broad shoulders, and large, strong hands. He was using all his facial muscles to glare at Corcoran.

"I'll keep them simple, Jake," Corcoran said almost getting a little snort from Lou Foster. "When Heckman came in to meet with Shorty Duggan and his bunch, who else sat at the table with them?"

"What makes you think there were others?" Jake smiled and tried to offer a snicker.

"Let's just say I do know there were others, I just don't know who, and I'm sure you do. This isn't a game, Jake. Too many people are dead, and those who don't cooperate with my investigation might find themselves charged as being complicit. Understand words that big, Jake? Or should I spell it out?"

Foster saw Jake start to reach for the shotgun under the bar and tensed for the fight, but Jake eased off. "You got a lot of nerve, Corcoran. I don't like being threatened."

"Then answer the question." He looked around and saw only two or three people in the saloon, one of them, at the bar, being the retired Wells Fargo agent who busted Shorty Duggan's head. He nodded to the man and asked him to come down to the bar and join the conversation.

"Mr. Diddy, if I'm not mistaken," Corcoran said. Diddy squeezed in between the two deputies. "Mind answering a question or two?"

"Not at all, Corcoran. This have to do with Jackson's murder?"

"Indeed. Do you remember Heck Heckman meeting with Duggan and his bunch in here?"

"Duggan was in regular but never had any money," Diddy laughed. "Then all at once showed up with a Double Eagle. That's the day I knocked him out. Go ahead."

"Duggan had a regular group, Pete Chambers, Jake Hubbard, and a kid named Jonas Johnson, right?"

"That's them," Diddy said.

Corcoran turned to Jake Flint. "See how easy this is? Now, I'm going to ask again, when Heckman met with Duggan and the gang, was there someone else involved from time to time?"

The question was aimed at Flint, but it was Diddy who answered. "Yeah, Corcoran, that saddle-maker, can't think of his name, joined the group often. He bought the drinks," Diddy said, and chuckled. "Sure as hell, it wasn't Duggan or Chambers buying."

Corcoran tried not to react to the comment about the saddle-maker. He remembered when the man came to town and fought so hard to get a shop and get it open. *Tommy told me he didn't do business with Jackson's bank, but I remember that he did. Jackson wasn't willing to give him a loan to open his business, but eventually did. Need a lot more to learn here.*

Corcoran turned to Jake Flint. "What do you know about Tommy Lane, Jake? Come in here regular, did he?"

"Who drinks or comes in here ain't none of your business, Corcoran. You ain't got no business in here, either."

Diddy spoke up. "Mr. Lane comes in here often, Jake. You know that." Diddy turned to Corcoran and Foster. "He was always complaining that Jackson was going to evict him if he couldn't raise some money. That's when he started drinking with Duggan and that bunch."

"Why don't you go home, old man," Jake Flint said. "You're talking out of line. Ain't none of your business what goes on in my saloon. Shut your damn mouth."

"That's enough, Flint," Foster said. "This is our investigation. Corcoran has the authority to shut you down if you interfere again." Foster stood to Flint's left and Corcoran and Diddy a couple of feet off to his right.

"Don't you mouth off to me, kid. Go wipe your nose and get the hell out of my saloon." He stood behind the bar ready to make war with the Eureka County Sheriff's office, and Corcoran stepped in.

"Don't make this worse than it already is, Jake. This is a murder investigation, and it involves you, your saloon, and patrons of your saloon. Can I make it more clear?" He stood at the bar, his hands in plain sight, never looking at anything other than Jake Flint.

"What Deputy Foster just said is the truth. Cooperate, Jake, or I close this place down, and arrest you as being complicit. Do you understand what I just said?"

"Ain't nobody arresting me, Corcoran. I'll shove that badge somewhere you won't like. Ain't nobody closing this joint, either." He did the unthinkable in Foster's opinion and made the quick move for the shotgun. Foster was faster and put two bullets through the middle of Jake Flint, driving the man backward.

Flint was like a barrel and fell back into shelves filled with bottles of whiskey, scotch, and gin, breaking many of them. He, broken glass, mixed alcohols, and broken shelving fell to the floor. Flint still had the shotgun in his hands, and as he fell, fired off both barrels.

His eyes slowly turned dull as his last breath wheezed out. Diddy was on the floor moaning, and when Foster turned him over, he found the man had been grazed by just one buckshot and was bleeding hard.

"Better run for Dr. Whidby, Lou. I'll do what I can for the old man." Corcoran pulled his kerchief and knelt down next to Amos Diddy. "You'll be fine, Mr. Diddy. Just a scratch."

"Hurts, Corcoran."

"I'm sure it does. Tell me about Tommy Lane, will you? Did you know him well?"

"No, other than when we were here." He grimaced in pain, closed his eyes for a moment, and started talking, "He'd take that table over there," and Diddy pointed at a table the farthest from the bar. "Them boys would huddle, actually talk in whispers, and look about to make sure no one was close."

"Didn't you wonder what that was all about?"

"Well, I guess I did, but knowing it was Duggan and Chambers, well, I just tuned 'em out. Lane had his problems with the banker, and I just figured they was making bad talk about him."

Corcoran couldn't help remember that Tommy Lane had told him that he hadn't had any problems with Jackson. *Are Mr. Diddy and I talking about our missing man? Was Lane the mastermind behind the kidnapping plot? Was it Mr. Lane who shot Jackson? How does Heckman fit into all of this?*

"Let me make sure I understand, Mr. Diddy. Lane was having trouble with Jackson?"

"Seemed so," Diddy said. "Lane always seemed to have money when he came in here, but complained about Jackson demanding money. Seemed odd to me."

"And to me," Corcoran said. *Lane had trouble getting a loan but told me he wasn't having trouble with the bank. Now, Diddy says he was always having trouble but had money in hand to spend in the saloon.* Corcoran looked at the Wells Fargo agent. "Sounds like the kind of man who doesn't know how to take care of his finances."

His thoughts were interrupted as Foster came in with Dr. Whidby. "Two men shot and there's Mr. Corcoran," he said without a smile.

"And Mr. Corcoran's gun is cold, Doc. I'm afraid Jake Flint is dead, but Mr. Diddy here does need a good going over by Eureka's finest doctor."

"Finest and only," Whidby said. He cleaned up Diddy's scratch and had Foster help him get Flint's body in the buggy. "You're keeping me and the undertaker busy, Corcoran. You can stop now."

"I'm locking this place up," Corcoran said. "Go and get the sheriff, Lou, and Mr. Diddy, I'd appreciate it if you would join me at that table over there. We have some more talking to do."

CHAPTER THIRTY-SIX

FOSTER and the doc wrestled Jake's body out, and the young deputy went to fetch the sheriff. Corcoran looked at the mess behind the bar and walked to the far table, a scowl on his face as he sat down. This idea of the saddle-maker being involved in the Louisa Jackson kidnapping really caught the big guy by surprise.

The man deals in leather all day, making saddles, harnesses for big teams. I wonder if he also works with buckskins? I wonder if he wears buckskins from time to time? He turned his attention to Diddy.

"Mr. Diddy, I need to have you tell me as much as you can about Tommy Lane. His financial troubles, his dealings with the Shorty Duggan crowd, everything."

Diddy sat down, feeling much better after Dr. Whidby cleaned up the deep scratches. "He's a bit of a showboat, Corcoran. Wears those fancy shirts of his more often than not, likes to flash just a bit of cash. He spends some of it, but seems to get more out of showing it off than spending it."

Corcoran chuckled at the comment. "I've seen those types," he said. "What are you talking about his fancy shirts? I've never seen him in anything but a work shirt in his saddle works. What kind of fancy shirts?"

"I called 'em show-off buckskin shirts. Some with fancy beadwork, some with deer or elk horn button closures. Duggan and his bunch loved 'em. I guess, for real, I did, too," Diddy said with a halfway hidden smile.

Corcoran didn't say a word, just looked around the saloon. *I've never seen Tommy Lane in anything but a work shirt. Mr. Diddy just described our missing man. If Lane put together the attacks on the stagecoaches and the kidnapping of Louisa Jackson, was he also the man who shot Enid Jackson?*

"Thank you, Mr. Diddy, you've once again been a big help. I may have a few more questions, but I think I hear the sheriff and Mr. Foster riding up. Go on home and take good care of those wounds."

He watched Diddy make his way out of the Flint Brothers Saloon as Ed Connor and Lou Foster walked in. "Pardon the mess, Sheriff. Come on in."

———

"IF IT WASN'T for Lou, I'd be dead," Corcoran said, the three of them sitting at a table in the Flint Bother's Saloon—Corcoran, Sheriff Connor, Lou Foster, the heart of the Eureka County Sheriff's office. "Never saw it coming. Too interested in Mr. Diddy."

The blast from Flint's shotgun had been heard by someone on the street and reported to the sheriff who made his way to Flint's place, meeting up with Foster.

"With Jake dead, this place now belongs to his brother Justin, so we won't be shutting it down," Sheriff Connor said, "as much as I'd like to."

"I agree," Corcoran said. "Let's concentrate on what we know about Thomas Lane." He looked at Lou. "You two better just sit still and listen to what that old man had to say," and Corcoran outlined what Diddy told him about Lane and his buckskin shirts.

Sheriff Ed Connor sat, almost with his mouth open, as Corcoran spelled out what he knew. "I've known the man from the day he arrived. I've never seen him dressed in buckskin,

Terrence." He looked back and forth between his two deputies. "I know he had trouble getting his loan to get that saddle shop opened, but I haven't heard a word about financial problems. That's a busy shop."

The sheriff shook his head, got up, and eased behind the bar, coming up with an unbroken bottle of whiskey. He grabbed three beer mugs off the bar after finding all the glasses busted up, and returned to the table. "Might be here for a while," he joshed. "You had dealings with Lane?" He asked Foster.

"More than once, but not that often. He made fine harnesses, but was an angry man most of the time."

Strange. Corcoran thought. *He's always been so pleasant, upbeat. Love his leather work. Why did he go out of his way to tell me he hadn't had problems with the bank, yet complain often about those problems at the saloon?* Corcoran held in a chuckle. *Establishing a story, eh, Mr. Lane?*

Corcoran sat back, looking into his glass of whiskey. "I wonder if Mr. Lane wrote that note to the Simpson kid? He's got to be working hard to keep Heckman from talking. What do you know about him, Sheriff, and you, Lou?"

"He's a quiet type, Terrence," Connor said. "What you've said makes me think he has to be our missing man."

"That would implicate him in the two stagecoach holdups and the kidnapping but not necessarily Jackson's murder," Lou Foster said.

"That's exactly where I am, too," Corcoran said. "Does he hunt? Have a decent rifle? Either one of you heard or seen anything about rifles?" Neither man said a word. "Right now, Heckman and his Henry repeater are at the top of Jackson's case, and Lane is at the top of the stagecoach problems."

The sheriff sat quiet, almost staring at the table top. He looked up and looked into each man's eyes before speaking. "Mr. Lane is a dangerous man, Terrence. Hear me out." He poured himself a fresh drink before continuing.

"I don't think he's the Jackson killer. He's had every opportunity. No, he wanted the old man to be hurt. Badly hurt. That was the purpose of the kidnapping. Steal the girl, hold her for a high ransom and kill her once it's paid. I'll bet that it was Lane himself who ruined the plan by not having food and water close for the bandits."

Corcoran sat back, a slow smile coming across his ruddy face. "He was to get half the reward and the other half was to be split between the gang, but it ended up that there was no reward. It's logical to me that he would, in turn, shoot Jackson."

"It would seem so," Connor said. "But it was Heckman who had the bigger hate for the man. Lane would more than likely put together another plan to get money, and Heckman wanted the man dead."

Another round was poured, each man around the table giving deep thought to the problems. "I don't think we have enough proof right now to arrest Mr. Lane," Corcoran said. "And, I think we'll need more than one of those fancy buckskin shirts, too. We almost need a confession."

"That's exactly what we need," Connor said. "I think our candlemaker is off the hook, for the time being." He looked around. "Let's call it a night, boys. Lock this place up. One of us, and it won't be me, has to tell Justin about his brother."

"I'll do it," Corcoran said. "And I'll want you with me, Lou. First thing in the morning, and then we'll have a talk with Tommy Lane."

"We're leaving Louisa out of all of this," Foster said. "Do you suppose she had any contact with Lane? We know she did with Heckman."

"You can handle that," the sheriff said with a chuckle. "Let's get out of here."

———

CORCORAN AND FOSTER rode out of the county stables just after eight o'clock the next morning. Corcoran had ridden in on Dude, but Foster kept his horse there. "Justin Flint is quicker to lose his temper than his brother, Lou, so we have to be as gentle as possible with this. If he'll even let us. He's known for just erupting in anger and has been involved in at least three killings at the saloon. He's been cleared of all three by old Judge Peters. Peters loves the idea of self-defense."

"I've never been to their home. I wonder why they didn't just build it behind the saloon."

"They came here as prospectors, made a fair strike, and used it to build that big house of theirs. They sold their claim to Eureka Consolidated for a hefty sum, and built the saloon. It's been successful since the day it opened. They've never had a hired hand, either."

"You know a lot about those brothers," Foster said.

"They've been difficult to get along with from day one," Corcoran said. "Don't have much use for the law and don't care which side they're on either."

The Flint brothers built a large home in the Victorian style. Two stories high with the bedrooms on the second floor. They had a carriage house but no carriage that anyone had seen. A barn was only used for hay storage and stalls for two horses. There were no hogs, no chickens, no milk cow, and no kitchen garden, which would be found at almost every home built out of town.

The brothers lived as if they were camping out, but in the splendor of their Victorian home. The home sat on large acreage, almost ten miles from the heart of Eureka, but the land was never touched by cattle or horses. "They are a strange pair, eh?" Foster said, as they rode up the pathway to the home. They stepped down and tied off.

"Don't walk too close, Lou. Don't make it easy on him." Foster caught the quick smile and held back a step or two, and the men walked toward the large front porch.

"That's close enough, Corcoran. You're trespassing. Get off my place."

Justin Flint was standing at the top of the stairs, a lever-action rifle cradled comfortably in his arms. "Have some bad news to pass along, Justin. Need to talk." Corcoran stopped, held his arms wide from his body.

"You got nothing to talk about with me. Get off my place or die."

"Anything you say," Corcoran turned and motioned Foster to follow. They got about two steps when that rifle sounded off and a bullet drove into Foster's shoulder, knocking him face down in the dirt.

Corcoran spun, his Colt in his hand and cocked it fast. As he jumped to the ground, he got one shot off, which passed through the middle of Justin Flint's head. There was no need for a second shot.

The big deputy was at Foster's side immediately. "Let's see how bad this is," he said, easing the man into a sitting position. "Shot you in the back, old man." He ripped Foster's shirt away from the wound. "That pretty much means he was afraid of you, Lou." He untied Foster's neckerchief and used it to cover the wound. "Think you can ride? Got to get you to Dr. Whidby's."

"What about Flint?"

"He's dead. Up now, on your feet." Corcoran helped the deputy up, and the two worked hard to get him in the saddle. "We'll walk these boys, Lou. Just hang on." Corcoran rode alongside Foster, and it was a long ten-mile ride to Dr. Whidby's office/hospital.

Foster was young and tough as they come, but the combination of a loss of blood and the shock of being shot, forced him to fight hard just to stay in the saddle. "You might have to tie me off, Corcoran," He tried to josh more than once on the ride.

"Damn you, Corcoran. Now you're shooting your own deputies? All right, let's get him in here," Whudby said. Foster was just barely conscious and needed help getting off his horse and into the building. "Any others?"

"Take it easy, Doc. Justin Flint shot him in the back. You'll need to recover Flint's body at the ranch. Let's get Mr. Foster put back together first."

Whudby grumbled and groaned, made a few more comments about Corcoran shooting people, and got Foster undressed and in bed. "Bad," he said, cleaning up around the wound. "Back shot, that bullet done some bad damage here. Tore this boy up bad. Get out of here, Corcoran and check back later."

CHAPTER THIRTY-SEVEN

CORCORAN'S first stop was the Jackson home. *Such an attractive home, but it's filled with so little warmth. Old man Jackson, angry all the time, unable to even have a friend, but was able to produce a wonderful daughter. This life we live is strange sometimes.*

He took the stairs two at a time and gave a solid knock on the hardwood door, which opened immediately. "Hello, Terrence. I was just leaving." Louisa didn't see the flash of a smile she expected. "Is something wrong?"

"I'm sorry to just show up like this. Lou has been hurt, Louisa, but Dr. Whidby is sure that he will be fine. Just sore for some time." He didn't go into any detail, *not up to him*, he thought, but did say he was at Whidby's and she would be able to drop in and see him.

Louisa tightened up but relaxed some as Corcoran talked. "Thank you, Terrence, for coming by. You look like you have something else on your mind. Does all of this have something to do with Dad?"

"More to do with you, possibly. Do you know Tommy Lane?"

"He seems to think that since my father gave him a loan to open his business that we should be friends. I've never met him in person, Terrence. That's what is so strange. I was already in California when he arrived in Eureka." She stepped out on the porch, closing the door.

"He wrote me almost every week while I was going to school. Very strange, in my opinion. I was flattered at first but then was more alarmed at where it all might lead and quit accepting his letters." She had a scowl on her face.

"Let's go in the kitchen, have a cup of coffee, and I'll tell you all bout the man." She led them across the living room and into the kitchen.

Corcoran joined her at the kitchen table and took a drink of hot coffee. "He made advances by post? That's a bit unusual. Did you tell him to stop?"

"I did," Louisa said. "I haven't seen or heard from him since coming home, either." She had a sad look on her face and continued. "He's not a bad-looking man, but tries to overwhelm someone instead of just being friendly. Did he have something to do with Daddy's killing?"

"I'm reasonably sure he had something to do with all of this. Lou will keep you up to date as much as possible." He took a sip of his coffee and smiled at the lady. "One request, though. Could you look at Lane's file with the bank, and if you find something that maybe shouldn't be there, let me know?"

"If there's something off, I'll let you know. Mother

and I are doing well down there, and I haven't run into any problems with existing loans. My father's personality wasn't right for dealing with people. Always angry, it seems."

She escorted Corcoran to the door. "I'll get down to Dr. Whidby's right away. Lou's going to need some serious nursing, I think." Corcoran caught the red flush on her cheeks and turned to walk down off the porch.

"I'm sure he will," he mumbled, stepping into the saddle for the short ride to the office. "Come on, Dude, things are fine at this end."

———

"FOSTER GOT his broken arm all healed up, and now he has a busted-up shoulder, eh? What are we gonna do with that boy, Terrence?" Sheriff Ed Connor said as he and Corcoran were seated in the Bonanza Club café, waiting for a platter of pork chops, eggs, biscuits, and gravy to come out of the kitchen.

"Louisa's story about our Mr. Lane is more than interesting. She shut the man down, and that's probably when he started planning for his big payday and her death. We've got ourselves tied up, Ed. How the hell do we prove any of this?"

"When we're through here, let's pay the man a visit. You and Lou were going to do that anyway, weren't you?"

"Yup," Corcoran said. "There's something strange about those buckskin shirts of his. Why would he only wear them at night, visiting with Heckman, Shorty Duggan, and company? The way Mr. Diddy described them, they would be a standout at his shop. He apparently likes them but only under certain circumstances."

"We're dealing with an unstable mind, Terrence. Making a pass at Louisa by mail, not having ever met the girl in person? That's more than strange," the sheriff said. "Being turned down by the lady, by mail, and conjuring a way to get even with her and hurting her father at the same time? Equally strange."

Corcoran shook his head slowly and reached for his coffee. "How did this artisan, this man who is an artist with leather, get mixed up with Pete Chambers and Shorty Duggan? His business, making saddles, tack, harnesses, is the job of an individual, Ed," Corcoran said. "He's alone all day in that shop, working his leather. It's not like a hardware store, a grocery store, or a saloon. There aren't a lot of people coming through those doors all day long. With a slightly off-center mind to start with, I would bet his conversations with himself are wild."

Connor was laughing right out when sweet little Cindy Cook arrived with platters of food that came out from the kitchen. "Oh, Terrence. You didn't come by like you promised. I have so much love for you."

The platters safely put on the table, Cindy settled into the big deputy's lap, her arms wrapped tightly around his neck. "So much love."

Connor's laugh continued as Corcoran worked to get free. He gave her cute little bottom a pat or two, she gave him a lingering kiss right on the mouth, and she danced her way back to the kitchen.

"You do have a way with the women, old man," Connor said. "Let's eat and talk about Tommy Lane."

"There's several ways of approaching the man, I think," Corcoran said. "Directly, as if we already know the answers, and hope he follows through with a confession, or as if we know nothing and need his help."

"He had to learn that Louisa was going to be staying in Austin for a day or two from Heckman, even if Heckman said he didn't know. Nobody else in that crowd would have known." Connor stabbed another pork chop and poured gravy over it. "Only thing better than this for breakfast is more of it."

Connor cocked his head to one side as if thinking about something. "Have we gotten one word of truth from Heckman? About anything? He and Lane, and Shorty Duggan, but Duggan isn't around to talk to."

Corcoran nodded his agreement. "Based on what we know happened with the stagecoach stops, Lane isn't the smart man he thinks he is. Had the boys rob a stage that Louisa wasn't on. Left food and water far beyond where the gang could ride to following the kidnapping of the girl. Yet gives the impression that he considers himself most intelligent. I think we can use that in our questions."

"I do, too," Connor said. "Your idea of letting him think we might be able to use his help might be the right way. I don't think he killed Jackson, though. I believe that was Heckman. Does Lane have a heavy-duty rifle?"

"Don't know," Corcoran said. "Don't even know where he's from, how he ended up here? Never really had a conversation with the man."

"Nothing like going in blind, eh? Wish Foster could be with us. He has a quick mind, like you, Corcoran."

CHAPTER THIRTY-EIGHT

I<small>T WAS</small> a short couple of blocks to Lane's harness and saddle shop, the late morning sun bleaching the rocks and simmering those out walking. "If this continues, I'm moving to Arizona so I can cool off," Sheriff Connor joshed. "I'd welcome a February blizzard right now."

"Saw in the paper that there are thunderstorms around Winnemucca. Might come this far south, if we're lucky."

Tommy Lane's door was opened in the hopes of a breeze, and the two walked in. The man had his leather etching tools laid out, and he was working on the skirts of a new saddle. "Fine work, Tommy," Corcoran said, watching the knife and hammer closely.

"Hello," he said, and laid the tools down. "Looking for new saddles, are we?"

"Not today, Mr. Lane," Connor said. "Got time for a little talk? Won't take long."

Corcoran saw the smile disappear, saw the hands

tighten up, and felt certain they had the right man. *He knows why we're here, so we'd best ask the right questions.* "Do you remember telling me the other day that you and the banker weren't having any problems?"

"Sure. He's a jerk from the first word, but not with me. Is this about his killing?" Lane looked back and forth at the two lawmen before continuing. "I didn't kill the man, but there have been times I gave it some thought. Understand his daughter has the bank now. She'd be just as bad as the old man."

"Oh?" The sheriff said. "I thought you had eyes on the lady. Wrote letters to her, even. What changed your mind?"

"I don't think that's really any of your concern, Sheriff. Awfully personal, sir. She has a nasty temper, like Jackson, and those of us who have loans with that bank will suffer from it."

"I was talking about letters of possible romance, not loans or mortgages. You and she have a breaking up?"

"As I said, far too personal, Sheriff. Bluntly, none of your business."

"I'm not sure of that, Mr. Lane," Corcoran said. "You're known to be seen with the men who kidnapped Louisa. Your relationship with the lady is important."

It got very quiet in the already quiet saddle shop, and Sheriff Connor watched as Lane's eyes darted about the store, as if he might be looking for something. They settled on a cabinet along the far wall. It stood about five feet tall and was attached to the wall, about two feet off the floor.

The cabinet had matching doors that opened from the center, and was highly tooled. Connor thought for sure that one could easily store a rifle or two inside. Lane turned away quickly, and he settled on looking at Corcoran. "If you're suggesting that I had anything to do with that, you're wildly mistaken. Yes," Lane said, "Miss Jackson and I had a falling out, and she has become rather nasty with me, but I still have strong feelings for the girl."

Sheriff Connor edged his way across the floor, crowded with three beautiful saddles on display, toward the cabinet. The woodwork tooling was well done, and Connor let his fingers follow some of the etching.

"This your work, Mr. Lane?"

"It is," he said. "But I prefer working on leather. I did that years ago. Stay out of it."

Connor let his fingers continue to follow the woodwork, looking to see how the doors were latched. He knew he didn't dare open it, since Lane had said no, but he wanted to know how, anyway.

"Fancy work," he said. "Always wanted to get involved in cabinetry, but the way of the badge has interfered. Tell us about this falling out you had with Miss Jackson. Do you still have thoughts of rebuilding that relationship?"

Corcoran almost chuckled at the comment. *Relationship? He wrote letters and she rejected him. I wonder if he'll try to conjure up an answer?*

"I think it's time for you gentlemen to leave. My relationship with the woman is none of your business." He stood straight, and his eyes burned with anger.

"Well, Mr. Lane, your relationship with someone who

was kidnapped to be held for ransom is very much our business," Connor said. "Your relationship with the men who carried out that kidnapping is very much our business. Your relationship with a woman whose father was recently murdered is very much our business. Answer the question, please."

"No," Lane said. "I don't think I will. Get out of my store."

"If we leave, Tommy, I'm afraid you'll be coming with us. We're investigating the kidnapping of a woman and the killing of her father. You have had a relationship with the father by way of loans for your business. You have had a relationship with the woman by your own comments. You have had a relationship with the men who kidnapped the woman, as told to us by a man who witnessed your meetings.

"You can answer these questions here, in the friendly confines of your own shop, or behind the bars of our not-so-friendly jail cells." Corcoran worked a smile across his face and took a quick step toward Lane, who backed up quickly. "Now, tell us about your current situation with Louisa Jackson."

"There is no current situation," the man said. Corcoran scowled a bit.

"She has rejected your advances is the way I've understood it. What is your reaction to that? To being rejected by the banker's daughter?" Corcoran was casually standing next to a saddle display, letting his fingers move about the beautifully carved leather. "For an artistic man like yourself, it must have taken a toll."

"Damn you, Corcoran, what would you know about

it? How dare you! She has no feelings for anything but herself. Self-centered, living a warm, rich life, never being denied anything she wanted. What would you or her know about losing something?"

Ah, now we're getting somewhere, Corcoran thought. He caught a quick smile that flashed across the sheriff's face and continued. "Your loss is more than just romance, I take it. A little of the easy life to go with a lovely lady's love? Well, that's your loss."

Corcoran turned to Connor. "Is it love and money, or is it desire for money? How is it you became friends with Heck Heckman, Mr. Lane? Was it to get closer to Louisa? Closer to that good life?"

"Mr. Heckman is one of the most intelligent men I've ever met," Lane said. "His personal library exceeds many schools I've known. He suffers from personal losses most would not understand."

"His desire to have relations with young girls, Lane? That kind of personal loss? What about your kind of personal loss? Wealth, is it? A great desire to be wealthy, and here was the lovely Louisa, the banker's daughter, and she rejected your advances. So you dreamed up this idea of taking care of both problems?"

"What do you mean *both* problems?" Lane blurted out.

"Her father's continuing harping on your loans and her rejecting your romantic advances. Kidnap the lady and hold her for ransom, and rip that money from old man Jackson's hands. Would you then kill the girl?"

"It will be a long, cold day in hell before you can

prove anything as wild as that. Arrest me now or get the hell out of my store."

Corcoran smiled, feeling that he hit the right button and that now was the time to leave. He nodded to Connor, and the two walked from the store. It was still hotter yet outside as the two moved down the street, slowly.

"Think he'll bolt?" Connor took a look behind as if he expected to see Lane running away. "I'd sure like to know what's in that cabinet."

"My guess it's those fancy buckskin shirts we've heard about." Corcoran smiled and continued. "He and Heckman came together somehow and tied a knot, a partnership. Probably in hatred of Jackson at first, and then in how to gain from him and hurt him at the same time."

Connor chuckled softly, catching Corcoran's attention. "What do you find funny in all this?"

"Well, Chief Deputy Sheriff, it's now up to you to prove all of this. I'll be looking for your report."

Corcoran chuckled. "I'll be back to see Mr. Lane, Sheriff, and my report will hold his confession." Connor saw the set of Corcoran's jaw, the power in the man's walk, and agreed with him by way of a nod.

It was a quiet walk back to the office, but Corcoran's mind was explosively busy. *I'm still sure that Heckman is the man who killed Enid Jackson, and I'm equally sure that it was Lane who brought the gang together to kidnap Louisa and demand money from the banker.* He chuckled softly and took a quick look at the sheriff, who was smiling as they moved through the town's busy sidewalks.

You're right, Sheriff. All I have to do is prove all of this. Maybe another talk with Amos Diddy, but he's already laid out how Heckman, Lane, and the gang got together often at the Flint Brothers Saloon.

His conversation with himself continued the rest of the way, never reaching a conclusion.

CHAPTER THIRTY-NINE

SHE HEARD the little bells tinkle and saw Corcoran's hulk move through the door. "I'm glad you're here, Terrence." Molly Malone looked around to make sure the store was empty of customers. "I have a great need of your arms wrapped around this little waif."

"Waif, is it? I'll do my best, pretty Molly." He wrapped his big arms tightly around the lady and held her for a long time, kissing her right on the mouth. "Actually, I'm here looking for some help."

"You've come to the right place. Coffee?"

"You've lit a fire in this heat?"

"A charcoal fire out the back door. Follow me." She walked around the counter and out the door to kneel down to where a coffee pot sat in a bed of coals laid out in the dirt. He had to chuckle as she brought the pot back into the store. "Sugar and cream?"

"Irish sugar, my dear."

He wasn't even surprised when she reached under the counter and brought out a bottle of Irish whiskey. "I didn't mean to seem like I was pressing you last night, Terrence. We had such a wonderful relationship before, and I ruined it. I'd like to give it another go. You mean so much to me."

His mind was alive with those same wonderful memories and clouded at the same time, knowing that the life of a lawman wasn't one most women would be comfortable living. Would he make it home after his shift, or would she be called on to identify the remains? Yet, he knew for a fact that he wanted to spend the rest of his life nestled in her warmth.

"And you to me, Molly." He took a long drink of his toddy, smiled, and gave her a peck on the cheek. "It's my work. I hope you understand that. Most women don't."

"I'm not sure I ever will, but at the same time, I want us to be more than just good friends, Bucko. Your work scares me, Terrence. We couldn't be married. I'd die a thousand deaths every day you walked out the door to go to work. Would you still be alive that evening?" She took in a deep breath, closed her eyes, and tried to hold back the tears she could feel gathering.

"That's exactly what I'm talking about," he said. He felt her tighten up almost as if she was fighting to not say *this is the end of the line*. "Let's take the time we need to discuss all this, maybe tonight, after supper. I'm still fighting my way through a kidnapping and murder."

"I know," Molly whispered." She had her fingers grasping his shoulders so tight she was sure she would rip his shirt. She felt him tighten up, which told her the love scene was over. He was already back at work.

"So, little darlin', I need to talk about what I'm

working on, and you might have some answers. About Heck Heckman, about Jason Matlock, and about Tommy Lane. I think they all do business here."

She sighed and eased away from the big man. "They do, Tommy, more than the others. What do you need to know?"

She walked them over to the cold wood stove and they sat down with their coffees. "I'm relatively sure that Heck Heckman is the one who murdered Enid Jackson, but right at the moment, can't prove it. And I'm more than positive that Tommy Lane put together the plot to kidnap Louisa Jackson and hold her for ransom. But lovely lady, I can't prove that, either."

"I can't see where I can help," Molly said.

"What can you tell me about Mr. Lane?"

"Tommy's an angry man, Terrence. Has been from the day he moved here. He has a hard time making friends or keeping friends. He takes every conversation as being personal, sometimes as a personal threat, even. I don't think he's the kind of man to kill someone, though."

"I don't either, but I'm sure he planned to have Louisa kidnapped and killed. Just not do it himself. How about Heckman?"

"He's a customer, but that's all." She took a quick glance around the store. "I don't think I've ever held a conversation with the man. He plunks what he wants on the counter, I tell him how much I want, and he pays for it. That's the sum of our relationship," she said, and laughed. "Not much help, I'm afraid."

She looked at Corcoran and smiled. "I have some sliced lamb that we were supposed to have sitting in the spring house, Terrence. We can have it with fresh bread and a cold salad tonight. I'd really like that."

He stood up and bowed. "I can't think of anything I'd rather have, than maybe a long hug from you." She jumped up and wrapped her arms around his neck. He kissed her long and soft, and finally let her go. "Seven."

————

"HELLO, Jason. Miss Clymer said she thought you'd be awake. Got a couple of questions."

"Always more questions, eh, Corcoran? Well, let 'em fly." Jason Matlock was still in bed, still suffering from his beating by Corcoran and the Heckman gunshot wound. "What is it you want?"

"What kind of relationship did Heckman and Tommy Lane have?"

"Relationship? Two angry men have a relationship?" Matlock laughed, but it was a derisive laugh, not humorous. "Lane made the harness for the Jackson teams, and Heckman helped with the fittings, and that's about it."

"They had drinks together often, at the Flint Brother's."

"Heckman doesn't drink, Corcoran."

"Afraid you're wrong about that. He and Lane met with Shorty Duggan and his gang regularly, and he very well does drink. You didn't know any of this?"

"First time I've heard it. What are you leading up to? You seem to have as many answers as you have a lot of questions."

Corcoran had to laugh right out. "I do, Jason. I do

have a lot of questions. You visited with Heckman and Lane, too, by way of his work. Anyone else come by?"

"Heck is not a friendly man. People shied away from him. Interesting that you say he and Lane had a friendship. Lane, too, is an angry man with few friends. I can't picture the two of them meeting up with Shorty Duggan, unless it was to hurt Enid Jackson or his family. That's where their anger originates."

"Thank you, Jason. Get well." Corcoran left the man's bedroom and the store and found himself just walking along the streets in Eureka, talking to himself, arguing even. "Matlock didn't know that Heckman drank regularly at Flint's? That Lane was with him often? That they met with Shorty Duggan?" Eventually, he made his way to the office.

"Heckman still alive?"

Sheriff Ed Connor snorted and pointed to the cell block door. "Dr. Whidby is back with him now. You don't look like a happy man, Terrence."

"Not Ed. Lane plotted the kidnapping, Heckman shot Jackson. Nobody has a clue about either man or either crime. The men were drinking associates and only Mr. Diddy knows that." Corcoran unstrapped his gun belt and hung it on a hook near the rifle and shotgun racks.

"Doc won't like this."

"I'll be gentle," Corcoran said with a snicker as he walked back to the cells. He found Dr. Whidby outside Heckman's cell, not inside.

"Problems, Doc?"

"Glad you're here, Corcoran. I need to examine his wounds, but he's fighting me all the way."

"Well, let's see what we can do about that." Corcoran pulled the cell keys from a wall rack and opened the cell door. "What's the problem here, Mr. Heckman? You want to fight the doc? How about fighting me instead?"

Heckman's head was wrapped in a bloody rag, as was his shoulder. His eyes were swollen and discolored, half closed, Corcoran saw. Was the man fighting the doc because of pain, or anger? "So, my friend, the pain's got you cooked up, eh? *He knows if I smack him a good one, it will probably kill him. His skull is already fractured, so it wouldn't take much.*

"When you and Tommy Lane had drinks at the Flints, what did you talk about? Harnesses for the Jackson horses?"

Even Dr. Whidby had to snort on that question.

"Who says we had drinks?" Heckman seemed confused with the question, and Corcoran wondered if this, too, was a ruse.

"Several people who were there, Heckman. It's well established from several sources that you and Lane drank together often. What did you talk about?"

"Don't recall drinking with the man. Why would I?"

"Maybe to put together a group of men to rob a stage-coach and kidnap a young lady, Heckman. Tell me about those meetings."

Dr. Whidby had entered the cell and was working on Heckman's shoulder, which had taken a terrible beating and was raw meat.

"What do you know about robbing a stage, Heckman?" Corcoran saw Heckman pull back just a bit. Was it from pain from Dr. Whidby's care of the wounds, or from the question?

"I know you knew Louisa was coming home. You knew she was stopping in Austin, but didn't know she was staying over a night or two. I know that you and Tommy Lane planned on stopping that stage and kidnapping the girl, but she wasn't on the stage, was she?"

"No, dammit. Duggan got it wrong." He stopped immediately. Dr. Whidby straightened up, his mouth wide open in surprise, and Heckman started cussing like no man has ever cussed.

"Remember what you heard, Doctor," Corcoran said. "Thank you, Mr. Heckman. I'll see you in court."

Corcoran helped get the doctor out of the cell safely as Heckman continued his rage. Corcoran was smiling as he walked back into the office. "One down, one to go," he said. "Join me for a cold beer, Sheriff?"

"You go on. I'll wait until the doctor is through, but tell me what happened."

"Heckman just confessed to the planning of robbing the stage and kidnapping Louisa, and implicated Shorty Duggan as well. Did it right in front of Dr. Whidby. Good as gold in court, Sheriff."

"Didn't get him to confess to Jackson's murder, though?"

"No, but we'll get that, I'm sure. I'm going to have a beer or two and plan how to attack Tommy Lane again. Having Heckman's confession will have an impact on the man, I'm sure."

"Get into that cabinet if you can," Connor said with a chuckle. "And, Corcoran, we might be wrong, you know. It might be Lane, with a gun we don't know about, who killed Jackson."

————

Corcoran let that thought linger as he walked across the street to have a cold one at the Bonanza Club. *Of course that's possible,* he thought. *At this point we don't even know if Mr. Lane has a rifle. Thank you, Sheriff, I'll surely keep that in mind.*

"Afternoon, Jimmy, even the rocks out there are complaining about the heat. Pour a cold one, will you?"

"Thank you for being easy on that young man. He's been a good worker, and I hope you find out who set him up."

Corcoran looked at his old friend and smiled. "You old softy," he said, and chuckled. "Larry Simpson is a fine boy, takes wonderful care of his mother, and you help him along just fine. We had a good talk and I'm pretty sure I know who set him up and who beat the hell out of Mr. Heckman, but I'm not saying who, just yet."

"So, Heckman's still alive, eh?"

"You'll hear from Dr. Whidby before long. Even the doctor learned some new curse words. One more cold one, Jimmy, and I'm going to try and wrap this case up." He watched Henderson refill his mug. "Heckman and Lane drank regularly at Flint's but didn't you tell me they didn't drink here?"

"Not together or alone, Terrence."

"One thing missing from my investigation, so far, Jimmy, is, I don't know if Lane is a hunter or even has a rifle."

"Can't help you on that one, Pard. He doesn't even eat in our restaurant. I wouldn't argue about owning one of his saddles, but I'm not sure I would ever end up being the man's friend."

Corcoran nodded his agreement, thinking how nice Dude would look sporting one of the sloped fork beauties. "I'll tell him you said so. By the way, pass the word that Lou Foster is going to be fine. Shot in the back but alive and kicking."

CHAPTER FORTY

"YOU'RE BECOMING A PEST, DEPUTY CORCORAN," Tommy Lane said as the big lawman entered his store. The door was standing open but there was no cooling breeze. Corcoran noticed the back door to the store also stood open. If the slightest breeze stirred it might find its way through the store.

"That seems to be the consensus when I'm working on cases like the one I'm on. Tell me about your meetings with Mr. Heckman and Shorty Duggan. Did you talk about hunting?"

"Hunting?" Lane seemed confused by the question and Corcoran pressed on.

"Yes, hunting. You are aware that Heckman has a fine Henry repeater, aren't you? Being friends, I figured you probably hunted as well. What kind of rifle do you use? I prefer my Winchester, myself."

Would this work? Corcoran was leading the man right along. Would Lane follow? "I usually take someone along each fall when I go deep into these Diamond Mountains for elk and deer."

Lane had questions written all over his face and Corcoran wondered if Lane even knew what he was talking about.

"My father and my brother were killed in the big war between the states, Deputy. I hate guns. Don't own a one."

"I'm terribly sorry for your loss, Tommy. Let's get back to you and Mr. Heckman. What did you talk about?" Corcoran let out a deep breath at Lane's answer. *He evades questions so easily, I wonder if this is the truth? Or is it designed to shut me off on weapons? Lane has too many pat little answers to tough questions.*

"To be as honest and frank as I can, Corcoran, Heckman and I often talked about the many different ways we would like to see Enid Jackson die. We had to change the subject when Shorty Duggan joined us once in a while."

That, Mr. Lane is a lie, but how do I break this feller? He's been doing this for a long time, evading the truth, not answering questions. "Did one of those situations involve standing behind a tree and shooting the man while he sat at his desk in the bank?"

"No, Corcoran it didn't. You'll have to talk to another of those who hate Jackson about that."

"Both you and Heckman had great amounts of hate for the gentleman, and you discussed how to kill him? How about how to harm him the most?"

"Such as kidnapping his daughter?" Lane asked, a smirk on his face.

"Exactly," Corcoran said. "The first effort failed, but people died. Heckman knew Louisa was supposed to be on that stage, Lane. What went wrong?"

Lane stood behind his counter, a small hammer in one hand and a leather knife in the other. He set the two down, uncoiled like an athlete, and made a dash for the back door of his shop, just two steps away. He was out the door and into his adjoining cabin before Corcoran could vault the counter and follow.

"Stop or die," Corcoran shouted, leveling his Colt at the fleeing man. Lane never slowed and Corcoran fired once. The bullet took a chunk out of one of Lane's ears as the man dived and rolled through the door and into his living room.

Corcoran spotted the Winchester lever-action rifle leaning against a couch, which also had a buckskin shirt laid out. Lane grabbed the rifle as he rolled up, had himself kneeled down and was aiming at the door as Corcoran flung himself through it.

The sound in the small cabin was brutal, and the bullet would have done terrible damage if Corcoran hadn't been rolling on the floor as the lead passed over his head.

"Give it up, Lane. You've got nowhere to run." Corcoran had the Colt in a two-hand hold, lined front and back sights up on the man, crouched near the fireplace, but didn't fire. "Give it up now, or die."

Lane's face was covered in blood from his missing ear, and fired from the hip, not caring where the bullet went, and made a charge at the back door of the two-room cabin. He didn't try to open the door, rather put a shoulder down and rammed his way through, splintering the simple framed door, and fell down going through.

Corcoran took three steps and was out the door, seeing Lane just yards away, and put a forty-five-forty bullet into the dirt, inches from Lane's head, which stopped the man's efforts to get away. "I hope the judge agrees with what Amos Diddy has to say about all this," he murmured.

Corcoran pulled Lane's hands behind his back and attached the cuffs. "Let's go back inside and do some talking, eh Mr. Lane?" He had to half drag the man back inside and shoved him into a chair. "For a man who doesn't even have a gun, this is a nice rifle, Tommy." He held the lever action up to give it a good look. "Glad you can't shoot straight."

Corcoran grabbed the only other chair in the cabin and pulled it up so he sat facing the saddle-maker. "Before we go any further, you're under arrest. And," he said, "I guess we need to get that blood flow slowed down some."

He pulled a rag from the counter and used it. "Hold this tight against the wound, and you'll be fine," Corcoran said. "Now, tell me about how you and Heckman put that attempted kidnapping together. Don't bother saying you didn't, because Heckman has already told me you did."

"Bastard," Lane said, and Corcoran wondered if he was talking about him or Heckman.

"Why would you say that? It could have been a good plan."

"It was a fine plan," Lane said, "if Shorty Duggan had

done his job. I helped with the plan, Corcoran, so that's all. I wasn't any where near the site of the hold up."

"You think being an accessory will get you off the gallows frame? You're wrong, Lane. You're an accessory to murder. People died because of your plan." Corcoran sat back in the chair and looked as Lane absorbed what was said. He saw the shoulders slump, saw the head slowly fold down to his chest, and saw the eyes close.

"Isn't a pretty sight is it, seeing the steps up to a hanging rope waiting for you? Is that why you beat Heckman to death? So he wouldn't testify against you? Sending the note to Smiley to get Heckman's meal was pretty sharp, too. The judge won't like it, though."

Lane just sat with head down, breathing hard but not talking. "Let's take a little walk, Mr. Lane. Need to get you behind bars. Don't worry, I'll bring the rifle along. You'll need to get an attorney, though. Maybe Larry Simpson can run a message for you. You remember Larry, don't you?"

Corcoran chuckled. "The boy who was supposed to deliver Heckman's supper? He doesn't much care for you, nor does his widowed mother. Let's go, Tommy, on your feet."

"It was Heckman's idea," Lane blurted out.

"But your plan?" Corcoran asked. Lane mumbled something that seemed to say yes and Corcoran smiled. "So, it was Shorty Duggan's fault the plan failed?"

"Stupid bastard, yes," Lane said.

All the time they were talking, Lane was holding a bloody rag trying to stem the flow of blood from his missing ear. Corcoran ripped a strip from the sheet on the bed and tied it around Lane's head. The man cried out when Corcoran tied it tight.

"You ain't gonna die, Lane. We got a little walking to do, so buck up, lad."

It was quite a procession down the streets of Eureka, Lane walking in front and Corcoran, a rifle in one hand, aimed at Lane's back, and Dude's reins in the other, the horse ambling along peaceably. There were the usual cat-calls sent Lane's way from bystanders, and a few *at-a-boys* offered to Corcoran.

"This might just wrap it up, Sheriff. Mr. Lane would like to sit at your desk for a couple of minutes to write out his confession to being an accessory to the stage coach robberies and the kidnapping of Louisa Jackson."

"He can gladly take my seat, then," Sheriff Ed Connor said. "Good news from this end, too. Lou Foster is on his feet. Can't come back to work yet, feeling much better." Connor wagged his head. "A bullet to the back and no vital organs damaged. He's one lucky deputy."

"Going somewhere, Sheriff?" Corcoran asked as Connor strapped his gun belt on.

"When Mr. Lane is finished writing his confession, lock him up tight and join me at the Bonanza. I have a great thirst because of what you've done." He was chuckling softly as he walked out the door.

"Be with you shortly," Corcoran said, and took his chair to sit in the open doorway to wait for Lane to finish writing.

———

"THAT MAN WAS SLOWER in his writing than any third grader, Sheriff. I almost offered to help."

"His attorney would have loved that. I sent a note to the district attorney that we would have copies of the confessions sent over as soon as possible. We might be going to trial quickly on this one."

"Such a terrible waste, Ed, and it could have been ever worse. Stagecoach people dead, gang members dead, and the Jackson family without a father."

"Worse? How is that?"

"It could have played out," Corcoran said. "Both Heckman and Lane are intelligent and cunning. Their educations wasted by all this, but what if they hadn't depended on Shorty Duggan and done some of the work themselves? Knew Louisa would not be on that first stage, we would not have had any idea that she was in any danger."

Ed Connor stood at the bar and flagged Jimmy Henderson for another couple of beers. "Don't want to think about things like that. You're right, they could have pulled this little caper off. Damn."

The two lawmen were well into their second mugs of beer when Smiley came rushing into the saloon. "Trouble, Sheriff."

CHAPTER FORTY-ONE

SHERIFF CONNOR, Dr. Whidby, and Terrence Corcoran sat at a table in the courtroom of the District. Judge Stan Carroll, who just rapped for quiet, and Deputy Sheriff Lou Foster, still sporting plenty of bandages, sat behind the little fence next to Louisa Jackson. He was sure to be called as a witness.

At the prosecutor's table, sitting alone, was District Attorney Tony Petri.

"This is a hearing, not a trial," Judge Carroll said, quietly. "Sheriff Connor, why isn't Mr. Heckman or Mr. Lane present?"

"I'll let Dr. Whidby explain that, Your Honor."

The judge coughed softly, glared at the sheriff for a moment, and addressed the courtroom, "Unusual, Sheriff. I was explicit in my order for this hearing. I don't like changes from my orders without my okay." He let his gaze move to Dr. Whidby. "This better be good, Doctor."

Whidby smiled and stood up. "Mr. Heckman's injuries from the beating he took are such that he might not survive spending hours here, Your Honor. He suffered a fractured skull along with other wounds and broken bones. I'm afraid he'll need several more weeks before he could attend court."

"And Mr. Lane? I don't recall hearing about him suffering injuries other than that to his ear?" Judge Carroll was an older gentleman, skinny as a rail, his face almost skull-like, his sunken eyes probing the doctor.

"Mr. Lane may not be with us much longer," Dr. Whidby said. "After being booked and put in his cell, the man ripped his mattress apart, made a rope of the material, and hanged himself. The deputy was able to free him and keep him alive. He'll be able to stand trial within a week at the most."

"Mr. Petri, what are your thoughts on all this?"

"We will alter our schedules, Your Honor. It appears that both men will be charged as accessory in the stagecoach robberies and the attempted kidnapping, and a second charge of murder in the death of Enid Jackson for Heckman." He shook his head and tried to hide a smile. "Dr. Whidby and your clerk will have to set the dates for trials."

"And, this hearing?"

"I ask for a postponement, Your Honor, until the defendants can be present."

The judge almost growled when he accepted the plea and called it quits, storming off the bench.

"If this doesn't call for a cold beer, I don't know what would," Sheriff Connor said, leading the Eureka County Sheriff's office out of the courtroom. Lou Foster stayed behind with Louisa who had asked him to have lunch with her at the Jackson house.

———

"WILL you be able to face those two men at trial, knowing they were plotting your death?" The couple were sitting at the kitchen table at the Jackson home. Louisa had a platter of smoked meats, some sliced cheese, freshly baked bread, and various jams and jellies. "This smells so good," he said.

"It won't be easy, Lou, but knowing you're there with me, I'll be fine. I have some interesting news for you. Mother and I have been talking with Father's attorney. He arrived two days ago from Reno."

"You've been busy," Foster said. "Are you and your mother going to be able to keep the bank open? This is a growing community with many successful businesses, not to mention the Diamond Valley ranches, and the active mines and mills. That bank is a necessary business in this county."

Louisa reached across the table and took his hand. "What I'm about to tell you is almost word-for-word what our attorney told us." She looked down at the table for a moment before continuing, "You've told me several times how you feel about your job as a deputy, and how being married and having a family would be difficult."

"Yes," he said, feeling a touch of anxiety flow through his body. "I want to be with you for the rest of my life, but I could never ask you and our children to have to live with that constant fear of me not coming home some night."

"I want the same thing, and without that fear. However, Mr. Lou Foster, how would you feel not being called Deputy Sheriff Lou Foster, and instead being called Mr. Lou Foster, President, Eureka National Bank?"

Lou sat bolt upright, his eyes wide open and brighter than Louisa had ever seen them. "I'm not qualified to do that," he said. "My god, Louisa, I finished high school, barely. How could that happen?"

"My degree, you might remember, dear man, is in economics. I can have you up to date as bank president within a year. No one but us would ever know."

"Giving up the badge in order to marry you and be the bank's president?" He sat back, took a long sip of coffee. "Corcoran told me he was willing to give up the badge, marry a wonderful girl, buy a ranch, and settle down."

"Why didn't he?"

"She was abducted and killed," he said, his face wrapped in grief at the thought.

"Oh, dear. That poor man."

Lou stood up and walked around the table, got down on one knee and took Louisa's hands in his. "Louisa Jackson, I don't have much to offer other than a strong back, a few pounds of common sense, and unlimited love for you. Will you marry me?"

She tore her hands loose and fell on him, wrapping her arms around his neck, kissing him all over his head and face. "Oh, yes I will," she cried out.

It was quite a scene Louisa's mother walked in on, the

two, on the floor, their arms wrapped around each other. "This is not proper behavior. Let go of my daughter," she said.

"He can't," Louisa said. "I won't let him. He's about to be my husband, Mother. You'd best get used to this beast of a man, he's going to run our bank, too."

————

"I WANT you to be the most successful banker in Nevada, Mr. Foster, but I can't let you go until these court cases are wrapped up." Sheriff Ed Connor was sitting behind his desk and his chief deputy, Terrence Corcoran was sitting alongside the desk. "Two men have been charged with being accessories to murder and kidnapping, and I'm going to need your testimony."

Foster started to say something and Corcoran cut him off. Too much of this case will depend on our testimony. We've lost too many witnesses. Duggan's gang, for instance, and the fact that Heckman and Lane may not testify against each other since they were partners in all this."

"I understand all of this," Lou said. "I'll be happy to stay on but I think you understand that I will also have to assume my office at the bank. So much depends on keeping it open and operating smoothly."

"And right in the middle of all this is you and Louisa are getting married," Smiley said. "Ain't never heard nothin' like this. Just ain't never. Who's going to be your best man?"

"I haven't asked him yet," Lou said, looking straight

at Terrence Corcoran, who shuffled his feet a bit, looked at the floor, and burst into smiles and laughter, reaching out and slapping Lou Foster across his broad shoulders.

"Damn right I will," Corcoran said. "You kids picked a date?"

"Judge Carroll wants to officiate well before the upcoming trials. He picked a date two weeks from now. Louisa will be wearing her grandmother's wedding dress and the tailor says he'll have my wedding suit done in plenty of time." He chuckled, got up and walked around the small office. "I've never been so nervous in all my life."

"Let's buy this man a cold beer and talk about the trial," the sheriff said, getting up from the desk and heading for the open door. "We've got a couple of men who need hanging and a judge waiting to get the job done."

CHAPTER FORTY-TWO

"I DIDN'T MAKE a mess of it, did I?" For the first time in two weeks Lou and Louisa were not surrounded by people constantly telling them what to say and what to do. They were sitting at the kitchen table at the Jackson house, together and alone. She was still in her wedding dress and he in his new suit, starched collar and all.

"You were wonderful, Lou. I'm still shaking."

"I'm sorry we have to postpone our honeymoon," he said. "Judge Carroll wants these trials to get started immediately. Maybe we can run away at Christmas."

"That would be nice. Where would we go?"

Lou sat back in his chair after taking a sip of coffee, smiled and reached for her hand. "I've never seen the Pacific Ocean or San Francisco."

Louisa squealed and jumped up and plunked herself in Lou's lap. "It's a magic town at Christmas, Lou. Oh, yes, it has to be San Francisco." She tightened up and almost scowled. "Mother is going to want to come, and I don't want that."

"We'll work it out," he said. "I also think we should move into a home of our own. Your mother needs her own space."

Someone walking by the large Victorian building would smile hearing Louisa's laughter ringing out. "How long will these trials last?" she asked.

"Carroll is making it into one trial and he said to expect about two weeks. I would think longer, but he's probably right. There's almost no one alive who was a part of the crimes. Your testimony will simply be about what happened and there won't be any cross-examination since none of the gang is alive either. It will be quick."

"I didn't realize it was so late," Louisa said. She started to light a lamp and Lou took her hand.

"I think we can find our way up the stairs," he said, and heard a delightful tinkle of laughter.

———

THE HEADLINES in the *Eureka Sentinel* spread across the top of page one: *Heckman and Lane, guilty as charged.*

Sheriff Connor was in the lead as Corcoran and Foster followed him into the Bonanza Club. "You were right, Terrence. That DA knew what he was doing. Got those men so angry at each other that they let the whole nasty story unfold in that courtroom." The sheriff raised his glass to his chief deputy.

"Next order of business is to find a deputy. We can't replace you, Lou, but we need to fill the void you're leaving," Corcoran said. He looked around the table and slowly shook his head.

"So many people dead. The entire gang, the banker, stage coach men. Terrible, and all for a few thousand dollars. Are you sure you want to give all this up, Lou?"

"I've learned more in the last few weeks about banking than I ever thought about. Jackson was a tyrant and I'm vowing right now, in front of my best friends, that I won't be. In fact," Foster said, "I'm reinstating Mr. Matlock's loan, but with one caveat. He cannot make anymore lanterns. He can make all the pretty glass pieces and candles he can sell, but no lanterns."

"That's the best news I've heard in a long time," Sheriff Ed Connor said. "You'll do a fine job with that bank, Lou. I think you've found your real calling. We're losing one of our best deputies ever to serve in Eureka County, but the county is getting the services of a community bank and banker. Good luck, son, good luck."

A LOOK AT: A TANGLED WEB OF FRONTIER LIFE

Brookside, Oregon Territory Book One

**Life in the Oregon Territory frontier village of
Brookside is drastically changed when schemes and
frauds turn violent. Families are split apart, and good
citizens die in this first novel in a continuing series of
life in Oregon's frontier period.**

Brookside, Oregon Territory in the late 1840s is a ranching and
timber producing village made up of those willing to face the
dangers and hardships of frontier life. Some are honest,
hardworking, and family oriented while others become
criminals, killers, and opportunists.

Farmer and rancher Jacob Hoagland works through a rough
period and, into the new year, is faced with a growing family
relying on him, an opportunity for farm growth, and a
community that finds it needs him, too.

Irene Creighton is married to an animal of a man who believes
it is a man's right to beat on his wife at will. After years of
abuse, she fights back with a cast iron pan. Her husband's death
leads to the discovery of his participation in land fraud within
the territory.

Ben Thorndyke is the village's most successful businessman.
His company builds the tools and appliances needed by the
timber industry and by the farmers and ranchers in the little
valley. In turn, his retail farm and ranch supply emporium sell
what he builds along with seed and other needed supplies. He is
a community leader and friend of the governor.

The county constable, Tobias Kennedy, came to America from
Ireland and landed in Brookside. He gets his information
through the menacing use of an oak walking stick, a constantly

questioning mind, and a distinct desire for Irish whisky and Oregon brandy.

These lives, along with the loves, joys and hardships accompanying them, will bring questions of criminality to a conclusion. But not everyone's life will take a turn for the better...

AVAILABLE NOW

ABOUT THE AUTHOR

Johnny Gunn has worked in print, broadcast, and internet, including a stint as publisher and editor of the *Virginia City Legend*. These days, Gunn spends most of his time writing novel-length fiction, concentrating on the Western genre. Otherwise, you can find him down by the Truckee River with a fly rod in hand.

www.ingramcontent.com/pod-product-compliance
Lightning Source LLC
Chambersburg PA
CBHW011514240626
47154CB00010B/3031

```
9 798889 567310 2
```